A SECRET to Tell

An Ari Adams Mystery

Ann Roberts

BELLA
BOOKS

2017

Bella Books, Inc.
P.O. Box 10543
Tallahassee, FL 32302

Printed in the United States of America on acid-free paper.

First Bella Books Edition 2017

Editor: Katherine V. Forrest
Cover Designer: Judith Fellows

ISBN: 978-1-59493-546-6

Books by Ann Roberts

The Ari Adams Mystery Series
Paid in Full
White Offerings
Deadly Intersections
Point of Betrayal
A Grand Plan

Romances
Brilliant
Beach Town
Beacon of Love
Root of Passion
Petra's Canvas
Hidden Hearts
The Complete Package
Pleasure of the Chase

Kickin' on 66 (Fall 2017)

General Fiction
Furthest From the Gate
Keeping Up Appearances

Acknowledgments

The idea for this novel emerged after my brother David purchased a home that had sat vacant for nearly thirty years. Little did he know I had grisly designs on it as the setting for a murder. I'm grateful for his help and knowledge of all things historic, especially the Catlin Court Historic District. As always, my wife Amy is the first reader and usually my harshest critic. She catches my continuity mistakes and tells me when I've given a character a ridiculous name. During the writing of this novel, she shouldered a huge load as we prepared to sell our house. I'm so lucky she's put up with me for twenty-two years. Without Linda Hill and Bella Books there wouldn't be a book. I'm incredibly fortunate to be a part of the Bella family, and I very much appreciate their support through the process. Finally, I am indebted to my editor, the great Katherine V. Forrest. I have learned much from her about writing and editing, and she always holds my feet to the fire about police procedure. If I drift off into circumspect TV crime drama behavior, she's quick to put me back on track with reality. This novel and the entire future of the series benefited from her observations and suggestions. Thank you, Katherine.

Most of all, thanks again to the loyal readers who continue to follow Ari and Molly on their adventures. I am humbled that you devote your money and your time to my writing.

About the Author

As of this book's release, Ann Roberts will have recently relocated to Springfield, Oregon, with her wife Amy. No doubt getting there was an adventure as they moved with Duke the Dog and his nemesis, Ferrill the Feral Cat. A life-long educator, Ann retired last year to devote her full attention to writing and serving on the Board of Directors for the Golden Crown Literary Society. Please visit her website at annroberts.net.

Dedication

For David and Susan

PREFACE

Victor Guzman, Esquire, halted at the sight of a gunman in his firm's law library. He'd momentarily returned to his office for a file, and as he returned to the library, movement caught his eye through the glass walls. In the split second it took for him to process imminent danger, the shooter turned, saw him and fired. He covered his ears as glass exploded around him. He didn't realize he'd started running until he saw the red exit sign above the east stairwell door. He barreled through it and headed up the stairs. Before he reached the first landing, he realized his mistake. He'd opened the door, seen the ascending steps and run up instead of down.

He'd never been in the stairwell. He always took the elevators from the fifth to the tenth floor where the other half of the law firm lived, and he'd been conveniently absent from the monthly fire drills. Now he was regretting those choices. While he easily powered up the first two flights, by the time he reached the seventh floor, he was gulping for air and his legs felt like sandbags.

He paused long enough to jiggle the doorknob, but it was locked, as it should be. A company badge only opened the door for the floors rented by that company. Yet sometimes doors were unlocked if the badge reader was broken. But not tonight.

He heard the fifth floor stairwell door crash open. The shooter was following him and he still had three more flights to go. Each step was one step closer to the tenth floor. He was out of shape, and he never should've given up that gym membership after the divorce.

Two more flights.

He whipped around a corner, using the handrail to pull himself up. He glanced down. The shooter leaned over the side, pointing the gun upward. He pushed away from the railing just as the shot reverberated throughout the stairwell. He jumped and grabbed his ears. It was so loud! He hugged the wall and turned past the ninth floor door.

One more flight.

If he didn't get through the door before the shooter reached the last landing, he'd be dead, shot in the back. He stumbled, the toe of his dress shoe catching a step. He stayed upright but his heart pounded in his chest, pleading for him to stop.

And the shooter was gaining on him.

He saw the door above. He focused on the black number ten spray-painted on the center. Three, two, one. He was there! He slapped his badge against the key reader and pushed open the door as a shot exploded above him. Tiny fragments of concrete rained on his head. He slammed the door shut behind him and glanced left and right. He went left, hoping the shooter would make the opposite choice. The floor was designed like a square donut with the elevators and stairwells in the center. An employee stretching his legs could make a complete circle and return to his starting point. A sea of empty cubicles filled the southern square footage, each one housing a paralegal or a legal assistant. He ran to the center of the maze and dropped to the floor just as the shooter burst through the stairwell door.

He closed his eyes and listened for footfalls but heard nothing. The shooter had gone to the right, toward the conference rooms and kitchen. Victor knew he had a little time before the shooter circled to the south side and began searching the individual workstations. He crawled toward the back corner cubicle, putting as much distance as possible between himself and the stairwell from which he'd just come. He was also closer to the other stairwell, but he didn't think he had the energy to power down ten flights. And he couldn't outrun a bullet.

He crawled past several workstations, noticing his paralegal hadn't bothered to shut down her computer. He needed to call the police, but his phone was in the law library. It suddenly dawned on him that each desk was equipped with a landline. He used the desk phones so infrequently that he'd forgotten they existed. He closed his eyes and listened but heard nothing.

He read the nameplate of the nearest cubicle: Sadie Adelstein. He didn't know her, but judging from the green cardigan hung on the back of her chair, he guessed she was older. He slowly sat up and peered onto her desk. Sadie's phone was out of reach, shoved behind her computer. Apparently, she rarely used her desk phone either. To grab the handset he'd have to stand and pull it toward him, pushing aside five different photos of two young boys Victor imagined were her grandchildren. He frowned. They had a policy about personal photos.

He slowly lifted his frame over the desk, but his large belly prevented him from leaning over the lip of the tabletop. Swift footsteps approached, but they sounded like the click of a woman's heels and not the smacking of soles against concrete he'd heard in the stairwell. He dropped to the floor. The heels disappeared, and he heard the stairwell door latch softly engage. It wasn't the shooter but someone else. Who was here this late on a Tuesday night? She had come from the direction of the conference rooms. She must have heard the gunshots, but she'd managed to escape. She'd call the police! He just needed to stay alive until then.

A loud crash from the kitchen sent him scampering along the back wall. The shooter had finished the search of the north side and would start to comb through the cubicles. Victor peered between two workstations and looked longingly at the elevators. They were ridiculously slow and provided nowhere to hide while he waited. If he tried to cross to the north side, to the conference rooms the shooter had already searched, he'd be seen for sure. His choices were to follow the Lady in Heels and dart down the west stairwell or find a secure hiding place. There was a short hallway that led to the storage room and the executive washroom, both potential hiding spots.

He heard the shooter rustling through the aisles between the workstations. Chairs toppled and the violent clatter of personal items hitting the floor suggested the shooter was as interested in vandalism as he was in murder.

He quietly crawled toward the hallway. Sweat burned his eyes and his shirt was soaked. He glanced over his shoulder. As he turned down the hallway, there would be a second when he was in plain sight. He lifted his head far enough to see the hooded figure turn to inspect a back cubicle.

Go!

He hustled around the corner, and once he was far enough down the hallway, he stood and sprinted to the storeroom. He fumbled with his keys, cursing Isabelle, the office manager, for talking him into regular doorknobs instead of the keypad entry ones he'd wanted to order.

"It's a money saver," he mocked quietly. "How about a lifesaver?" His hands shook as he tested each key. He knew he had one but he never used it. That's what subordinates were for. He jammed key after key against the lock's face but none of them worked.

"Shit."

As he stared at the ring, he finally remembered he'd given his storeroom key to Hannah, his personal assistant. He glanced down the hallway and saw the executive washroom and the west stairwell. He had to make a choice: Hide in the bathroom or try to chug down ten floors of stairs before the shooter caught up to him. He thought about the Lady in Heels. Certainly, she'd call the police.

He decided on the washroom. The door was solid oak with a deadbolt to ensure only those with the proper key could rest in luxury. After flipping the deadbolt latch, he slipped inside the stall. He sat down on the toilet and checked his watch—exactly nine thirty. This was his punishment for working so late. The property managers had made it very clear to him and his partners that they didn't pay for late night or weekend security. If you had a heart attack working at your desk, you'd better have your cell phone with you because there wouldn't be anyone nearby to help. That had certainly been true for his partner who'd died at his desk.

He clutched his chest and steadied his breathing. There was nothing he could do now except wait and hope that the police arrived quickly before the shooter found him and broke down the bathroom door.

He wiped his brow. *Hurry, hurry.* How long would it take them? What if the Lady in Heels didn't call the police? What if she wasn't real? He closed his eyes and bit his lip. *I didn't imagine her, did I?* No. He'd distinctly heard the click-click of her shoes. He clasped his hands together, praying she would help him. Whoever she was, she'd get a raise.

The smell of industrial cleaner was giving him a headache. The cleaning crew was done and gone by nine, even that slow pig Iselda. Why did the company keep her?

Nine thirty-one.

For a fleeting second he wondered if he should change locations. He was a literal sitting duck in the bathroom, but his logical lawyer brain told him this was the best he could do. The police would be here soon. Maybe they were here now. Some would come up the stairs while another group would take the elevator. He imagined a gunfight might ensue, or a more likely possibility would be that the shooter would flee. His attempt at killing Victor certainly hadn't gone as planned.

He pondered the identity of the shooter. The list of people who held a grudge against him was long. He'd made enemies as a family law attorney and his recent divorce had been messy. His ex certainly wished him dead. He wiped the sweat from his face with a shirtsleeve. If he got out of this alive, he vowed to be different. He'd treat people better. He'd exercise. Maybe his son Miguel would join a gym with him. He needed to lose a few pounds. He'd stop chasing tail and maybe his ex would take him back.

He glanced at the oak panels of the bathroom stall. This was safe—somewhat embarrassing—but safe. He'd send the Lady in Heels some flowers. It was the least he could do since she saved his life.

He checked his watch again. Two more minutes had passed. Where were those cops?

Then he heard a click and the hinge squeak he'd reported to maintenance three times. He'd forgotten one thing: the shooter might have a key to the executive washroom.

CHAPTER ONE

Perfect, Ari Adams mused. It was the most appropriate description of the glorious March day. She stretched her long legs and sipped the best coffee she'd ever tasted, thinking that her surroundings complemented the beautiful weather. The patio at the Groove on Grand was a blend of desert plants and flowerbeds bursting with color. She knew the marigolds, snapdragons and petunias were short-timers in Phoenix. Once the temperatures reached triple digits, the delicate flowers would wither, but for now the patio could be featured on *Houzz*.

She gazed across Grand Avenue at the O.S. Stapley Building, the new home of Southwest Realty. The sign painter had finished adding Ari's name just yesterday, listing her as a broker alongside the company's founder Lorraine Gonzalez. With a third business partner, they'd purchased the historic Stapley Building in addition to the Groove, an eclectic collection of structures that included the coffeehouse Scrabble and four brightly colored, identical cabins.

In a past life, the cabins had been located at a WWII internment camp on the outskirts of Phoenix, but now each one housed a different business. She loved that something from such a dark time could be repurposed in a positive way. The red cabin was The Pocket, the smallest bar in Phoenix, possibly the world. Ari's best friend Jane Frank owned it and had emailed *The Guinness Book of World Records* to see if she could make such a claim about her two-hundred-square-foot bar. A jewelry designer worked in the yellow cabin and the lime-green cabin was an art studio. She heard the blue cabin's front door close, and she smiled at the approach of Molly Nelson. Molly's shirt was the same royal blue color as the cabin, and the words Nelson Security were embroidered on the front.

Molly carried her own cup of coffee and her portfolio. She leaned over and kissed Ari before dropping into a patio chair beside her. Their fingers automatically entwined and Ari smiled at the touch. Their relationship was nearly as perfect as the weather. They had been through a lot over the past two years, including a terrible breakup, but now they were stronger than ever. Ari credited their therapist with nudging them toward the answers that could make their relationship work.

Molly caressed the red tourmaline gem on Ari's left ring finger. She'd given the ring to her for Christmas. Passing her broker's exam before the holidays had been a great present, but the ring meant much more. It wasn't an engagement ring. They were both clear on that point. That wouldn't come for a long while if Dr. Yee got her way, and Ari was fine with that. Still, she wore it on her left hand to keep the men and women from hitting on her too much.

She and Molly were exactly six feet tall, but their height was their only physical similarity. Her own hair and skin were dark from her Mediterranean roots, and she'd been told she should've been a model since she was blessed with her mother's exquisite long nose and high cheekbones. Molly's pleasant face and curly blond hair had ensnared many women during her single life, but those days were over, as was the heavy drinking that accompanied the parade of women who'd left her apartment, a different one nearly every night. She was a recovering alcoholic, and the time she'd once devoted to clubbing was now spent working out. She was lean and toned, and when they went out together, women ogled both of them.

"When's the interview?" she asked Molly.

"Not until nine." Molly checked her watch. "I'm not worrying about it too much since I don't think they'll hire us."

Ari cocked her head to the side. She knew Molly's pessimism was a defense mechanism and Dr. Yee had encouraged her to challenge it. "Why not?"

"Their last P.I. was a one-man show and he charged a lot less. I'm not sure how because they're a law firm of twenty-three attorneys, and they need a full-service investigative firm. I won't do it any other way since I'm still establishing my brand and my reputation."

Ari nodded. Nelson Security was a fledgling company, but it had gained positive notoriety after a former employee made headlines for saving dozens of lives. Although the employee had quit, Molly's phone hadn't stopped ringing, and she already needed to expand. They expected the business to outgrow the little blue cabin by the end of the year.

The backdoor of Scrabble opened and the manager, Chynna Grove, brought them a fresh pot of coffee and a carafe of creamer. "Knew you'd need a refill," she said with a wink.

Chynna was part hippie and part punk rocker. Her retro sixties clothes were the real artifacts. Today she wore jeans with peace sign patches and a tie-dyed tank top. Her hairstyle and hair color changed monthly. Since it was March, her hair was green. When she bent over to fill Molly's cup, Ari realized she could still see the Stapley Building through Chynna's ear gauge.

Once the coffee was poured she said to Ari, "Something I need to tell you." Molly's phone rang and she excused herself to take the call. "That woman from the health department came by again yesterday right before Happy Hour started at the Pocket. Muriel somebody."

"Oh really? What did she want?"

"She said there were still matters to discuss. I told her Jane wasn't going to be in for the rest of the day, but instead of leaving, she ordered a seltzer water and sat herself down at this very table."

"She was just hanging out?"

"I wouldn't call it hanging out. She sipped her seltzer and wrote in a notebook. She watched the people and faced only the bar. She never got up again. A few of the lesbian customers were freaked out. They thought she was stalking them, but I explained who she was."

"When did she leave?"

Chynna checked her phone. "She stayed until seven twenty-eight. I noted the exact time."

While Jane had been granted a temporary liquor license for her tiny bar, apparently Muriel, one of the division supervisors, didn't believe The Pocket qualified as a bar because of the very limited customer space (only three stools) and small square footage. She claimed there wasn't enough room to implement all of the expected food and beverage health measures. Ari had told Jane not to worry, but since Jane was also a real estate agent, she'd heard horror stories about inspectors. She felt they had reason to worry about Muriel.

"I'll talk with Jane today and let her know," Ari said. "Maybe we could meet with Muriel."

"Roger that," Chynna said. She offered a wave and returned to Scrabble. Rush hour had started and cars headed downtown made a pit stop for the best coffee in the area. Ari leaned back and sighed. Business was good. Her relationship was good. The weather was perfect. She was about to declare it a great day when Molly rejoined her and groaned.

"What's wrong?"

Molly took a final gulp of coffee and gathered her things. "That was Gloria Rivera, one of the partners with the law firm. There's good news and bad news. The good news is that Nelson Security is hired, no interview needed. The bad news is that the principal partner in the law firm, Victor Guzman, was murdered in the office last night. Gloria asked me to come right now. If you're free, wanna join me?"

They avoided the crime scene vehicles and news vans by parking on a side street. Ari followed Molly's truck in her 4Runner as she had an appointment later that morning. As they walked together, she craned her neck to see the top of the twenty-story office building at the corner of Indian School Road and Central Avenue. "What do you know about this firm?" She was certain Molly had done her homework to prepare for the abandoned interview.

"Guzman, Rivera and Dorn is a well-known family law firm. Less than a year ago, Richard Dorn had a heart attack and died at his desk. His wife still sits on their Board of Directors. Gloria Rivera was one of the first Hispanic females to pass the bar in Arizona. She joined forces with Guzman back in the eighties after she struggled to start her own firm. She's a great attorney, but she smacked against the glass ceiling and Victor offered to make her a name partner. Victor Guzman, the founder and the deceased, made his name via the good press he earned from arguing several unwinnable cases involving underdogs against big agencies. He took on Child Protective Services when they returned a five-year-old child to a sexual predator. He sued them on behalf of the aunt, who was the child's last upstanding relative."

"I remember that," Ari said. "And wasn't he the one who sued all those senior centers for elder abuse?"

"He was. He got ten million for the class-action suit that was distributed among eighty families."

"Sounds like a do-gooder," Ari concluded. "It's rather surprising he's dead if his press is to be believed."

Molly offered a sideways grin. "*If.*"

The uniformed officers managing the crime scene entrance let them into the courtyard when they recognized Molly. Lawyers from the firm had been herded there, and it was a sea of suits, cell phones, colognes and expensive leather briefcases. Although it was only eight a.m., the heat was taking its toll.

Several people fanned themselves with newspapers or file folders. March in Phoenix meant warm days and cool nights. Many of the men had their jackets slung over their shoulders with their ties loosened, although none of the women had compromised her appearance and could immediately walk into a courtroom for opening remarks. Ari knew from her experience as a police officer that women always had to be one notch better than their male counterparts. She imagined the legal profession was no different.

Most of the well-dressed people chatted in whispered tones, wearing serious expressions. They knew something tragic had occurred.

As she and Molly slowly drifted toward the entrance, Molly said, "Their business is shut down today. Wouldn't you tell these people to go home?"

"That's not gonna happen," a voice muttered.

They looked to their left and saw a fresh-faced Hispanic man who appeared to be right out of college. With his suit jacket draped over his arm, his red suspenders were visible. They were imprinted with white dog bones, and Ari imagined they hugged the line of acceptable dress at Guzman, Rivera and Dorn.

Molly faced him. "What do you mean?"

He looked surprised and then noticed the logo on her shirt. "Security? Are you the new P.I. we're supposedly getting?" She nodded and his gaze darted left and right. When he was confident no one of prominence was in earshot, he leaned toward them. "Isabelle the Hell will do whatever she can to get us back into the building ASAP. Time is money and several people are late for court. She'll have us sitting on the floor if necessary."

"Who's Isabelle?" Ari asked.

"Isabelle is the office manager. She rides herd on all of us paralegals, as well as the secretaries." He stuck out his hand in greeting. "I'm Xavier Yanez, one of the newest hires."

Molly glanced toward the entrance. "So, Xavier, what are your initial impressions of Guzman, Rivera and Dorn?"

He bit his lip and Ari guessed he was sorry he'd opened his mouth. When he spoke it was with great care. "They're highly professional and excellent advocates for the clients they serve. They're demanding, but that's because they represent their clients so well."

Molly smirked and replied, "Xavier, I wasn't asking for the company line. Your firm is about to become embroiled in a murder investigation."

He swallowed and pulled at the knot of his tie. "So it's true? Guzman's dead? That's the rumor flying around down here. A lot of people are talking and a few," he said, throwing his chin toward a group of suits on their cell phones, "are starting to call headhunters."

"It's a little premature to think people are going to lose their jobs, isn't it?" Ari asked.

He shook his head. "Oh no, they aren't worried about being fired. They're going to quit." He whispered, "Mr. Guzman's clients may have loved him, but he was…" Xavier paused before he said, "*difficult* to work for. Some of the serious expressions you see are because people think they'll be accused of the crime." He stuffed his hands in his pockets and glided away.

Molly exhaled. "Let's find the ringmaster of this circus."

They pushed their way toward the building entrance. Molly pointed at an older woman conferring with a much younger subordinate. Ari guessed this was Gloria Rivera, the only remaining name partner and the person with whom Molly would have interviewed. She looked out of place in a blue tracksuit and red baseball cap. Her eyes were puffy and Ari wasn't sure if she'd been crying or if she was exhausted.

As they approached, Ari heard her say to the younger woman, "Tell Leslie my gray suit is to the far right in the closet. Then she's to go to Eight C and bring me the flash drive in the top left drawer of his desk. That's where he kept it."

It only took a second for Gloria to recognize Molly. "Thank you for coming, Ms. Nelson. I'm Gloria Rivera and this is Brittany Spring, a paralegal. Please excuse my appearance." She looked at Ari and frowned. "I didn't realize you'd be bringing an associate."

"This is Ari Adams, a friend and part-time investigator. We often collaborate on various projects."

Gloria blinked, as if she thought she might know her. "Brittany, where can we have some privacy?"

Brittany, holding a clipboard pressed against her simple blue Oxford shirt, wore black Dockers and boots. She stood out as the only member of the firm not wearing a suit, save Gloria. The rest of her appearance was equally underwhelming. She wore little makeup and a unique butterfly pin held back her strawberry blond hair.

Scanning the courtyard and lobby, she replied, "I believe the area around the vending machines is open."

Gloria gestured for her to lead them inside. As they proceeded through the lobby, Ari's gaze flitted about the various crime scene personnel surrounding the information desk. The Chief of Police, Dylan Phillips, hovered over a computer monitor with an African-American man. When he lifted his head, she saw it was Andre Williams, Molly's former partner when she was a detective. They were too engrossed in the computer to notice her and Molly. She exhaled, grateful that the first time she was introduced to Chief Phillips wouldn't be at a crime scene. She knew, though, the time to meet her was fast approaching. The chief had been dating Ari's dad for nearly three months. Since Jack Adams was officially retired and only a consultant, the rules of fraternization didn't apply to him.

She glanced at Molly just in time to see her recognize Andre. She tensed and her lips formed a tight line. While Molly and Andre had remained close after Molly left Phoenix PD, they had never worked a case in their respective new roles. From the way Chief Phillips was speaking with Andre, Ari surmised he would be the lead detective on the Guzman murder. And Molly was the firm's new hired gun. *This could get interesting.*

They turned down a short hallway. Two young men Ari assumed worked for the law firm laughed and joked as they enjoyed Cokes and candy. When they saw their boss approaching, they quickly adopted somber expressions and hustled past her with a brief, "Ma'am."

Gloria turned to Brittany. "Please wait at the end of the hall and don't let anyone disturb us until we're allowed to go upstairs. And please text Leslie with those other matters." She turned to Ari. "I'm sorry. What is your name again?"

Ari smiled and hoped she sounded sincere when she said, "I'm Ari Adams. Ms. Nelson thought it might be helpful to have another set of eyes and ears given the seriousness of this morning's events."

"Yes," Molly interjected. "Who discovered the body? Have the police told you anything?"

Gloria shook her head. "All I know is the beginning. The office manager, Isabelle Medina, called me a little after six. She's usually the first one in the office, followed at six fifteen by one or two of the paralegals. They're responsible for making sure the attorneys going to court that day have everything they need. She found the tenth floor completely vandalized. Chairs and computers overturned, glass shattered on the floor in the kitchen, the copy machine destroyed. I told her I'd come at once. Then she called again, hysterical. She'd gone to the executive washroom because the hallway was flooded. One of the sinks had been plugged and the water on the floor had a red tinge." Gloria took a breath as she prepared for the last sentence. "When she checked the stalls, she found Victor. I threw on this lovely ensemble," she said, gesturing to the tracksuit, "and dashed here while Isabelle called the police."

At a commotion in the lobby, they looked down the hallway to see the coroner's stretcher pass. Gloria's gaze dropped to the floor as she composed herself. When she looked up, fierce determination had replaced sorrow and grief. She folded her arms and raised her chin. "Ms. Nelson, my expectation is that you are now the firm's advisor on this matter. I expect you to be a resource to the employees who might be interviewed, and since I've read your police file and know you personally apprehended dozens of criminals, I want you to investigate as well. I'll make sure the staff fully cooperates. You'll get whatever you need to find Victor's murderer."

"Excellent," Molly said. "I'm sure the police will ask you for a complete staff list with addresses and phone numbers, as well as full access to every employee's email."

"Of course. I'll get Isabelle on it immediately."

Brittany reappeared and said to Gloria, "The police are ready to escort you upstairs."

Gloria turned to Ari. "It took me a while to remember, but I've also read up on you, Ms. Adams. You may not be a licensed investigator, but you certainly get into a lot of trouble." Ari looked surprised and Gloria offered a sly smile. "I think that's a good thing."

CHAPTER TWO

Molly saw the look of relief on Ari's face when they returned to the lobby and Chief Phillips had already left. Perhaps this would push Ari to action, and she'd schedule the dinner she'd been avoiding for weeks. Her father had finally found someone he liked, but she'd admitted it was difficult to see him with anyone but her mother.

Molly had learned to listen and not to judge. She had an amazing family who'd adopted Ari as one of their own. But Ari's family wasn't anything like the large, gregarious Nelson clan. Ari had lost her mother to cancer and her brother to a gunman's bullet. All she had left was Jack, a father who'd disowned her years before over her sexual orientation. They had reconciled but the scars were deep.

They waited patiently for Andre to finish a conversation with some uniformed officers. Molly watched him closely with a mixture of pride and concern. He'd come a long way but she wasn't sure he was ready to run an investigation. *But my opinion doesn't matter*. He approached and after a congenial smile to

Molly and Ari, he introduced himself to Gloria Rivera. He was always a snazzy dresser, and Molly realized he looked more like an attorney than a detective in his matching three-piece gray suit. They rode to the fifth floor and he led them to the law library. Molly absorbed the scene: shattered glass in the hallway, a scattered file folder, a slug in the hallway wall.

"The coroner estimates time of death between nine and midnight. The last person to see Mr. Guzman alive was Maria Hernandez, a cleaning lady who works the fifth floor. She said hello to him as she made her rounds. She was done by eight fifteen, and he was still here."

He pointed behind them. "We believe he left the library and went to his office for this file." He pointed to the folder on the floor. "When he returned with it, he apparently saw the gunman who fired through the glass. Mr. Guzman dropped the file and ran to the east stairwell."

The table in the small library looked as if someone had left just a moment ago. A legal tablet sat next to Guzman's phone alongside an open law book and another file. On top of the tablet was an expensive pen and reading glasses. There was no blood and no sign the gunman struggled with Guzman, thus substantiating Andre's theory.

Ari pointed at the tablet on the table. "What was Mr. Guzman working on?"

"That's interesting," Andre said. "He was taking notes on child custody, a case that involved someone named Bambi Wilkerson. That's her file on the table." He looked at Gloria. "Ms. Rivera, does that name mean anything to you?" Then he bent over to read the tab on the abandoned file lying in the hallway. "Or Mackenzie Dearborn?"

She shook her head. "We have over two hundred clients, and in the interest of full disclosure, I'm semi-retired. I only work three days a week. We were in the process of adding another name partner who will eventually take my place. You should really speak to the two candidates. My daily responsibilities have been drastically reduced and I'm only working with our probate lawyers."

Molly flipped to a new page of her notebook. "What are the names of those two attorneys being considered for partner?"

"Brantley Dalton and Christine Pierpont. Victor was their direct supervisor. They've both gone to court today, and they're in the middle of a very important trust case. Detective, I'd appreciate you interviewing them last. I can't imagine either of them having anything to do with this."

"Of course." He pointed and said, "Let's go this way." He took them to the east stairwell. "When Mr. Guzman reached the stairs, we determined that he didn't go down, but instead, he went up."

"Why would he do that?" Gloria asked, exasperated. "There's no one here at night, not even security. He knows that."

"Force of habit," Molly offered. "When the brain moves to survival mode, it connects with whatever is comfortable and habitual. I'm guessing he often went to the tenth floor for various reasons?"

"Yes," Gloria agreed, rolling her eyes. "The attorneys are primarily housed here on the fifth floor with their personal assistants. The paralegals and secretaries live on the tenth."

"You don't seem to like that arrangement," Ari remarked.

"Not in the least, but Victor insisted. And since I'm a part-time employee..." She didn't bother to finish the thought. It was clear who was in charge. "He created a caste system where the fifth floor got the better furniture, the nicer kitchen, and newer computers, all because they were attorneys. But attorneys need their paralegals. It was a ridiculous set-up and I told Victor that." She paused and said, "That was actually our fight yesterday morning. But one other thing, he never took the stairs. He was overweight and didn't exercise. When he threw that stairwell door open, it was probably the first time he'd ever seen the building staircase."

They took the elevator to the tenth floor and Gloria groaned when she saw the destruction to the cubicles. She gestured to the mess. "Why? Why would someone do this?"

Ari exchanged a glance with Molly, but they deferred to Andre.

"More than likely, Mr. Guzman knew his assailant. This was personal. Whoever is responsible wanted to make sure your firm was punished as well."

Molly turned to Gloria. "Can you think of anyone who might have a grudge against you?"

"To do this? No, I can't think of anyone this upset. Although Victor has had many threats." Realizing she'd just contradicted herself, she said, "I don't know. Perhaps."

"You mentioned no one worked late," Ari said. "That surprises me since I know many attorneys who do."

Gloria nodded. "Of course. Sometimes they do, but we encourage family time and personal time, so most everyone is always gone by eight." She stopped short. Then she said, "Well, it used to be important when Richard Dorn was alive."

"When did he pass away?" Andre asked.

"About four months ago. Ironically, he was working late one night and had a heart attack at his desk."

Andre motioned for them to follow him. Passing the kitchen's overturned dining tables and chairs, they arrived at the executive washroom. From the doorway Molly scanned the pedestal sinks, the two solid oak stalls with carved doors, and the settee in the corner. A cabinet stocked feminine products, lotions and colognes. The executives had everything they could ever need during the workday. She also noted puddles of water on the floor.

"We also found the bathroom had been vandalized," Andre continued. "Mr. Guzman hid in the second stall, and the killer shot him at point blank range. Then he took off Mr. Guzman's tie and stuffed it into the left sink drain before turning on the cold tap."

Andre discreetly handed Molly his iPad, allowing her and Ari to scroll through the crime scene photos taken prior to the removal of the body. There was no damage to the stall door, so the shooter must have coaxed him to open it before he shot him once in the head. He fell sideways and his body slumped halfway off the toilet. His face pressed against the sidewall, as if he were listening to a conversation in the next stall.

"Ms. Rivera, since this is the executive washroom, can we assume there are a limited number of keys?" Ari asked.

"Absolutely. Victor insisted. Isabelle will know exactly who had a key, but I'd guess that if you find someone with a key who shouldn't have one, you've found your killer." She glanced at the carnage around her and wiped tears from her cheeks. "Detective, do you need me for anything else? I'll make sure you're provided with everything you request, but I should brief the senior associates, deal with Victor's ex-wife, and change my clothes." She touched her temple as if it hurt.

"There is one more thing I need to ask, Ms. Rivera," Andre said slowly.

"You need to know where I was last night," she said flatly. He nodded and she rummaged through her handbag. "I understand." She pulled out a ticket stub to the Phoenix Symphony Orchestra and handed it to him. "I was there with my neighbor, Mrs. Claris Dow. I'm frequently her guest, and we've struck up a friendship with the couple that has season tickets next to her. I'm rather certain you'll know the husband's name, Judge and Mrs. Gil Nolan?"

"Yes, of course I know Judge Nolan," Andre said.

"He will tell you we arrived fifteen minutes before the overture, had a lovely conversation about the birth of their fourth grandchild and enjoyed the entire concert together. At the conclusion, since he is a gentleman, he insisted on accompanying Claris and me to my car at approximately ten thirty-five."

Andre scribbled furiously on his tablet, capturing all of the particulars. "Can you think of anything else we should know right now?"

"Just one thing." She pointed at Molly. "As the authority for this firm, Detective Williams, I'm placing full trust in Ms. Nelson and her company. I authorize her to act as my agent and receive any and all communications you would choose to share with me. I can provide my wishes in writing if the police need me to do so." She raised her chin regally. "Are we clear?"

"Very much so," Andre replied. "I would trust Molly with my life." He gave her a wink and added, "In fact, I have."

Once Gloria excused herself, Ari turned to Molly. "What do you think? Is she a suspect?"

Molly and Andre both shook their heads. "No," Molly said. "She was genuinely upset by the vandalism, and she's so far out of the profile type. She's retired. She's got a good life. Victor Guzman's death only hurts her. She'll probably have to manage the firm for a while. I doubt that was in her plans."

"Of course, she could've hired someone," Ari speculated.

Molly made a face. "Doubtful, but I guess it's a possibility."

"I agree," Andre said. "I'll check with Judge Nolan, but I'm sure he'll corroborate her story." Molly pointed at him and he quickly said, "I won't forget. I really will call the judge *today*."

Molly grinned at the inside joke. When Andre was a rookie detective, he'd neglected to follow up on a witness who turned out to be the killer. "So what else do you know?"

Andre leaned closer and whispered, "We haven't talked to many colleagues who liked Guzman."

Molly nodded. "We met one guy downstairs who said several attorneys were probably going to quit now that he's dead."

"But why now?" Ari asked. "If they hated him and now he's gone, wouldn't that make them want to stay?"

"Good question," Andre said, noting it on his tablet. He took them to the stairwell. "Now that Ms. Rivera has left us, let me give you the full run-down of what happened." He pointed at the slug lodged in the cement above the door. "Killer shot at Guzman but he missed. Also, notice the badge entry. The killer had a badge. That's how he got onto both floors."

"This would point to someone who works at the firm," Molly stated.

Ari looked toward the corners. "Are there any cameras in here?"

"No," Andre said. "Only in the elevators, and we reviewed the tape. No one rode up to the fifth floor. Whoever did this knew if he took the stairs, he wouldn't be on camera."

"What about the lobby? There should be some footage from the entrance," Molly said.

Andre scrolled through his notes. "Yes. A figure in a hoodie approached the building at eight fifty-eight. After six p.m. you have to use your badge to open the front door, and that is the only way into the building. So he had one, along with a washroom key."

"When did he exit after the shooting?" Molly asked.

Andre sighed in disappointment. "We're not sure about when, but we have a guess as to where. There's at least one exit without a camera, the door at the most northeastern corner of the tower. The camera malfunctioned a few months ago and the property owner is finally getting it fixed, but they're waiting on a part. Emails notified all the building tenants about the work so everyone could avoid the door."

"The timing seems quite coincidental," Ari commented.

"Definitely," Andre agreed.

"Did anyone exit after nine p.m.?" she asked.

Andre scrolled through his notes. "A few people. We're still identifying them. I'll send you the footage."

"Is there a way to monitor the badge reader?" Ari asked.

Andre grimaced. "No. In fact, building ownership has changed hands twice in the past three years. They can't account for all of the badges." He cleared his throat and looked back at his notes. "So the gunman entered through the front door and turned right. That would've been where he accessed the east stairwell. From there he goes up to the fifth floor to Guzman's office."

They walked down to the ninth floor. Another set of techs had just extracted a slug from the stairwell banister. He displayed the evidence bag to Andre.

"A thirty-eight," Molly said, peering through the plastic.

Andre pointed down. "We know he fired up from somewhere between the fifth and seventh floors, but missed."

"The key is *missed*," Molly said. "This gunman missed a lot. He isn't a pro or an experienced shooter, which is why I'm doubtful Gloria Rivera or anyone would've hired him."

"That's what I was thinking," Andre agreed. "He was standing in the law library. He had an open door a foot to the left, but he shot through the glass."

"He was nervous and inexperienced," Molly concluded.

Ari studied the hole in the staircase railing. "This is desperation. He shows up thinking he's just going to walk in and shoot Guzman, but Guzman's not where he expects him to be. Then Guzman surprises him and he shoots and misses. Guzman takes off and now the gunman's chasing him. His anxiety and anger are increasing."

"Have you found any other slugs?" Molly asked.

"No," Andre said. "Just the three: the one outside the law library, the one in the railing and the one above the tenth-floor stairwell door."

"And the one in Guzman," Molly added. "Can we go back to that bathroom, please?"

They returned as the techs were wrapping up. Molly stood in the hallway and pointed toward the west stairwell. "Here's what I don't understand. You're Guzman and you know this guy is after you. If you've made it this far, why don't you run down the stairs rather than hole up in a restroom?"

They all pondered the question. It was an odd choice. Ari pointed to the deadbolt. "If he hid in the washroom, he probably engaged the deadbolt. He thought he was safe because so few people have a key, right?"

"But it's nine thirty at night," Molly countered. "There's no one here. If I know I'm alone, then my best option is to get out. If I stay here, he's probably going to find me."

Andre whipped open his iPad and pulled up a photo of Guzman that clearly displayed his enormous potbelly. "Probably is the operative word. Look at this guy. He's already tired from running up five flights. What's the chance he can run down ten floors of stairs and not have a heart attack or get shot in the back?" He waved his finger. "And that's another thing. The gunman is in decent physical shape. He walks up five flights, chases Guzman and destroys the tenth floor before he shoots him."

Ari shook her head. She couldn't understand Guzman's logic. "Still, why would locking yourself in a bathroom be the preferred option? Unless you thought someone would save you."

"But there was no one else here," Andre said.

Ari squinted and pursed her lips. She'd learned to question the obvious. "Are we one hundred percent sure of that?"

Andre's shoulders sagged. "This is going to be a bitch," he muttered. "Forty employees on this floor alone. I'll get the security footage for the whole evening."

Molly chose her words and tone carefully. "Besides the security footage, you might want to talk to their IT department. See if anyone was logged on an office computer after eight forty-five."

"We'd planned on it," he said, smiling. "One more thing I want you to see, but let's take the long way so we can look at the cubicles."

Several techs were taking videos and photos and dusting the workspaces for prints. Most of the chairs were overturned and personal effects like photos, stress balls and supplies covered the floor.

Molly motioned to an untouched cubicle that belonged to Devin Davies. "Are you keeping track of which desks were vandalized and which ones were not?"

Andre nodded. "We are."

Ari scanned the nearby nameplates. "Where does Xavier Yanez sit?"

"Let me check. They sent me a floor plan and said it was current." He tapped on his iPad and started to walk toward a corner. "There." He pointed to a clutter-free desk near the back windows.

"Huh," Ari mused.

"We met Xavier downstairs," Molly explained. "He's only been here a couple of months. I wonder if the same is true for the other newer employees. Were their desks skipped?"

"We'll check that out," Andre said as he scribbled on the tablet. "Now, let me show you what used to be the copy machine."

In the copy room the top feeder was bent backward and barely attached to the machine. The smashed glass looked like a spider's web. The front panel doors were open. A chair's legs had been stuffed into the machine's main guts, and the inside was covered in a sticky brown substance that had dripped onto the floor.

"That is some serious workplace anger," Molly said.

Ari pointed to the brown puddle. "What is that?"

"It's a Coke," Andre replied. "Someone shook it up and sprayed it inside. The killer was bent on destroying this machine."

Ari's phone rang and she ducked into an empty office. "This is Ari Adams."

"Ari, it's Scott."

She automatically smiled. Scott Long was her newest client and a childhood friend. He'd asked her to help him sell his family home. "Hi, Scott. Are we still on for ten thirty?"

"Actually, that's why I'm calling. I don't think we need to meet."

"Why not?"

"I just got a call from my half-brother, Barry. He told me his side of the family was pulling out of the deal. They're not interested in selling the house anymore."

Ari knew there was a complicated and thorny family drama involving Scott, his brother and three half-siblings. She'd only seen a small slice of it growing up three blocks away, but she'd heard it had become incredibly nasty after their father had died. Their house in Glendale had sat empty for twenty years while the family bickered over an estate that included the house and a million dollar soda pop company named Fizz. A judge had sent them all back to mediation.

"Why are they pulling out?"

"Barry got a call an hour ago from a paralegal that's handling our case. She couldn't wait to tell him that our mediator, Victor Guzman, is dead! Can you believe it?"

Ari thought of the suits pacing the courtyard and talking on their phones. Apparently one of them had shared the news of Victor's demise with Barry. "Well, it's terribly tragic, but certainly your case will be reassigned, right? There are other good attorneys who can mediate."

Scott retorted, "Doesn't matter. The new lawyer could be Perry Mason and Barry wouldn't be happy. Victor was good. We *all* liked him. He was actually helping us trust one another, and that hasn't happened since we were kids. Anyway, Barry called Cal and Nobel in Florida, and their Florida attorney told them not to do anything until he reviewed the whole case."

Ari knew Cal and Nobel were Barry's brothers and Scott's half-brothers. Whereas Scott and Barry lived in Phoenix, the rest of the siblings were out of state.

Scott groaned. "This is so ridiculous. We're back to square one. Barry will search for another mediator, but it will have to be approved by Nobel and Cal. My half of the family is going to get screwed. Maybe I just need to accept that we're going to lose everything."

"No, that's horrible," she said automatically. She looked over at Molly and Andre, who were conferring with a crime scene technician. "Isn't there anything I can do to help?"

Silence ensued and she heard traffic in the background. He was obviously in his car. He suddenly laughed and said, "Well, there's one thing that would cause a complete reversal of fortune, but I don't think there's anything you can do about it."

"What is it?"

"Prove that my stepmother killed my mother."

CHAPTER THREE

Ari slammed on the brakes as a small pickup truck crossed in front of her. The angry driver flipped the bird as he sailed through the intersection. She glanced to her right and saw the stop sign.

"Damn."

He'd had the right of way and she'd almost hit him. She took a deep breath to calm her racing heart and drove deeper into historic Glendale, a suburb of Phoenix.

She had a valid excuse for her distraction. Three blocks east was her childhood home, and a half-mile away was the boarded up convenience store where her brother Richie had been killed during a robbery. The clerk said the robber panicked and shot Richie when he came around the corner of the candy aisle and surprised the guy. His killer had never been caught, and for reasons Ari couldn't explain, she held the city of Glendale responsible. She rarely sought Glendale clients, and while she'd sold many Glendale homes, she was always relieved when those houses closed and she could take a respite from touring the familiar streets. She was happy to help Scott sell his family home, but she wished it were in a different part of town.

Now her curiosity about his mother's death counterbalanced her anxiety of visiting Glendale. He'd agreed to keep the appointment and explain what was going on. "Maybe it will be therapeutic for me," he'd joked.

She and Richie had been Scott's neighborhood friends during much of their childhood. They'd never gone to the same school, but they always played together after school, on weekends and during the summers. She and Scott were the same age, and although Richie was three years younger, Scott had always accepted him as one of the gang. Then there was Blythe, Scott's gorgeous sister. She and her twin brother Carlin had moved home when their mother fell ill. They were both in college, but Blythe always made time to hang out with the three of them. They had been best friends—until their families suffered similar horrific losses within two weeks of each other.

Just prior to Richie's death, Scott's mother Henrietta died from a fall down a staircase. Within a few months of her death, his father, Wilfred Long Jr. had married Millicent Farriday, a worker at Fizz. Ari had never met Millicent, as her friendship with Scott had dissolved in her grief for Richie. Seeing Scott was too hard. Then her parents decided to move. They couldn't live in Glendale anymore. Scott and that summer became a distant black memory until Facebook. Ari and Scott had become Facebook friends, vowing to meet for coffee but never finding the time.

Ari had assumed Henrietta Long's death was an accident. She also knew her own mother adored Henrietta but had never cared for Millicent. Ari remembered overhearing a conversation between her mother and father where she was quite candid about her feelings regarding Scott's new stepmom. She'd called her an ice queen and a gold digger. Ari wondered if her mother ever suspected Henrietta's death was more than an accident.

She pulled up in front of a large brick home, a marriage of the popular bungalow style with Tudor revival. The wide porch and large windows often found in historic bungalows joined to a roof with several gables, adding to its unique exterior. There wasn't another home in historic Glendale like this one.

From her title search she knew Wilfred Long Sr. had built it in 1928; the historic registry aptly listed it as Long Manor. The Long family still owned it, but no one had actually lived in the house for over twenty years. She'd never been inside, even as a child, although she and Richie would sometimes sneak around the back and peek in the windows while they waited for Scott to come outside and play.

A wrought iron fence followed the perimeter of the entire property. It had been built to keep looters and vandals away. At least the heirs could agree on security, if nothing else. She remembered riding past the manor with Richie when they were kids. Sometimes they would cut across the lawn or hide behind the big eucalyptus tree during a game of cops and robbers. She noticed a small hole where a basement window had been kicked out, and she wondered if there were some critters down there.

She strolled to the west side and peered between the bars at the backyard. It was two parcels of land and the largest property in the Catlin Court Historic District. A garage sat behind the main house with a sunroom above it. Long rectangular dormer windows on each side of the house circulated the evening air during the searing summer months. Sheets of plywood had replaced all of the windows. She imagined kids had destroyed the glass panes a few times before they were removed.

She frowned at the garage door, its wood splintered and brittle, the paint chipped and shriveled. While the house's red brick had admirably withstood eighty years of Arizona sun and monsoon rains, the garage was a testament to the true neglect and abandonment that had occurred. Anger and sadness filled her heart, and she hoped to be part of the process of restoring Long Manor to its previous greatness.

A red Corvette rounded the corner and parked behind her 4Runner. Scott Long emerged, his cell phone against his ear. He waved but stayed near his car to finish the call. Dressed in business casual of chinos and a yellow polo shirt, his close-cropped sun streaked hair and tan suggested he spent his free time outdoors. He was one of the few boys who'd ever kissed her, and for most of that summer long before she'd known she was gay, she'd referred to him as her boyfriend. He'd moved back to the Valley about a decade ago to serve as the CEO of Fizz, but then he'd quit abruptly. He'd alluded to her that his departure was another footnote to the family drama.

"This doesn't concern you, Barry," he said loudly. "I'll talk with you next week. I've gotta go." By the time he'd pocketed the phone and joined her on the sidewalk, his scowl had morphed to a broad smile. Tucked under his left arm was an old leather photo album. She gave him a hug and then he stepped back to look at her. "Ari Adams, you're absolutely breathtaking."

"You're very kind, Scott. You don't look so bad yourself."

"Thanks. I try to stay in shape, but this family crap is killing me. My teenagers are easier to handle than my brothers." He took a deep breath and exhaled. "How about I tell you a story while we take a tour?" he asked, holding up the photo album. "I even brought pictures." He held out a ring filled with ancient keys, but among them was a modern silver key that fit the west gate padlock.

"You know, I've never really been in the house," Ari said. "I think a few times we stepped inside the backdoor but that was as far as we went."

Scott gasped in surprise. "Really? Why did I think you, me and Richie played in my room?"

"I don't know. I remember we always stayed outside."

"Huh." He paused and nodded. "It makes sense. Linnie, our cook, always wanted us to be outdoors in the fresh air. Then when Millicent came into the picture, she just wanted us gone and didn't care where we went."

He opened the photo album to an old black and white studio portrait. An austere couple stared into the camera. He wore a morning coat and she wore a wedding dress. Neither looked happy. In the next photo, they stood on the front steps of the newly constructed Long Manor.

"These are my grandparents, Wilfred and Victoria Long. They're the ones who built this house in 1928 and started Fizz at the old factory five blocks away."

"That building is condemned, isn't it?" Ari asked.

"It is, but we still own it. And it's been the center of our biggest fight. About ten years ago, my stepmother Millicent found a buyer who wanted the land, but not the building. Blythe flipped out. She caused a media ruckus and moved to have it declared historic. When that happened, the buyer walked away and Millicent never spoke to Blythe again."

"I think I saw that on the news," Ari said.

"You and all of Phoenix. Blythe was one of the most determined and focused people I ever knew. She was more like Grandpa than anyone. Anyway, it caused a huge rift between the two sets of kids. Now, no one will touch the property because it's too expensive to retrofit. The city of Glendale continues to look for an investor because it's an eyesore. Any chance you and your business partners would be interested?"

"I think we've got our hands full right now with two historic buildings," she said, grinning. "No one's lived here for twenty years, right?"

He nodded. "We've been in and out, but no one's lived here since Millicent moved us to Florida." He waved his hand and added, "But I'm getting ahead of myself."

They headed up the steps and through the backdoor which opened into a small room. A thick layer of fine dust covered everything: a round oak table, four matching chairs, and a delicate glass bowl in the middle of the table. She envisioned it filled with fruit. In the corner was a china cabinet and she was surprised to see a complete set of china staring dimly back at them through the grimy glass doors.

A carved chair rail connected once-white wainscoting and badly faded flower-print wallpaper that was probably quite lovely fifty years ago. A long plaster crack ran diagonally across the back wall, tearing through the paper mercilessly.

Scott pointed to the gash. "This has happened throughout the house in nearly every room. Without any climate control, the cracks were inevitable."

Ari frowned and looked at him sympathetically. "That's going to be expensive to fix, but I understand why you wouldn't want to leave the A/C on for twenty years."

Scott snorted. "What A/C? I could never talk the award kids into installing it."

Ari knew "award kids" was Scott's nickname for his half-siblings, Barry, Cal and Nobel, who'd all been named after book awards. "I'm afraid you'll have to add A/C. No house is going to sell in Phoenix without it. Even the preservationists understand that."

"I understand it, too. It was my father who was the original holdout, and then no one would pay for it when we all inherited the place." He gestured to the dust-laden table. "You probably remember the breakfast nook. It attaches to the kitchen so Linnie could easily serve, but it's also fitted for privacy." He pulled out a pocket door from inside the wall. "Even though this was designed for breakfast, we kids ate most of our meals here."

He turned a page of the photo album to a picture from the early fifties. A young man wearing a letterman's jacket stared into the camera like it was his best friend. He was handsome and self-assured, and Scott looked like him.

"That's my father, Wilfred Jr. Everyone called him Junior. He was the only child of my grandparents and the heir to Fizz." Scott turned the page to Junior's wedding photo. "This is my mother, Henrietta."

Junior towered over his wife, who had flowing blond hair, warm eyes and a tentative smile. It was obvious she didn't enjoy being photographed, but from the way she leaned in to Junior, Ari could tell they were in love.

"They both look very happy. When were they married?"

He thought for a moment. "1967." He turned the page to a collection of school photos. She laughed when she recognized him. "Yeah, yeah," he said. "This was the three of us, Carlin, Blythe and me."

The boys possessed their father's strong chin and lopsided smile, but Blythe bore little resemblance to either Junior or Henrietta. She seemed to be a very serious person, and Ari imagined the photographer, who Ari guessed was Henrietta, constantly had to coax her to smile. Only in the candid photos with Carlin did she appear to be at ease.

"Carlin and Blythe were twins, right?"

"Yes, nine years older than me. I was the surprise."

Scott turned the page to a large photo of the entire family at Christmastime. The decorated tree stood to the left as the five of them gathered on the sofa. Henrietta and Blythe sat in the center while the three Long men stood behind it. Junior rested his hand on Henrietta's shoulder, and both sons mugged for the camera behind a laughing Blythe. Their languid poses telegraphed their ease with each other.

"You always seemed so happy. This picture proves it."

Scott pursed his lips and nodded. "Part of the reason we were so close was because we all ate together in here." He pointed to the china cabinet. "Mom and Dad rarely wanted to use Grandma's china. It was reserved for the dining room. Then, when Millicent came along, everything changed. She was all about the dining room and insisted Dad buy her new china."

He opened the pocket door and they moved into a dust-filled kitchen, leaving tracks on the floor of a room that had never been remodeled. The mint-green paint appeared to match the accent tile of the backsplash. The floor and the counters were the same small white hex tile customary of the nineteen twenties. The cabinets had glass fronts and small latch handles. Like the china cabinet, all of the dishes and serving bowls sat ready to be used, save the dust. He motioned to the original Round Oak stove. Even with twenty years of grime, it looked practically new, a testament to whoever had once cleaned it.

"This is gorgeous," she gushed.

"Look at these." He picked up matching salt and pepper shakers that were part of the stove and blew off the dust. Sitting between them was a built-in timer.

She glanced at the sink. As if recently abandoned, a hand towel rested on the tile counter and a bottle of dishwashing soap and a sponge were next to the faucet. The compounds that had created the soap had separated after two decades, the bottom of the bottle dark and the top light. Clearly the house hadn't been fully cleaned out. She imagined if she opened the drawers she'd find more towels, kitchen gadgets, utensils and original Tupperware.

"There's a lot of stuff here," she commented, trying not to sound judgmental.

"Yeah," he admitted. "That's part of the story." He held up the bottle of dishwashing soap. "There are several science experiments throughout the house," he joked.

"I'm surprised the kitchen hasn't been remodeled," she said.

"That was because of my dad. My grandfather was incredibly proud of this house, and when Dad inherited it, he was committed to keeping it as original as he could as a tribute to Granddad." He shrugged. "Maybe that's weird, but as kids we understood. So there's no garbage disposal, no big pan drawers and not enough clearance for one of those huge refrigerators. Honestly, if we ever get to sell it, I hope whoever buys it will keep it like this."

"Is your current house historic?"

"Hell, no," Scott snorted. "I like my disposal." They both laughed and he added, "There aren't a lot of places left in the valley that tell the story of the past, certainly not my home in Scottsdale. This place is different."

"I get that," Ari agreed. "That's why I love my historic home."

The kitchen opened to the formal dining area, via a swinging door. An antique chandelier, its crystal darkened with dust, hung over a long cherry wood table. A large built-in china cabinet and buffet behind the head chair provided servants ample space to stage the various courses during dinner. The mint green walls matched the kitchen. A picture window streaked with dirt afforded a view of the backyard and the west side of the house. Even with the neglect of decades, it was light and airy, and she remembered interrupting Sunday dinner at least once. She'd come to the window and waved at Scott. He'd shaken his head sadly and returned to his dinner.

Another wide plaster crack on the interior wall exposed some wiring and the studs that framed the house. She wondered if the house was actually habitable or if they should phone an inspector.

"I'll give you the name of some reputable A/C companies and I know someone who's amazing at remodel," Ari offered. "She could do your plaster work."

Scott blinked. "She?"

"She," Ari laughed, thinking of Jane's handy dyke friend Teri, who'd completely remodeled Ari's historic home.

"Thanks," he replied as they stepped into the main entryway.

Ari admired the beautiful beveled lead glass front doors. A symmetrical design of intricate swirls and loops ensured new guests were impressed when they arrived.

Scott entered the living room. Ari's gaze was drawn to the fireplace.

"That's Italian brick," Scott explained. He pulled out a handkerchief and wiped away the dust so she could appreciate the rose-colored bricks as smooth as marble. "My grandparents honeymooned in Italy and Grandma fell in love with the look when she saw it in the hotel where they stayed." He pointed to the modern gas element and fireplace fender. "We had this updated in the seventies. Mom and Dad wanted to keep the place as original as possible, but they gave in on points of safety."

Ari turned and gazed at the eclectic collection of furniture covered in dusty transparent plastic. The pink Queen Anne sofa was circa nineteen forty, and the coffee table was midcentury modern. The overstuffed pea-green velvet chair looked terribly out of place next to the long orange sofa Ari guessed was from the fifties. It seemed Wilfred Sr. and his wife Victoria had put their official and permanent stamp on Long Manor, and no one—not Junior, Henrietta or later Millicent—had dared to change it, even after their passing.

Ari glanced at the *People* magazines splayed on the coffee table. She chuckled at a July nineteen ninety-two edition featuring the Clintons with a headline about how they stayed in love. Another cover showed Princess Diana in mourning black, attending her father's funeral. The haphazard arrangement of the magazines and an ashtray half full of cigarette butts gave the impression that someone had left to run an errand but would be returning soon.

Scott stepped to a door that led out to the front porch. It was also as decorative as the main front door, but not as large. "My grandparents believed there were different types of visitors," he explained. "If you were extremely close or well-known to the family, you came to this side door because you knew it existed. If you were a stranger or a salesman, you'd knock on the main door. Where you knocked determined whether anyone would answer."

"I like it," Ari replied. She peered across the porch at an identical door. "What's that one for?"

"Follow me," Scott said. They crossed the entryway and headed into an expansive room with a corner window that wrapped around the south and east wall. "This was our father's office, and it was originally Grandpa's office, too." Ari peered out the windows that faced downtown Glendale and Murphy Park. "Grandpa wanted to watch Glendale grow, at least that's what Dad always told us. He also had his own exit. Sometimes it was impossible to tell if he was here or away, unless you went outside and walked to the window."

Ari raised an eyebrow. "No offense, but it sounds a little sneaky to me."

"It's interesting you mention that." Scott flipped the album open to a spread of photos showing Junior greeting employees, working at his desk and observing the assembly line. "My grandfather died in sixty-four, and my father became CEO at twenty-nine. My parents got married and we came along. It seemed like the perfect life for my dad. Everyone at the factory loved him. He'd walk to work every day and greet all of the shopkeepers. The story goes that he'd often chat with the mayor when he walked through the town square. He was an incredibly friendly guy."

She admired the old roll top desk and resisted the urge to pull up the accordion door and snoop inside. Offices were often the best places to glean secret information, but unlike the rest of the house, only the dusty shelves remained. The office had been thoroughly purged of documents and books.

"Did you ever meet either of my parents?"

She nodded. "Oh yeah. I met your mom the first day I ever knocked on your door. She asked who I was, where I lived, and who my mother was." They both laughed and she added, "They became friends."

His face brightened. "That's right! I went to the drive-in with your family a few times."

"Uh-huh. And I remember your dad playing catch with us sometimes. He invited Richie and me to tag along when he took you places."

He offered a sad smile and looked around. "Before we go upstairs, let's spend two minutes in the basement just so you can say that you've seen it. The smell is god-awful." They returned to the kitchen and went through a doorway into the laundry room. Scott opened a door and they descended the narrow stairs. The pungent odor of cat urine became almost unbearable by the time they reached the last step. The room was a long rectangle, hung with cobwebs, its floor scattered with feces. Ari imagined its only purpose was storage and laundry. A vintage washer and dryer sat against the far wall next to a metal door, which she knew was the laundry chute. A ray of light peered through the entry hole Ari had noticed when she arrived. She pointed it out to Scott as the reason for the overwhelming stench of cat pee.

Cardboard boxes filled the walls, the weathered wooden shelves sagging under their weight. It wouldn't be much longer before the entire structure collapsed. A few random boxes were strewn about the floor, as if someone had rummaged through them for something specific and hadn't bothered to put them back.

"This is where Millicent stashed the stuff she wouldn't let us take when we moved, as well as all of Carlin and Blythe's stuff that they left behind." He pointed to the boxes on the floor. "As you can see, over the years we retrieved a few things. I know Carlin's been down here once as well as Barry."

She peered into the box and saw several antique toys including a metal fire truck and a toy piano. "Were these your dad's? They're probably worth some money."

"Yup," he said, pulling an ancient cap pistol from one of the boxes on the shelf. "There's a lot of good stuff in here, but since all of us own it, anytime one of us wants or needs something from these boxes, it takes an act of Congress to grant permission for entry into the house."

"When did Millicent pass away?"

"About six years ago—brain aneurism."

"She was rather young, wasn't she?"

"Yeah, she was only fifty-two. Carlin said it was karma."

They climbed out of the basement, and she followed him up the main staircase. It opened to a long hallway that split the bedrooms between northern and southern exposure. "I know you'll remember this room," he said, leading her into the first bedroom next to the staircase, "or at least the window."

It had been his bedroom years ago, but more recently it had functioned as a sewing room. A sun-faded mannequin stood in the corner and a worktable filled half the space. Unlike the rest of the house, this room had been thoroughly purged. Only the large pieces of furniture were left behind.

"When Millicent arrived, I moved across the hall so she could have this room for sewing since it's a little bigger." Ari peered out the window at the ground below. When she and Richie came over to play, they would often stand in the yard and toss pebbles at the window until Scott appeared. His room faced the garage.

Another memory surfaced. "Didn't you have a relative that lived with you for a while?"

He laughed and ruefully shook his head. "Yes, our cousin Glenn came to stay with us that summer. His mother suddenly dropped him off and drove away. She didn't come back until Labor Day. Said she couldn't handle him. Mom and Dad couldn't handle him either until he found the movie camera and his obsession. He had that camera in his hand from sunup to bedtime. When Glenn left, Dad joked he had enough film to remake *Gone with the Wind*."

"He was…challenged, wasn't he?"

"Yes. Now he would be labeled as highly functioning autistic. His room was actually across the hall, but most mornings I woke up with that camera in my face. Scared me shitless. Sometimes he'd just sit on his bed and look out the window. I don't think he liked being alone. Eventually he moved in here but he was not a good roommate."

She reached back twenty-four years and saw a pudgy boy with sandy hair. She couldn't recapture his face, but then it seemed he always had the viewfinder against his eye.

"Whatever happened to Glenn? Do you still keep in touch?"

Scott lowered his gaze and shook his head. "No. His mom was my mother's sister. When she finally returned to take him home to California, she learned her sister was dead, and she was in quite a state. They left and I never saw Glenn again." He looked away. "I always felt bad for him. He was a great kid."

"So you don't know what became of him?"

He took a deep breath and said, "Several years after Blythe moved to California, she looked up my aunt. Glenn had moved into a group home when he turned eighteen. I don't know what happened to him after that. I think he's still alive, but I really don't know."

He led her past the other rooms. The two with the northern view were filled with boxes. The upstairs bathroom was painted a soft yellow, faded with age. A large makeup case sat on the counter. She pointed and asked, "Is that really twenty-year-old makeup?"

"It belonged to Blythe."

"Scott, I hope I don't offend you, but why didn't you guys finish cleaning this place out?" She gestured to the case. "Maybe throw away the makeup that no one would ever dare put on her face. Empty the ashtrays?"

"That would require us all to be in the same room or trust those leading the clean-up. We're not there yet. We'd hoped Victor could've helped us get to the point where we could empty ashtrays without supervision."

"I'm sensing some sarcasm and frustration."

"Just a bit," he said, laughing. He motioned for her to go into the last room, his parents' room. It enjoyed a southern exposure with wrap-around windows. French doors on the west wall led to a tiny balcony. She imagined the sunsets were beautiful back when the trees weren't quite so tall. She glanced at the Spartan furnishings—a dresser, a man's valet and two nightstands. A double photo frame sat on one of them, and through the dust she could see they were Carlin and Blythe's respective graduation photos. They wore their robes, but their expressions were completely opposite. He wore a broad smile while her lips remained in a tight line. Ari was momentarily reminded of Wilfred Sr. and Victoria's wedding photo.

"Where are your brother and sister now?"

"Carlin lives in Wyoming. Blythe passed away three years ago. She killed herself," he said flatly. "She always battled addiction and depression. Left behind two kids, but they're both adults."

"I'm so sorry to hear about Blythe," Ari said. "I only met Carlin once, but Blythe was always so nice."

Ari realized the graduation photos were the only pictures in the whole house. They had been abandoned, just like the kitchen cleaning products, furniture and miscellaneous. "I assume there's a reason these photos were left behind," she said gently.

"Yeah," he said. "Their graduation was really the beginning of the end for our family."

CHAPTER FOUR

"Scrappy" was the word that came to Molly's mind when Isabelle Medina joined her and Andre in the law firm's conference room. She was short and wiry. Her black hair laid flat against her head in a gentleman's cut. As the office manager, she had a position of power, but as she yanked the chair out from under the table, Molly pictured her dropping into it and draping one leg over the arm like a drug kingpin sitting on a throne. Her gestures and facial expressions lacked refinement and polish, suggesting she was just a step removed from being a badass on the streets. And when she fidgeted with her simple gold necklace, her shirt collar slid to the right and Molly saw the outline of a tattoo. She wondered how many tattoos covered her body and noted the long-sleeved dress shirt. They were interviewing her first since she'd found the body.

"Thank you for meeting with us, Ms. Medina," Andre began.

"Sure," Isabelle replied.

"Can you please explain how you found the body?"

She recounted her arrival at work and the discovery of Victor Guzman. As she spoke, Molly crosschecked her story with Gloria Rivera's and saw they matched.

"Please describe your relationship with Mr. Guzman," Andre continued.

Isabelle shrugged. "We were professional to each other."

"But you didn't like him," Andre confirmed.

When her gaze jerked up, Molly saw the look she'd seen so many times when she'd interviewed gang members—pure hatred of authority. It made her wonder how Isabelle had ascended ten stories to a prestigious law firm. She kept her hands folded in front of her, and Molly noticed several of her knuckles were bandaged.

"No," she said tersely. "I didn't respect him. He treated the paralegals and secretaries like they were crap." She turned slightly and looked at Molly. "I didn't wish him dead, but I'm not broken up about it."

"Where were you last night?" Andre asked.

"Out."

"Where's out?" he pressed.

Isabelle's shoulders tensed and she licked her lips before she said, "Just out. Walking."

"Was anyone with you?" Molly offered.

"No. I was alone."

Andre leaned on the table. "Where were you walking? Often we can pull camera footage and verify your story that way."

Her hard gaze met his. "I don't remember."

"Ms. Medina, I'm trying to help you, in case you don't understand that. The goal is to verify your alibi so we can remove you from the suspect list."

She drummed her fingers on the table and Molly pointed at her knuckles. "Bar fight?" she asked casually.

"No, I burned them on the stove when I was making tea," she said dryly.

Molly had seen bandaged knuckles many times. She pulled out her phone and played a hunch.

"Did you happen to be serving the tea to a guest?" Andre proffered. "Maybe someone who could verify your whereabouts last night?"

Isabelle scowled and turned away. "No," she snapped. "Do you have any other questions, Detective?"

"I want to know if you won or lost against Phoenix Fireball," Molly said, handing her phone to Andre. "It seems Isabelle the Hell is actually Ms. Medina's alter ego. She's one of Arizona's best MMA fighters." Molly looked at her with sincerity and said, "You've never lost. That's impressive."

Isabelle threw up her hands and popped out of the chair. She became a ball of nerves that couldn't sit still. She paced the length of the table and stared at the floor. "That doesn't have anything to do with the work I do in this law office," she insisted. "Please tell me this conversation doesn't leave this room."

"How long have you been cage fighting?" Andre asked.

She turned and pointed. "It's not cage fighting. We're not dogs or roosters. It's MMA, Mixed Martial Arts. And I've been doing it for about three years. I mean, I've been fighting for *money* for three years. I've been fighting all my life. It paid for college, and now that I've got my cyber security degree, I'll be hanging up my gloves for good." She turned to Molly. "And to answer your question, I won on Tuesday. Fireball's not in my league. I'm the second best in the Southwest, right behind Susan the Sniper."

"Look, Isabelle," Molly began, "we're not trying to get in your business or expose you. If you can account for the time, there's no issue. And we're not reporting this to Gloria Rivera."

Isabelle dropped into the chair. "I'm not worried about Gloria. She's cool. It's the Board of Directors. They're very conservative and they would find a reason to fire me immediately if they knew about my second job."

Andre looked at Molly. "Can they do that?"

"Of course," Isabelle answered. "This is a private company, and it's a *family* law practice. The board thinks that means we're all one big happy family. We play softball and work in the soup kitchen," she said in a singsong voice. "Richard Dorn wanted us to be one big legal version of *The Waltons*."

"Is there precedent for this type of firing?" Molly asked.

"Oh, yeah," Isabelle said. "There was an attorney who had a second job working at a strip club. He was dancing to pay off his student loans. A paralegal happened to come into the club for a bachelorette party and saw him."

"But it was okay for her to be there for the bachelorette party?" Molly countered.

"I know! Right?"

The room went silent. Isabelle rubbed her eyes as she decided how much to tell. She looked around the table. "Is this being recorded?"

"No," Andre answered.

"Here's the other problem," she said. "I didn't have my fight until ten. I was at the club, but everybody's in or out. I don't have a girlfriend or a best friend who was with me the whole time."

Andre slid a piece of paper and a pen toward her. "Write down a few names and phone numbers of anyone who can verify your whereabouts from eight thirty to midnight."

She opened her contacts on her phone and scribbled several names and pushed the paper back. "I don't know many phone numbers. It's not like they come over for tea."

All three of them chuckled. Molly made a note to check her background. "Can you think of anyone who had a serious disagreement with Mr. Guzman recently? Maybe shouting or verbal threats?"

She closed her eyes briefly and refocused. "There were two," she said, leaning back. "I go up and down the five flights of stairs all the time. As I was coming down last week, I heard one of the attorneys hoping to make partner talking on the phone in the stairwell. She said, 'If Victor thinks he's getting anything else, he's mistaken. I'll kill him first.' She saw me, said, 'I gotta go,' hung up, and scowled at me before she went back inside."

"Who else?" Andre prompted.

"The ex-husband of a current client. His name is Lonnie Wilkerson."

"That's Bambi Wilkerson's ex?" Andre confirmed.

"Yeah. He's left threatening messages for Victor. Said he was going to get him. Even showed up downstairs, yelling and screaming at security. The police removed him and the firm got a restraining order. Victor wasn't even here when it happened, but he got his jollies later watching the security video."

Molly flipped back a page. "What can you tell us about Mackenzie Dearborn?"

"She's a schoolteacher who hired Victor as her divorce attorney. I did the initial intake interview myself. She said she needed a great attorney because her ex-husband, a guy named Carlos Pino, was going to accuse her of child abuse. She said it so matter-of-factly I was stunned. And I've seen a lot. She immediately said it wasn't true, but she knew he wanted full custody, so she was sure he'd say anything. She said *he* was the abuser. Victor took the case and the hearing is in two weeks."

"So both the Dearborn and Wilkerson cases will be reassigned?" Andre asked.

"Yes. Probably to Christine."

Molly rested her chin in her upturned palm. "Where did you get the nickname, 'The Hell?'"

A real laugh cracked the tension in her shoulders. "Mr. Dorn gave me that nickname after he hired me. When I got here and saw how much wasn't getting done and how few rules people followed, I had this tendency to say, 'What the Fuck?' He suggested I change that to 'What the Hell,' which was more acceptable. So I did. Then I took it for my fighting name."

"So your job is to clean up the messes others make," Andre suggested.

Isabelle smiled, pleased by the summation. "It's part of what I do. No one was following office procedures. They weren't arriving on time or filing documents the right way. It was amazing the firm stayed afloat. But no one wanted to be the bad guy and call out the rule breakers. I don't have a problem with that."

Andre asked, "Is it your responsibility to issues badges and keys?"

"It is. I have some HR functions to my job."

"Is anyone's badge or key to the executive washroom missing?"

At the mention of the washroom, Isabelle stifled a laugh and bit her lip.

"Did I say something funny?" he asked mildly.

"Yes, but you don't know it," she retorted. "There are several missing badges, keys or both."

"Do you have a list?" Molly asked.

"Nope. No list." She looked directly at Molly and crossed her arms. "But if there were a list, Victor Guzman would be at the top of it. He reported his badge missing four days ago. I had to give him a temporary one."

"So Mr. Guzman's badge was missing," Andre confirmed.

"Yup. And as for the executive washroom, Victor may have thought only *executives* had keys, but really everyone on the floor had one." Isabelle smiled when their faces telegraphed their distress. "Sorry. I guess you'll just have to do your jobs."

Andre offered a stern expression. "Ms. Medina, you might not want to gloat too much just yet."

Her smug face turned suspicious. "Why?"

He leaned back and crossed his arms, mirroring her pose. "Well, if you're responsible for cleaning up messes, and if the killer knew you'd be the first person in the office, maybe he or she stuffed the tie in the drain and vandalized the copy machine to get back at you."

She pondered the idea and stroked her chin. "Hmm. Didn't think of that. I suppose that could be true."

"Who has a grudge against you?" Molly asked.

Isabelle looked through the glass and pointed at the maze of cubicles. "They all do."

"How likely is it that we'll find people at this club to substantiate Isabelle's alibi?" Andre asked Molly. He strode across the conference room to a snack stand for a bottle of water and some nuts. They were between interviews, waiting for Hannah Pence, Victor's personal assistant, to return from lunch.

"I'm not sure," Molly said, stretching. "But you need to run her profile. When she said she's been fighting all her life, I'm thinking she's a foster kid, which means it's likely she has a record."

"Could be," he agreed.

She held up her hands. "Oops. Sorry. I promised I wouldn't tell you how to do your job. My bad."

"It's okay," he said with a grin. After a pause he said, "I know I've still got stuff to work on, but I think I've really improved, don't you?"

"Yeah," she said honestly. "I do." She shifted the conversation back to business. "Have the techs found anything at Victor's apartment?"

He shook his head. "No such luck. The focus has been on his study, but there's nothing related to work. It's like he left it all here every night."

"Have they unlocked his personal computer?"

"Still working on it. Unlike most of America, Victor used a sixteen-character password he must have memorized. They haven't found a hard copy anywhere."

"Then there's got to be something on that machine that's worth remembering all those characters."

Andre smiled. "Absolutely."

"Did you get copies of the Wilkerson and Dearborn files?"

Andre nodded and sifted through several papers. He found both and handed them to her while he summarized. "Bambi's husband had one arrest for domestic violence. He's on the road as a truck driver most of the time, so that probably helps him stay out of too much trouble."

She skipped over the legal precedent Victor had included and found an ER report. "Most recently, it looks like Lonnie took their son Todd to the ER for a fractured wrist. The ER doctor, a Ross Bernard, noted multiple contusions near the break area."

"He's suggesting the mom grabbed him in such a way that he broke his wrist."

"Yes." She sifted through the rest of the paper. "Are there any photos?"

"No, and what's interesting are Victor's notes." He pointed to the comments and underlines Victor had made with a purple pen. "I think Victor was questioning whether this really happened. Take a look on the back flap," he directed.

An envelope was taped to the back of the thick file marked *Confidential*. She opened it and found a dossier from Daly Investigations. Pete Daly, a former Phoenix cop had served as the P.I. for Guzman, Rivera and Dorn up until his retirement. "This is interesting. Dr. Bernard is trying to finish his residency. He was dismissed from his last hospital for incompetency. He'd failed to order a test that the attending doctor requested. The next day the patient wound up in surgery because his appendix had ruptured."

She picked up the other file and read the initial notes. "Both are women fighting for custody of their children. Wilkerson's court date is still way out, but Dearborn's case goes to court in two weeks. There's nothing else at all." Her gaze flitted between the file folders. She closed them and held one in each hand.

"What are you doing?"

She set them down, side by side on the table. "Maybe it's nothing, but the Dearborn case is older and it's about to go to court. Yet, the file is half as thick as the Wilkerson file. Why is that?"

Andre's brow furrowed. He opened both files and they went page by page. "There's stuff missing from the Dearborn file," he concluded. "There's only a few notes from Victor and hardly any witness statements. Court is two weeks away and it seems like nobody's done any work on this case."

"So assuming they did the work for all of the billable hours listed here on the inside flap, where the hell is the rest of the file?"

CHAPTER FIVE

Scott led Ari across the dead grass toward the garage and continued his story. "So my mom got sick. She was diagnosed with colon cancer in November of 1991 and she was dead by August of '92. She'd never had a colonoscopy and it was stage four by the time she went to the doctor with symptoms. It had spread to her liver and lungs. She did the chemo and pills, but she just wasted away. Carlin and Blythe moved home to help Dad and me. Blythe gave up a scholarship at Berkeley to be here. That's how close we were." He exhaled and looked up at the sunroom. "Mom moved up there because she couldn't deal with the world and her pain at the same time. I'm sure it was hardest on my dad, but he did the unthinkable and took a mistress, Millicent, who later became his wife."

He glanced at her shocked face. "I know. We were too young to hear the sordid details, but that's why they got married so quickly after Mom died."

"That explains a lot," Ari said. "My mother wasn't very fond of Millicent."

He snorted. "She wasn't the only one." He opened the album again to a picture of a pretty redhead seducing the camera with her good looks. "Millicent worked in the factory, but she also had a part-time job as a waitress at the Gaslight Inn, the old historic hotel on Glendale Avenue. Apparently, my dad would show up after work but before her shift started. They'd spend an hour in one of the rooms and then he'd come home to us."

"How long did this go on?"

"No one really knows, and I'm guessing the owner of the Gaslight, a guy named Michaels, kept his mouth shut for the right price. People talked, but since Michaels and Dad were friends, it was never confirmed. Dad was in his early fifties and Millicent was only in her twenties. I'm sure Dad was lonely, but still…"

A metal clasp with a padlock had been added to the old door. He unlocked both, which opened to a steep staircase. "Before we go in, if you look at this wall, you'll see the remains of the original staircase. It used to be outside and there was a doorway right there."

She looked closely and could see the faint outline of the jamb. "Why did you move it inside?"

"That's part of the story," he said sadly.

He flipped a switch and an overhead fluorescent work light cast a dingy glow on the dusty space. The bottom floor was a garage with an old-fashioned wooden door that worked on a pulley system. A row of old paint cans lined the walls and three foldable tables and chairs were stacked in the back. It was mostly free from clutter except for some cobwebs in the corner.

They slowly ascended the steep staircase to the sunroom. The air immediately changed and a musty smell made her cringe. Dust swirled in front of her, as if it were upset that it had been disturbed. A smattering of what looked to be recent footprints on the dusty wooden floor suggested others had toured the property, perhaps even Victor Guzman.

Stacks of boxes created a maze. Someone had written a general description of each box's contents on the side. Most said *Photos* but there was a small stack of boxes labeled *Glenn's Movies*.

"This is where my mother spent the last year of her life. She came up here and became a recluse." He pointed to a door in the corner. "We had a small bathroom and sink installed, and Linnie brought out her meals and books to read. All of her friends abandoned her. No one came to see her. It was awful."

She remembered Henrietta staring out one of the big windows while they played below. "What did your father think about her moving out here?"

"He didn't seem to care," he said abruptly. "He had Millicent." They let the flurry of dust carry the statement away before he said, "Let's go back downstairs."

After Scott relocked the garage, he opened the photo album again and flipped through several pages until he found an old picture that showed the exterior staircase. "After my mom took ill and moved up there, she made a point to see us. Every morning she'd come down and join us for breakfast."

Ari noted the staircase was as steep as the interior one they'd just climbed to the sunroom, but it was rickety and splintered. She imagined what it would've been like for Henrietta to traverse the steps in pain.

"She'd have breakfast with us kids and hear about our day. Then she'd go back upstairs, and most of the time we wouldn't see her again until the next morning. It was a routine that never failed." He turned to her and asked, "Do you remember the walkway that cut through the yard and the rose bushes?"

"I do," she said, as the memory of the brick path came back to her. "We always played by the tree and Blythe would remind us not to hit the rose bushes with our ball."

"Mom loved her rose garden, but it was out in the front yard. She wanted roses in the back, so Dad had the walkway built and rosebushes planted. On the days when she felt well enough, which were few and far between, she could tend the roses. She belonged to the Glendale Rose Society for many years. She won awards for her flowers."

Ari looked closely at the old photo and saw the walkway between the rosebushes, but the yard now didn't yield a trace of either.

"At some point," Scott continued, "Blythe figured out Dad was having an affair, and she told Mom. Then Mom and Dad had a huge fight in the sunroom one day, but all the windows were open and Blythe just happened to be standing underneath one of them. Mom told Dad that if his daughter could figure it out, so could the town. It could ruin Fizz since the company billed itself as a wholesome family-owned business. Remember, back in the eighties, Phoenix was twice as conservative as it is now. Dad agreed to end the relationship, and Blythe figured Dad would just pay her off to get rid of her.

"Then one morning I came down for breakfast with Glenn and Mom wasn't there. When Blythe came down and didn't see her, she went out the back door and screamed. We ran outside with Linnie and found Mom in a crumpled heap at the base of the stairs. We hadn't seen her because of the rose bushes. Linnie immediately pulled Glenn and me back into the house. Then she called Dad who'd already left for work, and Carlin and Blythe stayed with her."

She touched her heart. "I can't imagine how traumatic that must have been for you."

For a moment he was unable to speak. He wiped tears from his eyes and composed himself. "Horrible for me, but worse for Glenn. At least I had the mental capacity to understand what happened. He went into some kind of trance." He took a breath and continued. "The coroner later ruled she died from a broken neck due to accidentally falling down the steps."

"Why was he so sure it was an accident?"

"Both Linnie and my father had seen her misstep and nearly fall before. They'd begged her not to go down the steps by herself, but she was stubborn. Every morning she did it alone. That morning there'd been one of the early monsoons peculiar to Phoenix. The wind was howling and the thunder and lightning were incredibly loud. There was water on the steps, too. So, it just seemed obvious that she'd slipped."

He sighed as he turned a page in the album to an eight-by-ten wedding picture of a middle-aged Junior and young Millicent. "Just two months after my mom died, Dad introduced us to Millicent and dropped the bombshell that they'd gotten married. He never talked to us about it. He didn't invite us to the wedding. They just went to the courthouse one day." He paused and wiped a hand over his face. "Carlin and Blythe had a terrible fight with Dad about a month after Millicent moved in. They left and never came back. I was too young to know any better, and Millicent liked me. I needed a mother, so we got along."

"And then your Dad and Millicent started a family?"

He turned to the next page of the album, which was filled with school photos of three children: three redheads with Junior's lopsided smile. "Yup. Three boys named after literary awards. Millicent loved books, especially children's books. The oldest is Newberry, but everyone just calls him Barry. Then there's Nobel and Caldicott, or Cal. Each one eighteen months apart from the next."

"They're much younger, right?"

"Barry's only twenty-four. He's the one who lives in Phoenix and works for a home health company. Nobel and Cal stayed in Florida with Millicent. Both of them are students at the University of Florida. We all got along okay. I was sort of a part of their second family, but I didn't see Carlin and Blythe for years."

He poked at a weed on the ground with his shoe and couldn't look at her. "Dad never got over what happened—Mom dying and then Blythe and Carlin leaving. He was heartbroken, even though he had three other children and a new wife. He was never the same. When he died in '96 , Blythe and Carlin didn't bother to call Millicent or me. They just showed up at the reading of the will. He left the soda company to Millicent, but he left the *house* to the six kids, with the stipulation that only adult children could participate in decisions regarding the house. Minors would be represented by Millicent until they came of age."

"So really, he left the house to Millicent, Carlin and Blythe."

"Yeah. The company was a mess. Dad started to lose it at the end. Carlin tried to run it after Dad died, but Millicent was always undermining him, so he left again and moved to

Wyoming. Then the economy shifted and now Fizz is a breath away from bankruptcy."

He sighed. "Back to the story. After dad died, Millicent just wanted out of Arizona. As hard as she'd tried over the years to break through to the upper echelon of Glendale society, she wasn't accepted. They all knew her as the gold-digging mistress. She wanted to sell the house, but Carlin and Blythe wouldn't agree. So she packed up the award kids and me, because I was only fourteen, and literally walked out. She left the dirty laundry, the cigarette butts, all of it."

"Including Carlin and Blythe's graduation photos."

"Yes. And once we all became adults, no one could agree about selling. No one wanted to live here so it's sat empty. Poor Long Manor has been the rope in an endless tug-of-war game."

She looked at the garage and said, "I guess you were stuck in the middle as well."

He shrugged. "For a while. But eventually it was the three of us against the three of them. I turned eighteen and headed to Wyoming to be with Carlin. Eventually I came back here." He closed the photo album and folded his hands in front of him. "Then Blythe committed suicide. She'd always been troubled and she just couldn't handle it anymore. She left two grown children who stand to inherit some of the Long estate if our side of the family can ever get anything."

"Why do you believe your mother was murdered?"

"I visited Blythe in California about a month before she killed herself, and she told me a story." He pointed to a yellow house across the street. "Do you remember who lived there?"

Her memory saw a balding man waving his fist. "I can't think of his name, but didn't he chase us out of his yard whenever we played cops and robbers?"

He nodded. "Ned Beaton. His son Garrett moved in when his old man took sick, and he kept the house after Ned died." They both looked over at the unkempt yard. The only green was the tall weeds that flourished after monsoon season. "According to Blythe, the day after Millicent married Dad, Blythe was outside unloading groceries from the car, and Beaton came across the street. He walked right up to her and said, 'You know, she killed her.' Blythe automatically asked, 'What are you talking about?' And he said again, 'She killed her.' Then he walked back across the street."

"I'm assuming he meant Millicent killed your mother," Ari clarified.

"Yes."

"He said nothing else, just that?"

"Blythe asked him to come back, but he just waved at her and said, 'I thought you should know.'"

Ari exhaled. "Wow. What did your sister do with that information?"

"Nothing. Until she told me. I guess she tried to talk to Beaton again about it, but he acted like he'd never said it. She let it drop and moved out. Went to California for a new life. I guess she figured it wouldn't have brought our mother back anyway."

"Did she say anything to Carlin?"

"No, I asked her that. Angry as she was about Dad's marriage to Millicent, Carlin was angrier. He would've probably killed Millicent himself. I think that's why Blythe never told him."

"How would Carlin react to the idea of me looking into your mother's death?"

Scott pursed his lips and shifted his feet. "I honestly don't know. I'll wait to see if there's anything to tell him."

"Will you tell the award kids?"

"I already mentioned it to Barry. You heard the tail end of my conversation with him. He was worried you'd steal something." Ari chuckled and he said, "None of them will care. They don't think you'll be able to find anything."

Ari tried to put all of the puzzle pieces together. "So you're wondering now if it really was murder. How would proving this help your situation with the house?"

"It would help the house and the company. Fizz is in trouble and Barry won't let me near it, since Millicent specifically gave it to Barry, Nobel and Cal in her will. They've hired various people to run it, but it's tanking. I've got my own data tech business, but the idea of Fizz going bankrupt just breaks my heart. If we could prove Millicent murdered my mother, my attorney thinks she could get the whole will thrown out and we would all inherit equal shares. That would include Blythe's two children who are over twenty-one."

"Ah," Ari said. "It's not six votes. It's seven. And you have yourself, Carlin, and Blythe's two kids. You have four of them."

For the first time since Scott had opened the photo album, he smiled. "I do."

CHAPTER SIX

The conference room door swung open and a woman with a long graying ponytail hurried inside. "I'm so sorry to keep you waiting," she panted. "I got stuck out by the elevators—I don't have my badge. I had to wait for someone to open one of the doors onto the floor." She took a deep breath. "Again, so sorry. Where would you like me to sit?"

"Right here is fine." Andre directed her to the chair Isabelle Medina had vacated. "This is Molly Nelson, head of Nelson Security."

"Oh, I know your company," Hannah said, shaking Molly's hand earnestly. "There's been a big brouhaha about what we should pay you."

"Oh, really?" Molly replied, unable to hide her surprise. "Then I'll hope it's the amount Gloria Rivera mentioned this morning."

Realizing her mistake, Hannah said, "I'm sure. Sorry, I just run amok sometimes. Confidentiality is my growth area," she added embarrassedly. "But I'm a go-getter. That's what Victor says." She folded her hands in front of her, adopted a serious expression and said, "Fire when ready."

Just as Molly was about to ask the first question, Hannah again jumped in, "I'm guessing you want to know where I was last night, right? What's my alibi?"

Andre nodded. "That's a good place to start."

She held up a finger. "I brought my date book."

Hannah lifted an enormous purse from the floor and dropped it on the table with a thud. She rummaged through it, tossing out a half-eaten candy bar with a long hair stuck to it, a Taser, an address book stuffed with so many extra pages it was bound with a rubber band, and a day planner.

When she continued to look after depositing the day planner on the table, Andre said, "Um, Hannah, is that your date book?"

She glanced up from the rabbit hole that was her purse and shook her head. "That's my day planner, not my date book."

She continued to search while Molly and Andre exchanged a look. Hannah couldn't be the killer unless she'd developed a highly convincing act as a scatterbrain. Molly couldn't understand why Victor would want her for his assistant.

"Ah, here it is," she said, pulling out a black journal with a red foil heart on the front. "Last night. That was Colby's night," she announced. "Four out of five stars."

"And what does that mean?" Andre asked slowly.

Molly stifled a chuckle, picturing this older hippie-type woman cruising for sex. Having spent a decade as a womanizer, she understood the star system, only she'd used cherries. After she cleared her throat she said, "I believe, Detective Williams, that Ms. Pence is referencing her sexual rating system."

Hannah nodded and smiled. "Yes, Colby's a dream."

Andre scratched the side of his head. "Forgive me, ladies, but I'm not making the connection. Is Colby your alibi? Is that what you're saying, Ms. Pence?"

"Yes!" Hannah exclaimed. She flipped back to the first page of the journal and handed it to him. "My star system is based on a rubric that includes the lover's endurance and prowess. It's not just about how long a partner can go, but how well he *or she* performs." She paused and added, "It's like the Olympics. Higher, faster, stronger."

Hannah's list included women as well as men, and a different person was listed almost every night. Molly glanced at Andre and tried to frame her question delicately. "Hannah, keeping in mind you're in the presence of a police officer, are you a call girl?"

A look of horror crossed her face. "Indeed, I am not! I'm an adult porn headhunter." Andre spewed water all over the table. "Oh, let me get that, son," Hannah said, jumping up. She crossed to a credenza and pulled out a few bar rags while Molly laughed and laughed. "You're not the first to react this way, Detective," she said gently. "It's fine."

"Stop laughing!" he barked at Molly, which only made her laugh harder. He finally offered a withering gaze and she quit.

"Let me explain my business," Hannah said. "I needed a second job. Did you know that Phoenix is becoming a satellite hub for adult films?" They both shook their heads. "Well, it is. I'm paid by several adult film companies to find new talent." She flashed a coquettish grin. "Colby's a new hire."

"So Colby is your alibi?" Molly asked.

"Yes, Colby as well as Mr. Fish."

Andre looked up from his iPad. "Who?"

"Mr. Fish is a jack-of-all-trades. He runs the camera, but more importantly, he makes sure the prospective talent is well-behaved."

"You'll need to give us their contact information," Molly said.

"I'll write it down for you." She reached inside her bag again. "I only need to find a pen and paper."

"Here!" Andre exclaimed. He whipped out a pen from his shirt pocket and yanked a sheet of paper from Molly's notepad, making no attempt to hide his frustration. Molly gave him a look and he took a deep breath.

When Hannah completed her task and set the pen down, Molly asked, "Can you tell us about your relationship with Mr. Guzman?"

Her pleasant demeanor disappeared in a frown. "Victor Guzman was a cheap, micromanaging prick, and anyone who doesn't tell you that is lying. The bastard even tried to control when people used the restroom. Thank goodness Isabelle didn't listen to him."

"You're referring to the fact that everyone had a key to the executive washroom," Andre concluded.

"Well, yes, but Mr. Guzman wanted all of the restrooms locked."

"What?" Molly asked, completely flabbergasted.

"It means when you needed to pee, you were supposed to check out a key from Isabelle. Time is money," she mocked. "The idea that grown adults need permission to tinkle is ridiculous. Isabelle kept one key on her desk so Victor thought we were following the rule, but really she had duplicates made for everyone."

"Can we see your key?" Molly asked.

Hannah bit her lip. "I can't find it. My cubicle is close to the bathroom, so I keep my key on my desk underneath my stapler. Everyone knows where it is, and a lot of people just take mine as they walk by. Most everyone is really good about returning it, so I'm hoping whoever took it will realize they have two."

"Did those keys open the executive washroom?" Andre asked.

"Yes. The same lock is on both sets of doors. This floor was originally designed for twenty people, but when GRD moved in, Victor wouldn't pay to retrofit the bathrooms. But he would pay to have two stalls cut off the existing bathroom and a door installed, so executives had their own place. It's an absolutely ludicrous idea since they don't work up here. Isabelle wouldn't stand for it, and she fixed the problem, just like she fixes everything."

"It sounds as if she runs interference for the employees," Molly suggested.

"She does," Hannah agreed. "She absorbs a lot of his wrath, at least she did. I imagine with him gone, her life will get easier." Instantly regretting what she said, she added, "But I don't think she killed him."

"Why not?" Andre asked.

"I don't think she could."

Molly circled her reminder to check Isabelle's background. "Ms. Pence, what do you know about the Wilkerson case and the Dearborn case?"

"Both so tragic." She pointed to the files and said, "Now, Lonnie Wilkerson, he could be a suspect for sure…" She trailed off and tapped her lip with her index finger. "Except he's not in town now. He showed up at my desk last week, demanding to see Victor before he went on a long haul. There's no way he could've killed Victor. He's clear across the country."

"That's easy enough to verify," Andre said, making a note. "Also, when we perused the Wilkerson case, we saw some of Mr. Guzman's notes—"

"You mean his purple postulations?" Hannah interrupted.

Andre glanced at Molly, who was equally confused. "What?"

Hannah waved her hands. "Sorry, in-house term. Victor wrote notes all over the case files. He always used a purple pen so they'd stand out." She took a big breath and her eyes narrowed. "On that file, if I remember correctly, his notes were mainly about the ER doctor."

Andre turned the file so she could see it. "Yes, Dr. Bernard. It seems as though he questioned whether Dr. Bernard's report was truthful."

"Victor was the king of conspiracy," Hannah said, chuckling. "He thought everyone was crooked, running an angle or trying to get him." She rolled her eyes for effect. "And it didn't help that Pete Daly, his investigator, fueled his theories." She looked at Molly with a serious expression. "Please tell me you're not like that."

"Uh, no," Molly replied. "So, whatever happened with Dr. Bernard?"

She shrugged. "As far as I know, nothing's happened." She pointed again at the files. "Lonnie Wilkerson is dangerous, regardless of what Dr. Bernard did. Victor is going to permanently remove him from Bambi's life." Her face colored as she realized what she'd said. "I mean, he was going to remove him," she whispered.

"What about Ms. Dearborn?" Andre asked. "Do you see her as being a threat to Victor?"

"No. Not at all. She's a little different. We hit it off right away because she's a schoolteacher like I was. A gentle and kind woman for sure. Similar case as Wilkerson. The husband, Carlos Pino, is abusive. This one's a slam-dunk, but I feel so bad for Mackenzie now. Her court date's going to get pushed back."

"Do you think Mr. Pino is a possible suspect?" Andre asked.

She cocked her head to the side, trying to picture the possibility. "Perhaps...but maybe not. We've had the Dearborn case for nearly three months, and I couldn't tell you what Carlos Pino looked like. But I know Mr. Wilkerson at twenty yards, and we're barely through pre-trial motions."

"What about the women?" Molly pressed, circling back to the question Andre had already asked. "Do you think either Bambi or Mackenzie is capable of murdering Victor?"

Hannah snorted and offered a dismissive wave. "Hardly. Bambi's got a bad back and never could do this much damage. And Mackenzie is the most unassuming quiet thing. She's been to our office many times with her daughter Gabby, and she's always the best mom. If I had a child, I'd want her in Mackenzie Dearborn's class."

Andre picked up both case files and showed them to Hannah. "Is there anything missing from the Dearborn file? As you can see, the Wilkerson file is much thicker, but it's a newer case."

Her gaze jumped back and forth between the folders. "That's odd." She shuffled through the Dearborn file. "You're right. It's missing documents. I know there were more witness statements, although I can't remember specifically who. I'd need to check my calendar. Would you like me to do that?"

"Yes, please," they said in unison.

She glanced at her watch. "Are we almost through? I have several phone calls to make, and Ms. Rivera has charged me with writing the first draft of Victor's obituary by the end of the day."

Andre shrugged. "I'm good." He deferred to Molly. "Ms. Nelson?"

Molly looked back in her notes. "Uh, just one more question, Ms. Pence. When you came in, you said you had to wait for someone to let you on the floor because you don't have your badge with you. Why is that?"

Hannah's face reddened and she assumed a penitent pose. "I can't find it. I'm hoping it will turn up."

"When did you lose it?" Andre asked.

"Last week. I noticed it was gone on Thursday or Friday morning when I went to swipe in. It's not in my bag and I can't find it at home. It's possible it fell into the trash." Hannah wrung her hands. "I haven't told Isabelle yet. I think she'll fire me. This is the third badge I've lost since I started working here."

"So your badge and your key are missing?" Andre clarified.

Hannah nodded sullenly. "For some reason, I lose more things here in the law firm than I ever did in my classroom."

"Maybe it's because you're balancing two jobs," Molly offered.

"Oh, no," Hannah scoffed. "It's not that. I started the adult porn headhunting gig when I was teaching. The only way to survive in education is to find a second income." Her smile morphed into a wide grin. "Now it's just a different kind of teaching."

Molly heard her stomach rumble and glanced at her watch. It was lunchtime, but Isabelle had scheduled their employee interviews back to back. Molly guessed it was her way of sticking it to law enforcement. She and Andre helped themselves to the small supply of snacks kept in the conference room, but they were out of water. On a brief break she went to the kitchen and found a stack of plastic cups in a cupboard. She didn't see a water cooler, so she settled for the terrible tasting tap water.

As she started back to the conference room, she saw Hannah Pence consoling a crying woman. Molly guessed she was one of Victor's clients.

"I promise you, Mackenzie, we'll reassign your case immediately," Hannah said.

Molly pretended to read a nearby rideshare bulletin board. In all probability, this woman was Mackenzie Dearborn. She wore Dockers and a T-shirt with a jaguar on the front, and "John Adams School" emblazoned on the back. Molly knew John Adams was a struggling school in South Phoenix. She looked to be in her mid-thirties with her hair pulled back in a ponytail. A girl, who Molly assumed was Mackenzie's daughter, stood by her side. She had long dark hair and seemed fascinated by her pink cast. Molly guessed she was about eleven. She wore a school uniform and the letters "PTSA" were embroidered in yellow on the front. Apparently, daughter didn't go to mother's school.

"This is so awful. Why does this stuff always happen to me?" Mackenzie whined.

"Oh, I know," Hannah sympathized.

"My court date is in two weeks. How is someone going to get caught up that quickly?"

"We'll get it done," Hannah assured her.

Molly felt a tug on her shirt. She looked down and saw two big brown eyes staring at her. She'd been so focused on listening to Hannah and Mackenzie that she hadn't noticed the girl had slipped away from her mother's side. The mother obviously hadn't noticed either.

"You're really tall," the girl said.

"I am," Molly agreed.

"Can I have a drink of water, please?"

She glanced at the cup she held. How could she refuse such a nice request?

"Sure." She handed her the cup and the girl drank greedily. "What's your name?"

"Gabrielle." She said it with a Spanish accent, and Molly remembered her father's name was Carlos. Most likely her father was Mexican. Gabrielle made a face. "This water tastes funny. You need to use the water filter. It's better."

"Oh," she said, surprised that Gabrielle knew her way around the law firm's kitchen. "You have a pretty name. What grade are you in?"

"Fifth." She looked at her mom, who still hadn't noticed she'd wandered off. "We're here to see Mr. Guzman."

"Oh," Molly said. Obviously, no one had told her about Victor's death, and Molly imagined that was probably for the best.

"Hey, what happened to your arm?"

Gabrielle took another sip of water. "My dad's a bad man and that's why we need Mr. Guzman."

"I see."

Molly watched her carefully. She hadn't answered her question, so either she was deflecting the truth, or she couldn't follow a conversation well. Having nieces and nephews, Molly knew either reason was a possibility.

Gabrielle handed her the cup as Mackenzie and Hannah approached. "Gabby, why are you bothering people?" her mother said sharply.

"Oh, she wasn't bothering me." Molly stuck out her hand. "I'm Molly Nelson."

"She's our new P.I.," Hannah offered.

Molly silently swore at Hannah. In an instant Mackenzie's demeanor shifted. "Nice to meet you. We need to go." She put a hand on Gabrielle's shoulder and turned her toward the elevator.

"Cute kid," she said.

"Yeah," Hannah sighed. "Her story's just so sad. Did she tell you about the cast?"

"Sort of."

Hannah watched them get on the elevator. When Gabby stopped to wave at both of them, they waved back. Hannah muttered, "It's too bad Victor didn't have the chance to put that slimy father away for good."

CHAPTER SEVEN

When Ari returned to the office tower armed with some lunch for Molly, the crime scene vehicles had left. It was after two p.m. and the line to the IRS assistance center went around the corner. April fifteenth was a month away, and the faces of the tired and hot taxpayers made her appreciate her accountant and her good fortune in life.

She was eager to dig into Scott's situation, but she had a house closing, and Molly had just texted with an SOS. Andre had left when a break on another case occurred, and Molly needed a second set of eyes and ears for her last interview of the day. She also wanted lunch, so Ari set aside her own plans to help her partner. Dr. Yee would be proud of her selflessness.

She entered the lobby and found the guard arguing with a uniformed man who appeared to be a hired driver. Next to him was a chunky boy dressed in a school uniform. On his backpack was a logo that looked like an atom, but Ari had never been great in science so she wasn't sure.

"I always bring him here every Wednesday. Mr. Guzman will be very upset if he finds out his son was not brought to him.

I have another client to pick up downtown in ten minutes." The driver's accent was thick, and he looked to be of Indian descent.

"Sir, I'm just a substitute guard. All I know is that no one is going up to the law office without an escort. I'll have to call, and someone will need to come down and fetch him."

Ari automatically stopped at the desk. Clearly no one had told the driver Victor was dead, and judging from the bored expression on the boy's face, he'd not been told either.

"Excuse me." They all looked at her, but she directed her comment to the guard. "I'm expected at the law firm. I'd be happy to take him up with me."

"I always wait with Hannah or Isabelle," the boy said. "Take me to one of them."

The guard nodded and the driver mouthed "thank you" as he ran out the door. Ari noticed the boy eyeing her lunch from In-N-Out Burger while they waited for the elevator.

"You're lucky," he said. "You got to go there for lunch."

"Your lunch wasn't so great?"

He sighed. "It's never that great. School lunches suck."

She nodded as they boarded the elevator. He pressed ten and continued to stare at her bag. She felt bad for him. He had no idea that his life had dramatically changed and he no longer had a father. She reached into the bag and pulled out her fries. When she handed them to him, his face lit up. "Thank you!"

"I'm Ari," she said gently. "What's your name?"

"Miguel," he said, shoving five fries in his mouth. "I'm Victor Guzman's son," he said proudly.

"Where do you go to school, Miguel?"

"Phoenix Technical Science Academy."

She was just about to ask him what he learned at school when the doors opened and he bolted from the car. "Thank you!" he called over his shoulder. He whipped open the front door of the law firm and ran past the receptionist. Her jaw dropped when she saw him, and a look of acute distress crossed her face.

She'd composed herself by the time Ari reached her counter. "Hi, I'm Ari Adams. I work with Molly Nelson from Nelson Security. As I arrived, a driver dropped off Miguel. Apparently nobody made other arrangements? The poor kid doesn't even know about his father." The receptionist immediately pressed a button and spoke with someone who apparently knew what to do.

Then she said to Ari, "I'm sorry. Who are you here for?"

"Molly Nelson. She's the firm's new investigator? She's interviewing employees."

"Of course. Down the hallway behind you."

"Thank you."

Despite a murder occurring in the office, everyone continued to work. Employees used their laps as makeshift desks, balancing tablets, phones and legal pads. She remembered what Xavier, the paralegal they'd met in the courtyard, had said. No one had gone home. He'd called it correctly. She weaved through the masses, hoping not to step on anyone. A few of the men stared at her lunch, coveting the In-N-Out burgers as Miguel had done. She found Molly in a tiny conference room. At the sight of lunch she groaned in appreciation.

"Babe, thanks," she said. They unpacked the food and Molly noticed they were missing a container of fries. Ari recounted her meeting with Miguel. Molly shook her head. "I can't believe his mother didn't pull him out of school to tell him."

"Me neither. But I can't believe those people out there are working."

"Anything for billable hours," Molly observed. "How are the interviews going?"

She summarized the morning interviews and her random meeting with Mackenzie Dearborn. "That daughter of hers is pretty cute, except for the cast on her arm."

"Who's left for today?"

"Just Brittany Spring. How was your meeting with Scott?"

Ari explained what Scott needed and Molly laughed. "That's a tall order. Solve a twenty-year-old mystery."

"Actually, it's a twenty-four-year-old mystery," she corrected. "I don't know if I can, but I'll try."

Molly leaned over and offered her a sweet kiss. "If anyone can pull it off, you can."

"How's it going working with Andre? Are you sticking to the pact you made with him?"

She nodded while she chewed. "He's asking good questions. I'm letting him take the lead. So far, so good."

There was a knock on the door and Brittany Spring opened it far enough to poke her head inside. "Is it time for me now? I'm probably early, but I've got a ton of copying to get done."

"Sure," Molly said, wolfing down the rest of her burger. "Please excuse the mess."

"It's fine." Brittany sat in the chair at the far end of the table, putting as much distance as possible between her and Molly. "We're really behind now, and we've got court deadlines to file and briefs to be copied. I don't know why anyone would vandalize the copy machine, but now we're stuck with a rental clunker for another week until the new one arrives."

"I take it the vandalized machine is beyond repair?"

"Definitely. The glass was shattered. The front panel was smashed, and the Coke they sprayed inside destroyed the drum and the gears."

"It sounds like you know a lot about copy machines."

She nodded. "I worked at a Kinko's through college, so I've become the resident expert when there are jams no one can fix. And I'm the only person who can be bothered to change the toner."

"I hear you," Molly said. "We'll go quickly." She gestured to Ari. "Hopefully you remember Ms. Adams from this morning?" Brittany offered a polite nod and returned her gaze to Molly. "Detective Williams had to leave, but he asked that I complete your interview and share it with him. Is it okay if I tape our conversation?"

"Sure."

Molly opened the recorder app on her phone and placed it in the center of the table. "Detective Williams might come back for a follow-up interview, if he has more questions."

"I get it," Brittany nodded. "I've dealt with enough witness transcripts to know most witnesses are only as good as their memory."

"So, are you studying to become a lawyer?"

"Oh no," she scoffed. "I have no desire for that kind of pressure. I'm a certified paralegal and I'm happy with that."

"And you most recently worked with Victor Guzman?"

"Yes," she said with a nod. "It was my turn."

"What was it like working for him?"

"Honestly, I dreaded every day. But it was my turn," she said emphatically. And *everyone* has to take a turn." She sounded robotic, as if she were reading from the firm's policy and procedure manual. She took a breath and said, "I don't mean to malign the dead. Victor was exceptional at analyzing evidence and asking questions, but he was incredibly demanding of himself and everyone around him. When he wanted something, he couldn't be bothered to ask for it politely. He thought his talent was an excuse for his vulgarity, boorishness, sexual harassment, and condescension." She took another breath and finished. "And God forbid you ever make a mistake."

"Like what?" she asked casually.

"Like a misspelling in a pleading or not following evidence protocol. And you'd be out of a job, if you ever missed a deadline. There was no mercy."

"It sounds like you're speaking from personal experience," Molly observed.

She sighed. "Since you've already interviewed Isabelle, she might have mentioned Victor tried to fire me. I made a huge mistake with a pleading and he looked foolish in court. He yelled at me in front of a room full of people and said the only thing I knew how to do was make copies." She glanced at Ari who saw tears in her eyes. "And he called me a dog. Said he didn't want to take anyone as ugly as me to court. He wanted jurors imagining themselves fucking a good looking broad when they tuned out the case."

"He said all that in front of other employees?" Ari confirmed, aghast.

She nodded. "Yeah. He told all the other homely dogs they needed to get a makeover ASAP. Then he barked at me before he fired me."

"He barked at you?" Ari asked.

"Yeah, he did. And now other people do it."

"I'm appalled by the barking thing," Molly said, "but moving to the part where you were fired, how is it that you're still here?"

She shifted in her seat, her agitation apparent. "When the firm's attorney found out what happened, he told Victor and Ms. Rivera they had to keep me or face a complaint to the state bar and possibly a lawsuit. Victor sort of apologized, said he'd lost his head and it wouldn't happen again. And it hasn't."

"Where were you last night?"

"Home. Alone. My son was with my sister and her kids. I had the night to myself. I drew a bubble bath and enjoyed the solitude. Unfortunately, no one can verify my story."

"Did you notice anything different about Victor over the last few days? Was he bothered or stressed?"

She nervously wrapped a strand of hair around her finger. "Not particularly. He's been working on a child custody case but it didn't seem to be terribly controversial."

Molly flipped back in her notes. "Was that the Bambi Wilkerson case?"

Brittany looked surprised. "Yeah, how did you know?"

"I saw the file. Can you tell me some of the particulars?"

"As you might guess from her name, Bambi is a stripper. She's got a seven year old named Travis. According to her, Travis's dad, Lonnie, got mad and twisted his arm so hard that it fractured. Bambi is suing for sole custody. Dad's shown up here and threatened Victor."

"How did Victor get the case?"

"Ironically, from me. I know Bambi. Her kid and my kid go to the same school. When she told me what Lonnie had done, I took it to Victor. I'm the president of the parents' organization, so I know she's a stand-up kind of person. Victor's son, Miguel, goes to school there as well, so Victor knows I've got the scoop on the parents. Bambi volunteers on a lot of the committees. She comes through for the school, so who cares what she does for a living, right?"

Molly picked up the Dearborn and Wilkerson case files. "Ms. Spring, as you can see, the Dearborn file is rather thin. It seems information is missing. Would you know anything about this?"

She shook her head, looking amused. "No, I don't have any idea, and I'd guess the only person who could answer that question would've been Victor. He routinely removed documents and added information. It drove Isabelle nuts. She had a whole system for organizing case files, and Victor would constantly interfere. But he'd explode when it wasn't logically organized. There was no way to win," she concluded.

Molly nodded. She glanced at Ari, her eyes asking if she had any questions.

Ari shifted in her seat and smiled at Brittany. "Ms. Spring, I rode up in the elevator with Miguel. He comes here on Wednesdays. Is that correct?"

Brittany's jaw dropped and she glanced at the door. "He's here? Nobody told him his father died?"

"That surprises you," Ari said.

Brittany thought about it for another beat and shook her head. "No, not really. He's an afterthought to both his father and mother. They're narcissists and Miguel knows it. He's not stupid. Gee, I wonder who'll get to break the news to him, Isabelle or Hannah?"

"Would that ever fall to you?" Molly asked.

Brittany snorted. "No, it wouldn't. And it would be a cold day in hell before I would lift a finger to help Victor Guzman."

CHAPTER EIGHT

Ari pulled into the Groove's small parking lot. Since it was Wednesday, only the Happy Hour regulars visited Scrabble or The Pocket, depending on their libation of choice.

After they'd finished interviewing Brittany Spring, Ari had rushed to a showing in the prestigious Willo Historic District while Molly returned to her office. Ari smiled, thinking of a potential commission. Her clients were interested in making an offer, but they wanted the night to think about it. She kept her fingers crossed that by tomorrow she'd be writing a contract.

She grabbed a sack of Glenn's movies and the movie projector she'd found in the basement. She hadn't thought of Glenn in decades, but what she remembered the most about him was how much he hated to be photographed. If Blythe or Junior tried to cajole him into a picture, he'd explode and run off. The only people who could get him to stand halfway in the picture were Scott and Richie. She wondered what kind of man he had become. She hoped he was alive and well.

She decided to go find Jane first and warn her about the health inspector. She quickly realized she was too late. A dowdy woman in a jungle-printed polyester pantsuit faced Jane outside the Pocket. Ari assumed this was Muriel, the health inspector. She held a clipboard so Jane could see it and pointed to something while she shook her head.

Jane also looked as if she was ready for safari, clad in a leopard-skin miniskirt that barely covered her bottom and a tank top that read *Pussy* in sequins. She'd teased her blond hair and wore enormous gold earrings that shimmered in the sun. Muriel read whatever was attached to her clipboard while she trailed her pen across the paper. Jane's gaze wandered away. When she saw Ari, she smirked.

When Muriel paused, Jane touched her arm and pointed at Ari, who felt obligated to join them.

"Muriel," Jane gushed, "this is Ari Adams, one of the owners of the Groove on Grand and a commercial real estate agent."

"Pleased to meet you," Muriel said in a no-nonsense way that suggested she was tired of Jane's nonsense and wasn't pleased to meet anyone since it was after five. "If you're the owner, perhaps you can explain the requirements for a property to be zoned for certain ventures, such as taverns or restaurants—"

"Oh, I wouldn't call it a restaurant and it's not a tavern," Jane interrupted. "I would never own a *tavern*." She looked repulsed and made a gagging noise. Ari glanced at Muriel, whose eyes continually strayed to Jane's voluptuous chest. Although her gaydar hadn't buzzed, Ari was rather certain Muriel was checking out Jane.

Ari offered a slight chuckle at her friend's hyperbole, but Muriel was not amused. "Regardless of what you call it," she said slowly, "it's not up to code."

"May I see that?" Ari asked, gesturing for the clipboard.

Muriel surrendered it but leaned closer and pointed to the middle section. "The problem is lack of adequate drying space for the glassware. With such a small square footage, Ms. Frank's back counter must serve multiple purposes, such as a staging area for liquor bottles. This means glassware could be exposed to whatever germs might have been left on the counter from the bottom of a box, crate, or what have you. It could be feces, dirt, chemicals—anything."

"Do you really think I wouldn't notice that?" Jane argued. "If there was a turd stuck to the bottom of a glass, I, or one of my bartenders, would probably rewash it— unless we were serving someone we didn't particularly like." She glared at Muriel, who scowled in return.

"I don't think public health is a joking matter," she said flatly. "And I'm sorry you do." She reached beneath the forms on the clipboard for a brightly colored sticker. She headed to the bar as Jane and Ari followed behind.

"What are you doing?" Jane cried.

"I'm shutting you down for now," Muriel replied. She approached the three customers sitting at the bar and said, "Folks, I'm sorry, but the Pocket is closed." She waved at Jorge, Jane's bartender, and said, "Sir, you need to step away from the bar, collect whatever personal belongings you have brought, and leave. Your shift is over."

"Wait a second!" Jane cried, stepping in front of Muriel. "You can't do this!" She turned to Jorge. "Don't move a muscle, Jorge. You stay right where you are."

Muriel glowered at Jane. "Ms. Frank, I suggest you heed my instructions, or I will add insolence to my report. If my superiors learn that you have been uncooperative and unwilling to support public health laws, they won't grant you a permit, even if you comply."

Ari thought Jane might slug Muriel, yet when she stepped closer, Muriel's gaze dropped to Jane's cleavage for a nanosecond. It wasn't lost on Jane, whose scowl morphed into a cat-like grin. Ari almost felt sorry for Muriel. Jane could turn most women into a blubbering puddle.

"You keep staring at my chest," Jane whispered breathily.

Muriel's eyes widened and she gasped. "I am not!"

"Go ahead," Jane encouraged. "You can look but you can't touch. Not unless you ask very nicely."

Muriel's gaze remained glued to Jane's face. She groped for her bag, which she'd set on the patio table, all the while staring into Jane's eyes. She suddenly turned on her heel, and with trembling hands, slapped the sticker on the Pocket's front door.

With her head down, she mumbled, "Since I consider your behavior to be combative, I will be sending a patrol car over in an hour to ensure you have closed the bar."

Jane put a hand on her hip and thrust out her pelvis. "Combative? Really? You can't even look at me." She slowly gyrated in a sexy dance that followed the pulsating music from the Pocket's sound system. Ari was certain Muriel's hooded eyes followed every one of Jane's lustful moves.

When the song ended, Muriel found her voice. As she looked past them toward the parking lot, she croaked, "I'll be back in a week to see how you've addressed this concern."

Jane lifted Muriel's chin with her index finger, forcing her to meet her gaze. "I'll be counting the days." Muriel made a squeaking sound and scurried to the Groove's exit while they watched.

"Do you think she'll really send that squad car over?" Jane asked.

"Probably," Ari conceded, "but I bet it will be Charlie. I doubt he'll shut you down."

"I don't think he will either, not if he wants to continue to partake in the red, white and blue price specials."

Jane had created a special Happy Hour pricing for firefighters, the red, teachers, who wore "white hats," and policemen and women, the blue. They were thrilled to have dollar beers and two dollar wine and well drinks. Consequently, every fire station, police precinct and school district within a ten-mile radius patronized the Pocket. Since owning a bar was only a hobby, Jane paid little attention to her bottom line. She made plenty as a real estate agent.

"I don't think you should push her, Jane," Ari warned. "I'll help you figure out this counter space problem, but you don't want the health department as an enemy. She might go back and file a sexual harassment report against you."

"Do you really think she'd do that?"

Ari shrugged. "I don't know. You freaked her out. I'm not sure if you surfaced her deep-seated lesbian feelings or sent her into shock."

She smoothed her skirt and adjusted her tank top. "I guess I'll find out in a week. Either she'll come back or she'll send some scowling old fart to take her place."

Ari heard the wistfulness in her voice and immediately turned stern. "Jane, you're not planning to seduce her, are you? I thought you and Rory were exclusive?" Rory was Jane's long-distance girlfriend, who, in Ari's opinion, was the best woman she'd ever dated.

"It's a long story," Jane said, batting away a few tears. "It's not that we broke up. We're just taking a break."

She pulled her into a hug. "How do I not know this?"

A foot shorter, Jane rested her cheek on Ari's chest. "You've been super busy with your life, and Molly, and your dad. We haven't had a lot of time together."

Ari kissed the top of her head. "I'm going to change that, okay? If you're near Glendale tomorrow, let's do lunch. I'll be in the area."

Jane offered a sympathetic look. She knew how much Ari disliked Glendale. "Definitely lunch. Now, I'm off to talk to Jorge and make sure he knows he isn't fired. He's often confused by any English that isn't the name of a drink." She kissed Ari's cheek and sashayed away.

Ari sighed and headed over to Nelson Security. Although the blinds were closed, a soft glow from Molly's desk lamp crept between the slats. She knocked four times rapidly, the special knock they'd agreed upon. More than once, Molly had opened the door to a drunken patron of the Pocket, the homeless, or potential clients who didn't believe in business hours. While she wanted more business and she didn't mind helping the homeless, her processing time was critical for a case and interruptions needed to be kept to a minimum.

It took her a minute to open the door and Ari immediately saw why. Stacks of banker boxes filled most of the room. One was open on Molly's desk. She'd written four names on the large whiteboard that covered most of the north wall. She'd also copied all of the crime scene photos and tacked them to the corkboard strip that ran the length of the whiteboard. Ari stared at Victor Guzman's death photo. He could've been sleeping, except for the gaping bullet hole in his head.

"Want a slice?" Molly motioned to the pizza sitting on a stool in a corner.

"I do. I'm starving since I only had half my lunch," Ari said, referring to the fries she'd given to Miguel Guzman. Ari set the pizza on one of the boxes and took the stool for herself.

Molly pointed at the movie projector. "Will we be watching movies?"

"Yes," Ari said with a smile, "But why don't you summarize for me while I eat?"

Molly nodded, and just as she was about to start, she said, "Whoa…Wait. Almost forgot." She crossed the distance that separated them and planted a sweet kiss on Ari's lips. "Thank you for coming to the law firm today and bringing my lunch. I know you had other plans, but I appreciated it."

"You're welcome," Ari said warmly. Dr. Yee had taught them the importance of showing gratitude and affection for the simple daily efforts they made toward each other. "Now, give," she joked, scarfing down a big bite.

Molly went to the whiteboard and the four names. "You'll notice all of the key suspects are female. We know this was personal. We know the killer was not a professional because *she* couldn't hit the target until she was less than six inches away."

"Do you really think it was a woman?"

Molly nodded, frowning. "After you left this afternoon, I went down to the café in the courtyard. I interrupted a few conversations with some of the paralegals who were on a break. I asked who might have been angry enough to kill Victor." Molly pointed at the first name. "Eden Venegas, ex-wife. An obvious choice. Divorce finalized five months ago, but both Victor and Eden have filed harassment charges against the other regarding Miguel. Both have claimed Miguel is not happy when he's with the other parent."

"Miguel doesn't look happy at all," Ari commented.

"Understandable. Everyone in the office hates Wednesdays because he can be a holy terror." Molly pointed at the second name, Isabelle "The Hell" Medina. "Either Isabelle or Victor's personal assistant Hannah was usually stuck with Miguel."

"Why isn't Hannah's name on the board?" she asked with her mouth full.

"She has an alibi." Molly couldn't help but giggle as she answered. "That's a good story for later. She's not the killer." She tapped Isabelle's name with her knuckle. "Isabelle hated Guzman for several reasons. In addition to having her workday hijacked every Wednesday when Miguel visited, apparently Victor was a horrible micromanager who constantly undermined her. The last straw could've been when she applied for a different job in the firm and Victor squashed it. According to the paralegals, it was down on the fifth floor, which is regarded as the superior floor. And the job was for nearly double the money she makes now. Apparently, she obtained a degree in cyber security that she'd like to use."

"Why hasn't she quit?"

Molly smiled. "She's an ardent admirer of Gloria Rivera and it's home. She wanted to advance in the company but Victor wouldn't let her. Her alibi is flimsy because no one was with her before her fight."

Ari raised an eyebrow. "She's a fighter?"

"Uh-huh. It's called MMA, or Mixed Martial Arts. Isabelle the Hell is one of the best in the state. She's a contender for the national championship this year."

"I wasn't aware such a thing existed," Ari confessed. "So I guess she has means and motive. And the physical capability."

"Absolutely." Molly adopted a lecherous grin and leaned over her. "Maybe we could take in a match? Watch a little girl on girl action?"

Ari closed the distance and kissed her hard. "Babe, I'd go anywhere with you."

Molly stepped away and looked at her watch. "I'm pausing that action. I'm going to finish this summation in five minutes, and then we will resume kissing."

Ari flashed her bedroom eyes and unbuttoned her shirt. "Finish in four," she whispered.

Molly groaned and turned back to the whiteboard. "Two clients' names are connected since touching their case files was the last thing Victor Guzman ever did. You heard Brittany mention one of them—"

"Bambi Wilkerson, the name on the folder in the law library."

"Yes, but Bambi and her husband Lonnie were working. Andre checked. Their story is somewhat connected to the other file, which I'm guessing is why Victor went to retrieve it before he was killed." She pointed to the third name on the whiteboard. "Mackenzie Dearborn is another suspect. Her file was the one Victor went to retrieve from his office." She handed Ari her copy. "Mackenzie hired Victor to obtain full parental rights of her daughter Gabrielle, claiming Dad, Carlos Pino, is abusive. Carlos maintains Mackenzie is the abusive one. So far I'm not seeing any follow up. There's no notes, no list of witnesses, nothing. It's almost like this isn't the real case file."

"Weird."

"Definitely. They go to court..." Molly flipped back to the beginning of the file. "In two weeks."

She grabbed another slice of pizza and asked, "But how would an outsider get in without a badge and a key?"

Molly offered a frustrated look. "Let's just say there's at least two employees whose badges are lost, and everyone has a key to the restrooms."

Her jaw dropped. "Really? There's no way to limit the suspect pool?"

"Not when it comes to badges or keys."

"But it would still be more difficult for a non-employee to take someone's key or badge, don't you think?"

"Probably," Molly acknowledged.

Ari read the fourth name. "Brittany Spring, Victor's paralegal?" She scowled. "Honey, after what she told us about Victor barking at her like a dog, I'm not surprised somebody murdered him, but she seems too meek to fire a gun."

"I hear you, but she might not be what she appears." Molly grabbed another piece of pizza and added, "Get this. After a paralegal does her month with Victor, she gets an automatic paid two-day vacation that doesn't count against her banked vacation days."

"It's like combat pay."

"Yup. And Victor's only stipulation is—"

"His paralegal has to be a woman."

Molly nodded and gave her a thumbs up. "He's someone who needs to dominate women. He's the definition of machismo."

So the four prime suspects are Eden Venegas, Isabelle Medina, Brittany Spring and Mackenzie Dearborn."

"And probably one more: Christine Pierpont. She's an attorney hoping to make partner. Her chances were pretty slim until Victor died." Molly recounted the conversation Isabelle overheard in the stairwell between Christine and her friend. "I didn't have a chance to talk to her today. She was in court."

Ari wiped her hands on a napkin and gazed at the boxes. Each one had a name on the end panel. "Are these his current case files?" she asked incredulously.

"No, these are cases from within the last year. I'm reading the summary notes and making a list of anyone we might want to interview because the case was especially nasty. The current cases and recently closed cases are being copied for me right now. Of course, they had to take them to a copy place because they're down to one machine."

"Yeah, what was that all about? Does anyone have a theory about why the killer vandalized the copy machine?"

"No, but have you ever worked somewhere with a poor copy machine? At the police station more than a few cops threatened to shoot the damn thing."

They both laughed and Molly leaned over and kissed her. "We've talked enough about my day. Tell me about yours." Molly glanced at her watch. "You have thirty seconds before I maul you."

Ari gave a short summary of the Long family and the mysterious neighbor who might've been an eyewitness. She grabbed her messenger bag and pulled out three eight-millimeter canisters. "How about we help each other? We can look through your case files while we watch home movies made by Cousin Glenn."

"Sounds exciting," Molly whispered in her ear. "And I can throw in some steamy security camera footage from the office tower." Molly parted her legs and stroked her thighs. She pushed up Ari's skirt and slowly slid her fingers beneath Ari's underpants.

"Oh, you're talking my language now," Ari murmured. She threw her head back as Molly entered her. She was suddenly a very different kind of hungry. Their detective work would have to wait.

Ari emerged from the blue cabin's tiny bathroom wearing only a short red silk robe.

"What should we watch first?" Molly held up a DVD of the security footage and a canister of Glenn's movies.

"Surprise me," Ari said, in a thick voice she barely recognized.

She cleared the couch of the boxes Molly had deposited there. Clad only in boxers, Molly unpacked the projector Ari had pulled from the Long's basement. As she bent over to thread the film, her sinewy muscles bulged. Ari resisted the temptation to jump up and trace each one with her lips. The afterglow lingered and she still felt Molly's fingers inside her and Molly's mouth tasting her nipples.

"What's that look for?" Molly teased.

"Just get over here," Ari whined. "I'm lonely."

Molly started the projector and joined Ari on the couch. They'd erased the whiteboard so it could serve as an impromptu screen. Without warning a plate of scrambled eggs came into view. A fork scooped up a mouthful and the camera followed the fork to twelve-year-old Scott's mouth. Glenn zoomed in on his jaws chewing.

"Really?" Molly said. "This is what we're watching?" She grabbed the film canister. "Aren't these labeled?"

Ari sighed. "No, Cousin Glenn wasn't intellectually equipped to label them and I doubt anyone ever watched them after he left. He was autistic. He showed up the summer Richie died. His mother dropped him off and went on a trip. Someone must have realized he loved the video camera, because he never set it down."

"Well, then he's certainly forgiven for not labeling his masterpieces, but I'm not thinkin' these movies will rival Spielberg."

"Let's see if it gets any better." She opened a nearby banker box and handed Molly a stack of files. "We'll multi-task and read while we watch."

When breakfast ended, the movie skipped to a trip to the market with Blythe, and then a game of horseshoes with Carlin, Scott and Junior. At one point, Junior encouraged Glenn to put down the camera and throw a horseshoe, but the camera shook left and right, as Glenn said no. Then the movie ended abruptly as a horseshoe sailed through the air. The image disappeared and the reel's tail flapped as it spun around.

"Okay," Ari said, untangling herself from Molly. "Nothing important on that one." Molly grunted as she closed one of Victor's case files. Ari glanced at her as she threaded another film. "Find anything interesting in those closed files?"

"Nuh-uh," she said, holding it up. "I'll give Victor credit for follow through. Not only did he have his paralegals document any threats made during a particular case, but also when it was over, he kept tabs on the people who'd made the threats. He noted whether they moved out of state, lost interest or became incarcerated. I can automatically disregard most of these files because the suspect is already in jail or has left Arizona."

"That's helpful," Ari agreed as the next movie began.

It started with sunrise over Murphy Park. She pictured Glenn's old bedroom that faced the historic downtown. Then it suddenly transitioned to a plate of waffles. This time Glenn recorded Carlin's eating habits and the scowl the teenager offered the camera. Suddenly children's legs ran in and out of the frame as they played a game in the backyard. Her gaze settled on a spindly set of legs in cutoff shorts. She knew those legs and the tube socks that came up to his knees. As the camera moved back and forth, sometimes the legs flew out of the frame, but just as quickly, they returned. She found her own legs, also in cutoffs but taller, minus the athletic socks. She willed Glenn to stand up but he remained seated on the grass, content to record the lower half of the neighborhood kids, including the spindly legs that belonged to her deceased brother Richie.

"Babe," Molly called from the couch.

"Huh?"

She couldn't take her eyes away. Richie was so close. She felt Molly's arms around her as they watched the end of the film. She didn't realize she was crying until Molly handed her a tissue. She wiped her eyes and smiled at her caring face. She'd mourned Richie's murder and thought of him often to this very day. But for the first time in two decades she was reminded of his life in such a way that almost made him real again. He'd been a happy, laughing, mischievous kid. Her heart hung over a canyon, the depth of her loss unfathomable. Yet, Molly's nearness provided ballast; her crystal blue eyes gave comfort. Only her mother had been able to pull her heart back from the edge after Richie had died. Until she met Molly. Whenever gloom threatened to rob her day because she couldn't beat the sadness, Molly always found a way to bring her back.

"You okay?" Molly whispered in her ear. She nodded and Molly said, "I guess we'll be watching more of those movies, won't we?" They both laughed and Molly joked, "I can't wait for French toast morning."

They burst out laughing, shattering the tension. She hugged Molly fiercely. "I love you so much."

"I love you, too. Forever."

Once she'd recovered, she stepped away, all business. "Okay, I think we've established what awaits us in Glenn's movies. How about we look at your security footage?"

Molly grabbed her laptop and pulled up the file. The lobby filled the screen and the camera focused on the front doors leading into the courtyard. In the corner, the time stamp read eight fifty-eight.

"Okay, here comes our perp."

A figure in a gray hoodie paused at the card reader outside and quickly yanked open the front door. Her head was down, but the curves of her body signaled female despite the nondescript sweatpants and baggy hoodie. "Certainly enough room to hide a gun," she muttered.

"Agreed," Molly said. "So she goes up to five. Andre also sent us footage from the two other cameras the property manager installed. Both are for the west side of the building, northwest and southwest. Those exits are closest to the IRS help center. In the event there was ever a bomb scare, or if a fight erupted between taxpayers waiting for help, they wanted video footage to cover their behinds."

"Has that ever happened?"

"Oh yeah, a few times. People are not happy when they come to that office tower to visit the IRS. Either they're going to the top floor because they're being audited, or they're waiting in the very long line that snakes through the courtyard outside because they don't understand how to file their taxes." She pulled up a drawing of the entire complex. "Here are the camera locations. Until recently they haven't been able to use the northeast camera. They sent out an email to the tenants, asking them to avoid using that exit for the next two weeks. They've been waiting on a part and they're fixing a wiring issue."

"So if our killer works in the building she knew it was the exit to choose because she got the email."

"Unfortunately," Molly sighed. She hit the fast forward button and time whisked ahead. At nine twenty-four a group of four women wandered into the frame, their backs to the camera as they headed out the front lobby doors. They appeared engaged in conversation as if they knew each other.

"Andre is identifying those women," she explained. "There are fifteen different companies and agencies in the building. Twelve of them routinely have employees who work late hours, although most don't work past nine."

Ari watched the women file through a single door. They were brunettes wearing dark overcoats to fend off the blustery March winds. Identifying them would be difficult. As the third woman exited, she leaned closer to the screen. "Wait. Back that up."

The lobby lighting was dismal, the architects depending on sunshine and glass to save costs during the day. But at night, the shadows distorted the images. The women again reached the door and Ari said, "Stop." The third woman was in the doorway and one of the few overhead lights was close enough to illuminate the back of her head.

"I'm not sure."

"What do you think you see?" Molly asked.

She shook her head. "Let's watch the footage from the other two cameras and come back to this one."

"Okay." She played the footage from the western cameras. No one used the southwestern exit during the window of time Andre had sent, and only two men used the northwest door, both hurrying toward the intersection. "They're probably hustling to catch the light rail," she guessed.

"Go back to the lobby camera, please," Ari said. Molly tapped the keyboard as Ari continued. "I remember the first real estate firm I worked for was in an office tower. After a while, you get to know people from riding the elevator together. You strike up conversations as you leave. So I don't think the four women walking out together necessarily *work* together. They might've met in the elevator. Let me control the mouse, please," she said.

She played the few seconds of the women exiting several times, trying to see the third woman. When she found the frame that gave her the clearest view, she sat back and pointed.

"I know it's really grainy, but look at the top of her head. She's wearing something in her hair."

Molly squinted and moved so close to the screen her nose almost touched it. "Maybe. What do you think you see?"

She pointed to a tiny speck of color on the screen. "Do you see that yellow curve there? I think that's the wing of a butterfly. When we met Brittany Spring, she was wearing a butterfly clip in her hair."

CHAPTER NINE

Ari wandered through Long Manor, trying not to sneeze from the dust. She'd told Scott she would search the house, peruse the family photos and interview some of the older citizens in downtown Glendale who might remember Junior, Henrietta and Millicent. She doubted she could prove what he needed her to prove. Yet she felt an obligation to try, if for no other reason than to help an old friend from childhood, someone who knew her family back when it was happy and whole. But as she sat in Junior's office, she worried this might be a mystery that should remain buried.

She sighed deeply and swiveled the chair around to face the desk. She rustled through the cubbies and tiny drawers. She found nothing important, only the expected detritus after years of use: random paper clips, dried out pens, old business cards and a cough drop that had fallen out of its missing box. She discovered one surprise in the bottom drawer—a Rubik's cube. He'd managed to get the yellow side finished, but the other three sides were a long way from completion. She wondered if he'd given up or if he periodically pulled it out and made a few more turns. She dropped it back in the drawer and headed for his office closet.

She was snooping, something she never would've done in front of Scott. Room by room she opened every drawer, searched through the closets and peered above every high shelf. She looked behind furniture, stood on chairs to see the tops of the window coverings, and sacrificed her clean sweatshirt and jeans as she crawled on the floor to look under beds. She even lifted mattresses to scan for tears or slits that could be a hiding place for secrets. Three hours later she had combed through the entire main house, uncovering amid the dirt and dust the weird, the disgusting and the laughable.

While searching the living room, she'd decided to check the fireplace flue, since valuables were sometimes stored in chimneys. She grabbed the poker and pushed it up the flue. It only traveled a few inches before hitting a barrier. A wadded piece of newspaper fell to the floor. She smoothed it and saw the date at the top, "November 8, 1997." She coaxed several more wadded paper balls from the flue until the entire collection landed in a heap on the firebox floor, along with the skeletal remains of two poor birds that had been trapped inside.

Scott had mentioned various science experiments around the house, and she found one underneath a twin bed frame upstairs. Thirty-four wads of bubble gum lined the bed frame rail. They had shriveled like multi-colored raisins but they still had some stick. She pictured one of the award kids spitting it out of his mouth before bedtime and sticking it on the frame before Junior or Millicent appeared to tuck him in.

The saddest discovery came in Junior and Millicent's room. Apparently, Millicent had never cleared out Junior's things from his side of the dresser. The three drawers were impeccably ordered, as if they would be subject to a military inspection. Musty smelling underwear and socks were folded and categorized by color in the first drawer. The second drawer contained a small assortment of T-shirts, also stacked by color. The third drawer held miscellaneous items like a bow tie and cummerbund, cufflinks, handkerchiefs and a small Bible. Certain passages had been highlighted including, "For whoever keeps the whole law but fails in one point has become accountable for all of it" from the Book of James. In the Book of Timothy she found, "But if anyone does not provide for his relatives, and especially for members of his household, he has denied the faith and is worse than an unbeliever."

The second quotation seemed to suggest Junior felt guilty about Henrietta's death. If in fact Millicent killed her, perhaps Junior learned of it later and held himself responsible. That would make sense since it was obvious he didn't stop seeing Millicent after the confrontation with Henrietta in the sunroom.

One of the last things she discovered was tucked away on a shelf in the room Glenn inhabited, the old camera he'd pressed against his face for most of that summer. It was rectangular with a handy grip so a child could easily use it. She pulled off the lens cap and pointed it toward downtown. She imagined the view he would've enjoyed in this bedroom, facing the Fizz factory and the town square. She returned the camera to the shelf and crossed the hallway to the sewing room, which had been Scott's room.

As she stared at the garage through the window, she realized from this angle the outline of the old staircase wasn't as faint as she originally thought. She could clearly see the old doorframe that would've opened to the landing. The angle of the railings and the stair steps depicted how truly treacherous it would've been for someone in failing health to descend the steps alone every day. She wondered why Junior hadn't insisted one of the children help Henrietta traverse the staircase each morning.

Perhaps such a thought had crossed his mind after her death. *For whoever keeps the whole law but fails in one point has become accountable for all of it.* Ari imagined him wracked with grief and guilt, barking at a hired man to dismantle the rickety stairs, pull up the bricks that formed his wife's special path to the breakfast room, and destroy the rose bushes that would be a daily reminder of her death. Everything was gone now, except the eerie outline of the staircase.

She scanned the interior of the sewing room. This was Millicent's domain, but when she and the kids departed for Florida, she left most of her things, including the mannequin, sewing box and pattern boards. Perhaps she had no intention of ever sewing again. She studied the Singer machine. Her mother had owned a similar model. She remembered her mother's sewing room, and a thought occurred to her. Sewing required good lighting. Her mother had put the machine near the window with a standing lamp nearby. Yet Millicent's sewing machine faced the interior wall next to the door—not the window—where there would have been better light and a lovely view of the trees in the backyard. Why would she want to stare at a blank wall while she worked? Wouldn't it have been too difficult to see intricate stitching or the eye of a needle?

Her phone pinged and she checked a text from Jane.

Sorry. Can't do lunch today. Buyer is certain she saw her dream property and wants a showing during her lunch break. Maybe see you and M later? xoxoxo.

She felt relieved. While she desperately wanted to catch up with Jane, especially if she'd broken up with Rory, she needed to search the garage and the sunroom. She sent a short reply and headed outside. Scott believed if clues existed, they would be within the family memorabilia. As she ventured across the grass, a tingle crept up her back. She had the odd feeling she was being watched. She furtively looked over her left shoulder just in time to see a tabby cat disappear around the house, toward the opening in the basement. She chuckled, thinking about the assortment of gadgets and knickknacks they'd seen the day before down there. She hadn't bothered to make a second trip to the basement, as she couldn't imagine how the boxes of toys and memorabilia would help her, especially Blythe's box of *Tiger Beat* magazines. Yet if she didn't find any clues in the sunroom, she supposed she'd have to brave the cat pee stench and wade through the basement boxes just to be thorough.

She opened the padlock and found the light switch for the garage. She took a long look up the steep interior stairs and ascended slowly. Fortunately, the switch activated the four industrial fluorescent work lights in the sunroom as well.

"Start in the corner and work my way across," she muttered.

Two hours later she'd divided the boxes into three groups: photos and films, important papers and house miscellaneous—which was the largest at twenty boxes. There were ten photo and film boxes to peruse and five full of bank statements, letters, warehouse requisitions, household accounts, bills and copies of wills.

She visualized a plan. She could set up her "war room" in the garage. The lighting was fine, and since it was March, the indoor temperature would be bearable. The folding tables would allow her to spread out and the boxes were close by. The only issue would be getting the heavy banker boxes down the steep stairs. She certainly didn't want to tumble to the bottom.

"Just like Henrietta."

She remembered there were some large baskets in the basement. If she could find some rope, she could lower each box from the sunroom to the garage.

She held her nose and was rewarded for her tenacity. The basement proved to be an old-fashioned mercantile. Not only did she find a basket and some rope, but she also found masking tape, thumbtacks, markers and paper.

Within an hour she'd transported all the photo boxes from the sunroom to the garage. She could feel the burn in her calves and knew she'd pay for it the next day. She thought about presenting Scott with a bill from her masseuse.

"And if he thinks I'm taking these back upstairs, he's crazy," she said as she climbed to the sunroom once more.

She assessed her progress. Only the boxes of Glenn's films and those filled with family documents remained. She'd look through the documents here, but she didn't want to watch the movies alone. She needed Molly beside her for the moment when Glenn captured Richie's face and not just his legs. She was sure she and Richie were featured in many of the films since they'd all spent so much time together that summer.

She glanced at her watch and saw that it was nearly two o'clock. She was filthy, but fortunately, she didn't have any client appointments that afternoon. She decided to keep working for another few hours, since she didn't know what the next day might bring. Such was the life of a real estate agent who lived at the beck and call of clients. She had the time today, so she should use it.

She trudged back downstairs and stared at the stacks of boxes, debating how to begin. She decided to take a cursory look to see what the Longs had bothered to photograph. The answer proved to be everything. She'd never seen so many pictures of a single family. In addition to capturing the customary holidays and birthdays, they recorded daily life. There were pictures of the children doing homework and playing outside. Often other people, such as the mailman and visiting neighbors, were included. Even camera-shy Glenn had his picture snapped a few times. She realized her heart was racing, anticipating the moment when she found pictures of herself and Richie with them.

It wouldn't surprise her if they had more photos of her than her own parents did. Jack and Lucia always seemed to forget the camera when they went on vacation, or they'd get caught up in the excitement of Christmas morning and forget to take any pictures. Then after Richie died, no one felt like taking pictures anymore. It was as if they knew the photo wouldn't look right.

She decided to create a family tree. Using the pushpins and the inside of the wooden garage door, she tacked up Wilbur and Victoria's wedding picture at the top of the tree. As she perused their boxes, she jotted notes on an old yellow legal pad, made yellower after twenty years in the basement.

Several facts emerged: Wilfred Sr. was quite proud of Fizz and there was almost an entire album devoted to the construction of the plant and its grand opening. Another album detailed the building of Long Manor. While Wilfred seemed to enjoy being photographed, Victoria rarely posed for pictures. When she did, it was usually holding Junior. Once he was upright and mobile, Victoria vanished from the photos completely.

Next came their only child, Junior. He had seven boxes all to himself, and each was labeled with a span of years. He had many friends and posed with different groups of kids, depending on the activity. Numerous photos showed him holding awards for sports, academics and Boy Scouts. He served on the Student Council and was elected Homecoming King during his senior year. In several photos he had a different girl on his arm. At the bottom of her notes, she wrote, *All-American boy*. Junior was quite the catch.

She found a small envelope of photos showing him at work. For her family tree, she picked one of him sitting at his desk at Fizz. His tie was askew and papers surrounded him, but he still smiled.

All pictures of Henrietta were in the box labeled *Married Life*. She was usually standing with her entire family, but Ari found one rare photo of her minus Junior, holding Blythe. She tacked it up next to Junior. She looked at the two of them side by side. They were both handsome and she knew they'd been completely in love.

Ari glanced at Junior's photo. "Then why did you cheat?"

She regretted the words before they left her mouth. She was not in a position to judge others about cheating. She chastised herself and went in search of a box for Carlin, Blythe and Scott. Since each had a stack of four banker boxes, finding photos was easy. She found a treat when she dug through Scott's box and came across a picture of her, Scott and Richie. They had been playing football, and she imagined Henrietta must have interrupted their game. Their faces were red and Ari's braid was half undone. They wore the smiles of youth. Glenn stood near Scott but half of his body wasn't in the picture.

She suddenly remembered a pretty woman holding an Instamatic camera, the one with the flashbulbs that popped off. Ari had completely forgotten Henrietta's camera, and she wondered if it was tucked among the pictures. She stared at every inch of the photo, trying to extract another lost memory of that day. It had been so long ago. She knew her memories of Richie faded with each turn of a calendar page. She wiped away her tears and stuck the photo in her pocket. She'd show it to Scott and ask if she could keep it.

She chose each child's high school graduation picture and finished the family tree, at least, the *first* family tree. She realized there were far fewer boxes for the family Junior and Millicent created. The reason became immediately apparent. Millicent preferred to be the subject of pictures rather than the photographer. She was in most of the photos and she posed for each—hand on her hip, right foot slightly turned, chin up and flashing a brilliant smile. She always stood on the left. Ari randomly pawed through a few dozen pictures to confirm her theory. She imagined Millicent orchestrated most of the photo opportunities, choosing her placement and capturing her best side.

She tacked up a photo of Millicent playing golf on the other side of Junior. Then she hunted for photos of the "award children," Newberry, Nobel, and Caldicott. Each one had a single box that was only half full. She found their graduation pictures and tacked them up on the tree.

She stepped back and admired her handiwork. "That was the easy part," she muttered, turning to the stacks of banker boxes. She realized she also needed to put a photo of Cousin Glenn on the family tree since he was there throughout that fateful summer when Henrietta and Richie died.

She found a photo of him in Scott's box and stuck it on the family tree, off to the side. She checked her watch. It was nearly four o'clock and she wanted to make a stop at the office before she met Molly for dinner. She trudged back up the steep stairs and perused the movie boxes, hoping a few of them would be properly labeled, but that was wishful thinking.

She heard a slight creak and froze. Someone was opening the garage door. If it were Scott, or Molly, or Jane, or anyone who knew her, they'd be calling to her. She swore quietly, realizing she'd left her purse—and her gun—downstairs. She'd been shot two years before, and because trouble tended to find her, she'd invested in a small handgun, a concealed weapon permit and a safety course. She moved against the wall, conscious of where she stepped. The old wooden floorboards would probably give away her position if she haphazardly waltzed across them. She'd just have to bluff.

She started down the staircase and said boldly, "I don't know who you are, but I have a gun. Please identify yourself now."

No one responded. She breathed deeply to slow her heart rate. She waited and listened intently. Whoever was downstairs had an incredibly light step or hadn't moved since her declaration. She imagined he or she would be studying the pictures on the garage door and the notes Ari had composed. The intruder might even take something essential if he knew what he was looking for. She needed to be proactive.

She couldn't see the garage door below from her limited vantage point, but the minute she put her foot on the first squeaky step, the garage door opened and light flooded the bottom of the stairs as the intruder fled.

She hurried down and grabbed her gun, tucking it in the waistband of her jeans. She charged outside but there was no one in the yard. She headed to the south side of the property and worked her way west. The only person she saw was a Hispanic teenager sitting at a bus stop across the street, scrolling through her phone. The girl looked up and Ari waved.

"Hi. Did you happen to see anyone come out of that house in the last minute or so? I'm worried I missed my sister. She might not have thought I was home, and she's bringing me some important medicine. Did you see her...or anyone?"

The girl looked at her suspiciously and shook her head. "No, I didn't see your sister, but there was a dude who went across the street."

"You saw a guy? What did he look like?"

She shrugged. "I don't know. White guy. Not really old or young."

Ari assumed she meant someone close to her own age. "Did you see where he went?"

She pointed to the Beaton's place. "Over there. To that house."

Ari reached into her pocket and pulled out a five. "Thanks for your help."

The girl shook her head. "Nah. I just answered a few questions. You don't have to pay me for being courteous."

Ari blinked and thought she might fall over. "Wow, that's really adult of you. What's your name?"

The girl smiled slyly. "I may be courteous, but I don't tell strangers my name."

"Thanks," she said with a chuckle as she headed back across the street.

She made sure she locked the wrought-iron gate behind her when she returned. She went into the main house and up the stairs. She'd found a pair of binoculars in the hall closet during her earlier snooping. She retrieved them and went to the master bedroom. The curtains were shut to block out the afternoon sun, but she opened them a crack and gazed across the street at the Beaton house. Ari remembered it was Mr. Beaton who'd accosted Blythe Long and said, "She killed her." He was dead now, but Ari imagined the bald man standing at the kitchen window and staring at the Long garage looked a lot like him.

CHAPTER TEN

Molly processed the information from Victor's case files during her thirty-six mile drive to Sun Lakes, the retirement community where retired P.I. Pete Daly lived. She'd called Andre last night and shared Ari's hunch that Brittany Spring, Victor's paralegal-of-the-month, might be on the video footage, leaving during the window of time when he was killed. She strongly urged Andre to visit Brittany as soon as possible. She hoped he'd listened to her. She exhaled, reminding herself she wasn't his boss anymore. She wasn't even a cop.

"But I still think like a cop," she muttered.

It drove her crazy that Andre didn't react quickly—to anything. She'd hoped he'd want to drive to Brittany's little apartment on the west side and roust her from her bed, which would've been the right move in her opinion. An interview with someone who was barely awake gleaned key pieces of information that otherwise might be guarded. She thought she'd taught him that rule, but he'd put off the interview until the morning.

"Let's just hope she's still in town this morning."

She shook her head and erased her frustration. She needed to focus on what she could control—her interview with Pete. He'd been a key player at GRD and one of Victor's most trusted colleagues. He'd counted on Pete to help him with some exceptionally messy cases.

She knew family law was often a volatile legal arena. Emotions ran high since children were involved. While Victor won more cases than he lost, whenever his client prevailed, it sometimes translated to an irate loser, usually the ex-husband or ex-wife of his client.

Over the years he'd experienced numerous telephone threats, and several people had tried to intimidate him as he left court. One irate ex-husband had tried to attack him in the court lobby, but none of those instances had ever led to further confrontations. He hadn't even filed an assault charge against the man who'd attacked him.

Molly and Ari had found only one case they felt warranted a second look. While representing one half of a lesbian couple in a nasty child custody suit, he'd been stalked by the opposing spouse during and after the case. A copy of the injunction was included in the case file. She intended to ask Pete about Gretchen Farmer, the offended spouse. Since the case had occurred three years prior, she doubted there was any connection to his death, but sometimes there were clues in the least likely places.

When she was on the force, she'd heard Daly's name mentioned periodically. He'd resigned and started his own company, but rumors suggested Internal Affairs had pushed him out over questions about his tactics and integrity. After reading through Victor's files, she had the same questions. She'd left Jack Adams a voicemail, hoping he could provide more information. An Internet search yielded nothing about other clients, and he didn't have a website or a Facebook page, which didn't surprise her. Pete was old school.

She pulled into the mobile home park and saw him in a lawn chair outside, smoking a cigar and drinking a beer. Since it was only ten o'clock in the morning, she chalked it up to retirement privilege. She parked next to his black BMW and deduced Victor paid him well, too well for normal P.I. work. If he could afford such a luxurious car, he had another source of income, or Victor rewarded him for unethical or illegal behavior to win a case.

"They better not expect that from me," she said through gritted teeth as she gave the BMW an envious look. Then she looked at the old mobile home. Clearly he didn't care enough to use any ill-gotten gains to improve his housing situation.

"Welcome, Ms. Nelson," Pete said, stuffing his stogie into the side of his mouth so he could shake her hand. He didn't bother to get up, and from his decent potbelly she guessed there was little that motivated him to rise from his chair. His short-sleeved plaid shirt was too small and clashed with his wrinkled Bermuda shorts. Only a wisp of white hair remained on his head, and a bandage covered the bridge of his nose. She wondered if he were being treated for skin cancer. "Please have a seat," he said, motioning to an identical lawn chair. He opened a small cooler between them. "Can I interest you in a beverage?"

"No, I'm good," she said casually. "I know you and Mr. Guzman were close, so please accept my condolences."

"Thank you. Victor and I were a good team."

"I appreciate you meeting with me and getting me up to speed."

He popped another beer and quickly sipped the foaming liquid before it dribbled over the side of the sweating can. He leaned back and crossed his legs. "There's really not much to get up to speed on. The firm hit a lull as I retired, and their cases were pretty straightforward. They didn't need much investigation. At least that's what Gloria Rivera told me."

From the cynical look on his face, she got the impression retirement had been proposed to him and not the other way around. "As I mentioned on the phone, I've been asked to investigate Mr. Guzman's murder. I was hoping you could share your thoughts about who might want him dead."

He laughed and shook his head. "That list is a mile long. Victor enjoyed confrontation in his professional and personal life. There was nothing he liked better than to watch the floor fall out from under an opponent during a cross-examination. Those smug assholes, usually a deadbeat dad, would tell some story, and then all of a sudden, bam! Victor would pull up some surveillance footage I'd found, or he'd whip out a phone recording and the other attorney would be screaming his objection. Victor and I, we made a great team," he repeated.

He kept laughing and she waited it out. When he nursed his beer again, she asked, "So, it sounds as if some people might've been upset with the methods he employed to win his cases."

He offered a sly smile. "Come now, Ms. Nelson, you don't need to be so diplomatic out here in Snoozerville. Did Victor ask me to break the law? Sometimes. Did he push the boundary of right and wrong? Absolutely. Morally, was he usually right? Yes." He shifted in his chair and leaned closer to her. "You heard about the CPS case? The one where we sued?"

"Oh yes. CPS blew it completely."

He jabbed at the air in agreement. "And the only way we were going to win that one was with a little sleight of hand and a lot of underhandedness." He looked up and added, "Sorry, Victor."

"I read he once had a stalker. Could she be a suspect?"

He grimaced and said, "I doubt it. That stalker-dyke, Gretchen whatever-her-name was, calmed down after she found another girlfriend. We never heard from her again."

She held her temper and crossed Gretchen Farmer off her list.

He took a big swig and set the can down on the cooler. "Here's what I think. My cop contacts already shared the details. This guy isn't a pro. It's probably a crime of passion, so it's someone in the office or a current client with a lot of access. Anybody from three or four years ago doesn't have that kind of rage."

She opened her notebook. "In your opinion, who are the suspects?"

He scratched the stubble on his face and said, "I'd say the office manager, Isabelle the Hell, Brittany Spring, Christine

Pierpont and Gloria Rivera. Outside the office, I'd pick Eden Venegas, Victor's ex-wife." He grinned. "You always have to include the ex as a suspect, right?"

His conclusions matched hers. "I can tell you've already been thinking about this."

"Oh yeah. The minute I heard about it, I started thinking about perps."

She flipped to a previous page of her notepad. "We interviewed Brittany Spring yesterday."

"Yeah, she shuffles between the attorneys. You may have heard paralegals were always temporarily assigned to Victor, but she's got her own problems. She makes a lot of mistakes and she's not his type of woman, you know?"

The hairs on her neck stood up. "What do you mean by that?"

"She's not girly. She never wears a suit. It's like she thinks she's working at Target. Except for the boots," he added. "She's got great boots. But Victor likes women to look professional and wear makeup. You know, doll it up. There's also her lack of ability as a paralegal. One time, she made a huge mistake on a complaint. Victor went through the roof. He called her a dog and started barking at her." He paused and asked, "Did she tell you this?"

She nodded. "Yes, and she said he had to apologize. She's clearly still upset about it."

"Damn right," he agreed. "Because it continues to be office gossip. People *still* bark at her, and all the new hires learn which paralegal is the dog." He frowned and she was pleased he disapproved.

"What about Christine Pierpont?"

"She and another guy, Brantley, are vying to be Gloria Rivera's successor. There was some hanky-panky going on between Victor and Christine."

"You think they were having an affair?"

He raised his eyebrows. "I *know* they had an affair. She thought sleeping with the boss made her the obvious choice to be named partner, but Victor was picking Brantley, not her. That would have made her mad enough to kill. She thought she'd earned it. Now with Victor dead, maybe they'll both get a spot."

She remembered the conversation Isabelle overheard in the stairwell. *If Victor thinks he's getting anything else, I'll kill him.*

"Wouldn't Ms. Rivera have a say about her successor, especially if Ms. Pierpont was the better choice?"

He puffed on his stogie and eyeballed her critically. "Can I trust you?"

She leaned forward, resting her elbows on her knees. "You can. This is confidential. I'm still on the fence about entering a contract with GRD. I've agreed to investigate Mr. Guzman's death, but nothing more."

He seemed pleased with her answer and leaned close enough so she could smell his beer and cigar breath. "Gloria Rivera owed Victor Guzman. She appeared to be a woman of steel, except when it involved going toe-to-toe with him. Anytime they disagreed, he always won. He never told me why, but when we'd be talking about her, he'd have a little smug smile."

He leaned back and said, "My money for succession would've been on Brantley, simply because he's a guy, and Victor Guzman was a male chauvinist." He looked up again and said, "Sorry, Victor. You know it's true." He met her gaze. "So, no, it didn't matter that Christine was the better attorney, at least not until Victor took a bullet in the head."

"So you're saying Ms. Rivera had a reason to kill Mr. Guzman?"

"She'd be my prime suspect."

She decided not to share that Gloria had an airtight alibi and changed the subject. "One of the employees we spoke to yesterday suggested people were contacting headhunters now, *after* Mr. Guzman's death. Would that be because he also had something on them?"

He sighed and looked away. "Still speaking confidentially, right?"

"Absolutely."

"Victor used people's secrets as leverage against them. One of my unspoken responsibilities when I did background checks on potential employees was to find their dirt. Victor tended to hire the candidate with the most vulnerability, not necessarily the most talent."

"Giving him the greatest leverage."

He nodded and finished his beer.

"So you know all of the secrets at GRD," she concluded.

"Most, but not all," he corrected. "I don't know what he has on Gloria Rivera."

"Isabelle told us about her side business. I'm assuming that's what he held over her."

"Ah, yes. Although she's not called 'Isabelle the Hell' for nothing. She makes everyone's life a living hell, but that's because Victor did it to her. Sometimes she was only the messenger. He'd put some ridiculous policy in place, like the one about the bathroom, and she'd have to enforce it. You've heard about that, right?"

"Yes," she said.

He looked around as if someone might be listening and said, "I was the one who made copies of the key for everyone. We kept that on the QT." He looked up again. "Sorry, Victor. All of the secrets are coming out today."

"What did he expect from Isabelle to ensure his silence?"

He shook his head and sat up straight, ready to give her a lesson. "Nothing. He had no intention of trading information for silence. Oh no. He held whatever leverage he had over the employee's head for the duration of their employment." He paused to allow her time to think of the ramifications.

"He created an environment of servitude," she murmured. "It's not that surprising he was murdered."

He nodded and grabbed another beer.

"Tell me about his ex-wife, Eden Venegas."

A wide grin spread across his face. "She's a looker. They were rotten to each other, but she should've gotten more than she did. He used all of his tactics to make sure she didn't get her half, even though this is a community property state. Not only did he hide some of his assets, but he also added a morals clause in the pre-nup. She could barely understand English when they got married. She had no idea what she was signing."

He leaned closer again and whispered, "I've heard she's found herself a young man, emphasis on the *young*. She was worried Victor would find out and invoke the clause. Then she'd lose the alimony and Miguel. Now I guess she's free to do what she wants."

"Tell me about Miguel."

"Such a sullen boy. Bright but sullen. Doesn't speak much. A mama's boy. He'd come to the office every Wednesday and drive Isabelle or Hannah crazy until Victor was ready to leave. Eden's life will be much easier without Victor, the least likely candidate for Father of the Year." He again raised his head to the sky. "Sorry, Victor."

"You've criticized him a few times now," she observed. "Did you ever tell him you thought his tactics were inappropriate? Did you advise him about other choices?" He seemed to withdraw. "Sorry, that wasn't my place to say."

He raised a hand, accepting her apology before he chugged his beer.

"What about Mackenzie Dearborn?"

He easily returned to the conversation when the focus shifted from him. "No, nothing there. That one's open and shut."

"There seems to be parts of the case file missing. Do you know anything about that?"

"Nope."

"Any other suspects?"

"Nope."

She didn't believe him but she didn't want to alienate him.

He pointed his cigar at her. "Definitely look at those folks I mentioned. And call me with questions. I'm sure this guy knew Victor."

She cocked her head to the side. "You keep saying 'guy' but all of the suspects you've mentioned are women."

He seemed taken aback as he thought about the statement. "Well, damn. I guess I'm a feminist after all."

She stood and thanked him for his time. As she turned to go he said, "Do you want to know the reason I didn't say anything to Victor about the way he treated people?"

"Of course."

"Because before he hired me, he hired someone else. And as a former detective, Ms. Nelson, I know you've heard the department scuttlebutt about my departure from the force. Who do you think knew all of *my* secrets?"

CHAPTER ELEVEN

Ari called Molly's cell, but it went to voicemail. "Hey, it's me. I'm leaving this message so you know I'm going over to visit the neighbor across the street from Long Manor. The last name is Beaton. In the event I don't return and you can't find my body, check the yellow house." She laughed and added, "Just kidding." She didn't mention Mr. Beaton had stealthily entered the garage and run away the day before. Those details would send Molly into action, and she didn't want to scare the guy off.

She decided on a peace offering of iced tea and oatmeal cookies from Coyote Oaties, a great bakery across from Murphy Park. When she'd picked up the cookies, she'd chatted with Kiki, the owner. She'd learned most of the businesses in downtown had changed hands multiple times since the Longs lived in Glendale. The only proprietor remaining who might remember them was Vada Michaels, the wife of the original owner of the Gaslight Inn.

Vada was already on her list to interview, but Garrett Beaton's behavior had immediately moved him to the top of the list. Armed with tea and cookies, she took a deep breath and started up the walk to the Beaton front porch.

The yard was nothing but dirt and patches of weeds that clung together for survival. The house was equally neglected. The yellow paint was so faded that the original deep pink color permeated the most sun-drenched spots and made the exterior look as if it had a bad case of acne.

While the house begged for remodeling, she noticed a speedboat and a late-model Chevy truck parked in the carport. She sensed a contradiction in lifestyle choices. She thought she saw the kitchen curtains rustle, so she was prepared when the front door flew open as she stepped on the porch.

"Good morning. It's Mr. Beaton, isn't it?"

He remained behind the old metal screen door. He was tall and imposing, and a slight tinge of fear kept her rigid, ready to toss the carrier holding the tea and cookies in his face and pull her gun from the back of her waistband.

She guessed he was about forty and had chosen to compensate for his bald head with facial hair, specifically long side burns and mutton chops. He had on a black Harley-Davidson T-shirt and jeans, and tattoos trailed down both arms.

When he failed to reply, she said, "I'm Ari Adams. I'm the real estate agent hired by Mr. Long. When I realized who you were, I wanted to apologize for threatening you yesterday. You surprised me, and when you didn't identify yourself, I got scared. Still, I certainly wouldn't want to offend a neighbor."

There. She'd said it all. She visualized the motions necessary to rid herself of the refreshments and pull her gun if he lunged at her.

"What kind of a gun do you carry?" he asked.

"Sig Sauer 9."

His stony expression shifted and he nodded, impressed. He opened the screen door and stepped aside, inviting her in.

"So, again, don't want to offend, but since our initial introduction was a bit rough, I'd like to enjoy the weather on the porch. Okay by you?"

He laughed, breaking the tension. "Understandable. Yeah sure."

Two old aluminum chairs and a metal card table were the only furniture on the porch. She set down the carrier and took the chair closest to the stairs. He dropped into the other one and picked up the cookie bag.

"Coyote Oaties makes the best oatmeal cookies ever," he said, as he fished two out.

"I've never had one."

He handed her the bag and she readily agreed after a few bites.

"I'm sorry for scaring you," he said. "When you mentioned the gun, I thought for sure I was dealing with a wacko. That's why I retreated."

She chuckled and relaxed. "Is your last name Beaton?" she asked as he dug inside the bag again. She was grateful she'd bought several cookies.

"Uh-huh. I'm Garrett Beaton. This is my dad's place. He was Ned. When I got out of the Marines, he was losing it, so I moved back. I'd lived in Vegas for years, but things weren't great there, and he needed me…" He let the sentence die in favor of finishing another cookie.

"Did you know the Long family?"

He shook his head. "My parents divorced when I was six, and my mom took me to Nevada." He glanced at her and added, "Actually, we ran away. Dad was abusive. He tried to find us a few times, but he never did. After I joined the Marines and grew up, I got in touch with him. I wanted to know why he'd treated us so badly. He apologized and we kept writing. I never told Mom before she passed. Eventually, I could tell he needed help. My mom was gone. I was an adult and a veteran. He wasn't going to pull any shit with me. And it was fine, except for the last six months of his life. Those were bad days."

"I know what you mean. My mom died from cancer when I was in my early twenties. It's hard to watch." He sipped some tea and offered her the cookie bag, which she declined. "Did your dad ever talk about the Long family or anything in the past about the neighborhood?"

He wiped some crumbs from his chops and pondered the question. "In the last two months he said a lot of stuff. Some of it made sense and some of it didn't. Most was about my mom and me. He never forgave her for leaving him." He shifted in his chair and pointed toward Long Manor. "Once in a while, when I'd wheel him out here for his breakfast, he'd stare across the street, point his finger and say something like, "That bitch was no better than your mother."

She felt a tingle down her back. "Did he ever use a name or did he just say *she?*"

"No, it was always just *she*, but it was odd because I got the feeling there were two people, or it was just one person with a split personality," he said with a laugh.

"Why do you say that?"

He poured the last two cookies from the bag into his large hand and tossed the bag on the table. "Most of the time, he was comparing my mom to the mother across the street, calling them both bitches, but sometimes he said the nicest things. Talked about how wonderful she was and the way she played with her children. He talked about croquet." He waved a hand. "I don't know. To be honest, I was only half listening. Those last few months he was really difficult to manage. I was up most of the night taking him to the john, so I was barely coherent in the mornings."

She smiled sympathetically. It had been very similar when she cared for Lucia at the end of her life, but her mother still had her faculties.

His eyes narrowed. "What's with all the questions? I mean, it's really nice of you to bring me cookies, but when you said you were a real estate agent, I figured you wanted me to keep an eye on the place or fix up my yard."

"Here's the thing, Garrett. The house sat empty for years because the heirs are fighting."

He snorted. "That figures. Rich people have time to argue." He gestured to the Long's yard. "And play croquet."

She let the comment go, imagining his childhood was far more difficult than most. But when she glanced at the expensive boat and truck, he noticed.

"Yeah, I probably shouldn't be throwing stones. I've done okay in the inheritance department. When you look at this place, who would've thought my dad had any money? Maybe that's why he did. He never upgraded a damn thing."

"Did he ever mention that Mrs. Long died in a terrible accident? She fell down the staircase that used to be on the outside of the garage." She paused while he searched his memory, but when he didn't say anything, she continued. "Mr. Long married another woman who was much younger than his first wife. There was talk they'd been involved before the first wife died. I heard your father believed the second wife killed the first wife. I've been hired by one of the heirs to see if I can prove his mother was murdered and your father was right."

Garrett leaned back in the chair, stared at her and exhaled. They listened to the birds chirp while he collected his thoughts. Eventually he nodded and said, "That actually explains something for me. A week before Dad died, he started to jabber incessantly. He'd talk about people dying and I thought he was talking about himself, trying to get prepared for what was coming. We'd have breakfast right here and he'd say things like, 'So much death…too much darkness.' One day he'd been going on for a while about death and the white light, and he suddenly dropped his fork and grabbed my hand. He was completely coherent and said, 'She killed her.' I just nodded, not knowing what he meant, but he pointed across the street. Then he started to cry. I'd never seen him cry."

They both automatically looked at the garage. As she sat on the Beaton porch, Ari imagined Ned Beaton's clear view of Long Manor before the wrought-iron fence had been installed. She wondered if, after his wife and son escaped, he'd fancied Henrietta Long and the life she had with her children. Maybe he'd become a voyeur and watched her from his porch. If he'd been an early riser, he probably would've noticed Millicent hurrying toward the staircase. Perhaps he watched her pour something on the stairs, already wet from the monsoon rains. If that was true, then why hadn't he said anything to the police? Lost in her own thoughts, she almost missed what Garrett said next.

"And I guess their mom wasn't the only neighbor to die. Dad went on about a little boy. He was nine."

Suddenly she couldn't breathe. She closed her eyes for a moment, and when she opened them she knew he was staring at her.

"Are you okay?"

She nodded but kept her head down. Mourning over Richie had ended years ago. She'd plastered an incredibly thick scar over her heart, but it wasn't something she could handle unexpectedly.

She raised her head and said flatly, "That boy was my brother."

He paled and his jaw dropped. "Jesus, I'm so sorry." He clasped her hand, but she automatically pulled away.

She stood and he followed her to the curb. Before she crossed the street, she turned to face him. "I'm sorry for the abrupt departure. Thank you for sharing those stories about your dad. And if you think of anything else, please let me know."

She handed him her business card, and he admired the ring she wore on her left ring finger at Molly's insistence.

"Hmm," he said. "Married?"

"Just about," she said.

"What's his name?"

She giggled. "Her name is Molly."

He threw his head back and laughed. "Oh, you're killin' me, Ari. You're killin' me. I don't even stand a chance."

"Nope," she called over her shoulder.

Ari stood at the corner of Glendale and Fifty-Eighth Avenue, across from the Gaslight Inn. Before she dove into the photo boxes, she wanted to know more about the drama that had split the Long family. Since the inn featured prominently in the affair between Junior and Millicent, she hoped someone would have some answers.

She already knew the Gaslight Inn was built in 1926, two years before Wilfred Long Sr. constructed Long Manor. Although the Michaels family wasn't the original owner, they had bought the place right after World War II. Ari had gone to elementary school with Luke, one of the grandchildren. He'd joined the Army after high school and perished in Afghanistan.

A flag was permanently displayed in the inn's front window in his honor.

Directly across from the front door sat a mint condition, banana yellow '66 Mustang. For a moment she felt sick to her stomach. She'd known someone with an antique Mustang who'd come between her and Molly. She quickly turned away from the car. A middle-aged woman swept the entry and quietly sang a song under her breath. Earbuds trailed out of her blond hair, tuning out the sounds of the street. She wore yoga pants and an Army T-shirt. When she looked up, Ari waved. She pulled a bud out and smiled.

"Hi, I'm looking for the owner." She held out a business card. "I'm Ari. I'm a realtor, but I'm not here about the property. I'm hoping someone might be able to answer some questions about the Long family and Millicent Farriday."

The woman's face fell. "Millicent. There's a name I haven't heard in decades."

"You don't seem thrilled."

"No, but it's not your fault." She stuck out her hand "I'm Deb. Let's go find my mom, Vada."

She followed her into a lobby that looked more like an old-fashioned sitting room. The overstuffed chairs and linen-covered tables established the early twentieth-century period. She admired a china cabinet filled with knickknacks from around the world. A high ledge displayed antique canisters, ladies' hatboxes and other period items. In the corner was a computer station ensuring guests benefited from twenty-first century amenities while enjoying the quaint, old-fashioned look of the inn.

Deb disappeared between a set of swinging doors marked "Employees Only." Ari admired the room until Deb returned with an elderly woman who used a cane. She wore black polyester pants and a T-shirt that read, "Former Hell on Wheels."

"Hello," she said in a scratchy voice. "I'm Vada Michaels. And you are?"

She had a warm smile and turned her head when she asked the question. Ari guessed she was also a little hard of hearing.

"I'm Ari Adams, Mrs. Michaels. It's very nice to meet you."

Vada blinked and turned her head so she could stare at her. "I know who you are. Adams family. You're Jack and Lucia's daughter."

"I am," she said, surprised. "I didn't realize you knew my parents."

"Oh, yes." Her smile faded and she said, "It was such a tragedy about your brother."

"Mom, why don't you sit down?" Deb suggested.

While she maneuvered her mother into a chair, Ari took a deep breath and composed herself. She wasn't accustomed to hearing Richie's name so frequently.

Deb asked, "Would you like some water, tea or coffee?"

"Water would be great."

"Tea, please," Vada croaked.

"I know, Mom," she replied, gently patting her mother's shoulder before she headed for the kitchen.

Ari guessed Vada was in her eighties, and the delicate way she set her knotted hands on the chair's armrests telegraphed her frailty. She knew it would be a brief interview, as Vada would tire quickly.

"I appreciate you seeing me, Mrs. Michaels."

"I don't get many visitors. This is a treat." She spoke slowly and took deep breaths, as if it were a struggle to do both at the same time.

"I wanted to ask you about the Long family. Do you remember them? They owned the soda pop factory a few blocks away."

"Of course. Junior and Henrietta, lovely couple. Junior was a regular at the pub."

"And do you remember Millicent Farriday? I believe she worked here back in the eighties?"

Vada shook her head and cupped her ear as Deb returned. "Millicent Farriday," Deb said slowly and louder. "You called her the floozy."

She laughed, slightly embarrassed, and Deb prepared the tea. "She'd come in late and act pitiful in front of my dad. He was such a sucker for a pretty face."

Vada raised her index finger. "That's true."

"Then she'd wink at me, like she was saying, 'See I know how to pull one over on your old man. You could learn from me.' She had one thing on her mind when she worked here, if you could call what she did *work*."

"What was that?" Ari asked.

"She wanted to find a rich husband, which is exactly what she did; only he was married to someone else."

"I take it you were around when she worked here."

"I was in high school." She narrowed her eyes. "You look familiar. Were we in a class together?"

"No, I was in school with Luke. We moved away when I was thirteen."

Vada touched Deb's arm. "Her brother was murdered," she whispered.

Deb's cheeks reddened. "I know, Mom."

"He went right after Henrietta passed," she observed.

"Yes," Ari managed.

"Your father was a great man," Vada said, pointing at Ari. "It was wonderful how he helped your mother deal with the cancer."

She froze and nearly dropped her water glass. She opened her mouth but couldn't speak. Her mother's battle with cancer several years after Richie's death had absolutely nothing to do with her father. At least, that's what she'd always thought. They had divorced and Lucia had moved to Tucson at the end of her life. Ari had moved to Tucson and joined the police force. They were a team, the two of them. As far as Ari knew, her father had no place or role in that part of her mother's life. Of course, Ari knew she'd traveled to Phoenix for some doctor appointments and some Hail Mary procedures, none of which stopped the aggressive cervical cancer. But her mother never mentioned seeing her father on those trips. Clearly, Vada was confused.

"Are you okay?" Deb asked.

"Yes. Vada, do you remember the last time my dad and mom stayed here?"

She stroked her chin. "Hmm. It was during dipshit Bush's first term. I remember talking to your father about him right here in this room. Both of us agreed that dust was smarter than that man," she said with a laugh. "It was right after nine-eleven, I think."

She tried to remember where she might have been, but Deb cleared her throat, and Ari was drawn back to the conversation. Her personal life would have to wait. "Getting back to the Longs, what can you tell me about Millicent and Junior?"

Deb answered first. "She started working here because she could only get on part-time at Fizz."

"She was a waitress at the bar," Vada inserted.

"Yup, that's right, Mom. And she was always hittin' on the guys. She just wanted to meet a man. Mr. Long started coming here on his way home from work. He loved his wife, but she was sick. I don't think he liked going home. Soon he was coming in every day, always sat on the same stool. Millicent waited on the other customers, but after she served their drinks, she went back to him like a magnet." Deb scowled. "Then my pop announces that Millicent's changing her shift. She's not starting until an hour later."

"Room four," Vada said.

Deb laughed and shook her head. "Great memory, Mom. You're right. Room four."

She looked from mother to daughter. Apparently, Junior's affair had been an inside joke for decades. "I'm guessing Millicent and Junior had a tryst in that room?"

"An *ongoing* tryst," Deb clarified. "Like that just became their bedroom. We took it off the list of available rooms to rent. Even if they missed a whole week, we didn't rent it out because the possibility existed that he'd want his pole greased at the last minute."

"Deborah!" Vada scolded. "Language, please."

"This was your dad's doing?"

"Oh yeah. Junior paid him well."

"Is he still alive?"

"No," Vada replied. "Heart attack. I always told him to lay off the fatty food but he never listened."

"How long was their ongoing tryst? And how long was room four unavailable?"

"At least a year. By then everyone knew. The only person who didn't know they were having an affair was Henrietta. At least I don't think she knew, but maybe she did. She was a smart woman and so sick."

"We took her soup," Vada murmured, her eyes closing.

Ari saw Vada was fading. Deb squeezed her mother's hand and her eyes opened again.

"When Henrietta died, did anyone suspect foul play?"

For the first time in the conversation, Deb turned to her mother to answer. Vada opened her eyes wide and seemed to completely comprehend the question. She looked over Ari's shoulder, toward the bar area.

"Mom?" Deb nudged.

"Nobody could prove it," Vada said finally. "And she was so sick. We all felt bad for her and those poor children."

"Do you think Millicent would've been capable of killing Henrietta?" Ari pushed.

"Yes," they said in unison.

"Tell her about the conversation Dad had with Millicent," Deb urged.

Vada looked confused. "Which one?"

Deb turned to Ari. "One day Millicent told Dad he could rent out room four again."

Vada nodded. "Yup. That happened."

"The thing is, Millicent had the conversation with Dad the day *before* Henrietta died."

Ari nodded slowly. "Like she knew something was about to change and they wouldn't have to sleep around anymore. Did your father tell the authorities?"

Deb snorted. "Nope, that wasn't gonna happen."

"Vroom, vroom," Vada added.

Ari looked puzzled. "What does that mean?"

Deb giggled as her mother continued to make the sound. "Mom, you crack me up." She squeezed her mother's hand and looked at Ari. "Did you see that Mustang out front?" Ari nodded. "That car and fifty grand is what Junior Long gave to my father as the price for his silence."

Ari strolled slowly through Murphy Park on her way back to Long Manor. She tried to stay focused on the case, but her thoughts returned to her own parents. Without knowing it, Vada Michaels had dropped an enormous bombshell, shattering Ari's understanding of a significant chunk of her past. Just as Vada relied so much on Deb, Lucia had done the same with Ari during her last year while the cancer choked the life out of her. Ari had stayed at her side when she wasn't working.

She suddenly stopped and dropped to a bench. She remembered a conversation with her mother about the cost of the aide who stayed with Lucia during the day. Ari had always assumed Lucia's health insurance covered it—until a bill arrived one day. She'd questioned her mother, and Lucia cut off the conversation. She demanded Ari hand her the bill, which she did. They never spoke of it again and no other bills appeared.

Ari closed her eyes. She'd been young and naïve about the ways of the world. She leaned back on the bench and exhaled, suddenly realizing that her mother didn't have insurance. She couldn't have had insurance. There was no job and no husband. Ari certainly couldn't afford a dependent on her own coverage. Jack paid her bills. That had to be it. She fought the urge to burst into tears. She wanted to go home and take a bath, but she had an appointment in an hour.

She took a deep breath, forced herself up and hurried back to Long Manor. As she pushed through the wrought iron gate, she heard the revving of a motorcycle. Garrett roared out of his driveway on a sleek Ducati motorcycle. He offered a wave as he passed. She admired the shiny chrome glimmering in the sunlight.

She pulled out her car keys and came around the corner to her 4Runner. Her windshield was shattered. There were three points of contact, and she guessed the weapon was a baseball bat. She noticed a piece of paper underneath the windshield—only it wasn't paper but the photo of Henrietta holding Junior, the photo Ari had used for her family tree on the garage door. On the back was written, "Let It Go."

Gripping her keys in shock, she looked around and gazed over at the Beaton's little yellow house. Garrett had seemed so friendly, but perhaps it was an act. Maybe his father was somehow responsible for Henrietta's death, and he worried the truth would jeopardize his inheritance. Perhaps he hadn't been the one to break her windshield. If not, she needed to ask him if he heard anything or saw anyone. She rubbed her forehead. A massive headache loomed, but she needed to deal with her windshield and cancel her afternoon appointment.

Once the phone calls were out of the way, she studied the garage. Nothing was missing or disturbed, except the empty space on her family tree where Henrietta's picture belonged.

She found a replacement photo, one of Henrietta with the children, and tacked it up. When the glass repairman arrived, she excused herself and headed toward the small coffee house a block away. The best remedy for a headache was indeed a bold espresso. By the time she returned, her windshield was fixed and her headache had disappeared.

As she pulled out of Long Manor, she cast a long look at the Beaton house. She knew how much Ducatis cost. And speedboats. And optioned-up trucks. She stared at the tired, decrepit little yellow house. She knew it hadn't always been tired and decrepit, but she remembered it had always looked creepy. Ned Beaton hadn't been a friendly man in public, and apparently he'd been a monster to his wife and Garrett. He'd been a loner, and maybe that explained his fortune. He was a cheapskate who never spent any money or had anyone to spend it on. But she wondered... She was certain the Beatons were somehow tied to the death of Henrietta Long.

CHAPTER TWELVE

When Molly saw Ari's text after her meeting with Pete Daly, she immediately called her.

Ari answered on the second ring. "I'm okay, honey."

She took a deep breath and didn't blurt her first thought. Dr. Yee had taught them the art of pausing before speaking. "Did you learn anything useful? Was he an SOB?"

"No, he was quite pleasant. Apparently, I scared him the day before when he came by."

Her brain went on alert. "What happened the day before?" Ari stumbled to explain and she frowned. "Honey, are you keeping something from me?"

Ari sighed. "Yes, I'm sorry."

She explained and Molly shook her head. "Well, if you're okay..."

"Thanks for understanding, babe. I'm wondering if there might be something to Scott's theory."

"Do you have anything concrete?"

"Well, now that you mention it, I do. And I'm only telling you this because I don't want to keep anything from you. I want—"

"Honey, just tell me," she said in an exasperated tone.

"I have a smashed windshield and a note written on the back of Henrietta's photo that says, 'Let It Go.' And I don't think they mean the song."

She offered a little laugh but Molly didn't join her. "What exactly happened?"

"After I visited with Garrett Beaton, the neighbor, I went downtown and spoke with the owner of the Gaslight Inn. I found my windshield smashed when I came back."

"Do you think Mr. Beaton did it?"

"I'm not sure. I'll tell you more about it later, and we can watch more of Cousin Glenn's fabulous movies."

"I can't wait," she deadpanned. "Stay safe," she cautioned.

"Yes, dear. And you're doing absolutely fabulous with tempering your anger." She hung up before Molly could respond.

On the way back to Phoenix, she tried to focus on her case and not worry about Ari. She pondered what dirt Victor would have had on Pete Daly. For a fleeting second she considered him a suspect until she realized he'd never make it up one flight of stairs. But could someone have used his inside knowledge about the firm and its secrets to serve her own murderous purpose? Possibly.

Her phone chimed with a text. Andre.

Can you meet for coffee at the Refuge?

She replied yes and headed toward I-10. She wanted to hear about his interview with Brittany Spring, but she knew he might not have conducted it yet. She felt as if she needed to constantly remind him about the loose ends. He struggled with following through—a concern Jack had mentioned to her a few months prior. He wanted Andre to succeed, but now that Molly was off the force and no longer his partner, Andre's shortcomings were obvious to the brass. And it didn't help that he hadn't been assigned a new partner yet. She knew he worked best with a collaborator, but the city was in an indefinite hiring freeze, which meant there wouldn't be any promotions in the near future since they couldn't afford to lose the beat cops. As it was, every detective spent a few days each month back on a beat in uniform.

He pulled in and she scrambled out of her truck to meet him. He'd barely shut his car door when she said, "Did you talk with Brittany? Did you find out anything from IT? Has she been arrested?" He looked guilty and couldn't meet her gaze. "Andre, what happened?" She couldn't help that the question came out in the same tone she used when she was the lead detective and he was the young upstart.

His shoulders sagged, as if he was about to confess his sins. "I haven't interviewed her yet, but we're absolutely certain she's not the killer." He barreled through the last part, hoping to avoid her wrath.

"Why not?"

"Can I get a coffee first?" he whined. "I haven't had nearly enough caffeine today."

They headed inside and the wonderful aroma of coffee greeted them. The Refuge was managed by several refugee organizations. Recent refugees from places like Somalia learned vital job training skills such as counting money, serving food and speaking English with customers. Molly and Ari frequented the place as often as she could since they served a variety of wonderful ethnic food depending on the current chef's country of origin.

Once they'd settled at a table with their coffees, Andre opened his iPad. Molly was pleased to see he had a list of things to share.

"Our tech is still trying to blow up that picture, but he's not having a lot of luck. It looks like there's something in her hair—"

"But no judge would ever issue an arrest warrant based on a fuzzy picture," she concluded. "What about the other women she left with? Can we identify them?"

He put up a hand. "Okay, hold on. We could but I don't think we'll need to. I think she'll talk with us because we know she's not the killer." She offered a raised eyebrow and he turned his iPad so she could see a screenshot. "The IT guy, Jean-Claude, confirmed that Brittany Spring was logged onto her work computer at eight forty-five, Tuesday night. When he checked her browser history, he found she'd spent time on one site not work related, the Phoenix Technology and Science Academy. Remember she told us she was president of the PTA."

"Right. But does he know when she went to that site?"

He shook his head. "No, she could've had it up all day."

"I doubt that, not with Isabelle the Hell on the floor."

His eyes got wide. "True that. She scares me. But she could've kept it minimized on her toolbar and it would still show up as active. We know she was on the school website at some point, but more importantly, he confirmed that Brittany sent a document to the copy machine at eight fifty-five, and it was a school flyer."

"She's not the killer," Molly said. "You gotta love technology."

"Exactly. She couldn't be entering the building at eight fifty-eight in a hoodie and working at her desk at the same time. I'm guessing she's been using the firm's equipment and supplies after-hours for her volunteer position as president of her daughter's school PTA."

"And that's probably enough to get her fired. But it means she was there. She probably heard the gunshots."

He pulled out his floor plan. "Here's her desk and here's the copy room. Notice they're both on the other side of the floor from the east stairwell, where Victor Guzman and his killer emerged. I'm thinking she got off the floor without the shooter seeing her."

Molly studied the layout, her mind formulating a series of events. "What if Victor went right and the shooter went left? She'd be searching conference rooms over here. If I'm Victor, I want to put as much distance as possible between me and that gun. I hide closer to the west stairwell, formulating a plan. Notice it's close to the copy room. I hear footsteps and I hear somebody push open the west stairwell door."

"So she gets away," Andre continued. "When we met her, I saw she wore her badge on a lanyard, which means she always has it with her. So she could've walked down to the fifth floor and hopped on the elevator, or she just walked to the ground floor."

"And when she got there," Molly continued, "she waited until she heard people getting off the elevator. She joined their group and walked out." Molly sighed and rested her chin in her upturned palm. "But why didn't she call the police?"

"That's a good question, one we should ask her soon. Because I'm thinking Victor heard her leave and assumed she'd call the police. That's why he made the choice to wait it out. He thought the cavalry was coming."

"It makes sense." Molly stirred her coffee. "For whatever reason, she didn't call, and then the killer left through the exit without a camera. You said we should ask her soon. Does this mean you *still* haven't gone to talk with her?" Molly knew she sounded frustrated, but Andre sometimes needed a kick in the behind.

He sat up straight and said, "Actually, Chief Phillips wanted a briefing on the case, and when I explained we'd learned Brittany couldn't be the killer, *she* made the call to postpone my interview."

Molly raised a hand in surrender. She'd been ready to bark at Andre, but she couldn't argue with him if he was just following orders. The brass had to be briefed at some point, but from a detective's perspective, there was never a good time.

She sighed and changed her tone. "Okay, so we know who didn't do it. What do we have on the suspects?"

He glanced at his notes. "I followed up with Judge Nolan, and he confirmed Gloria Rivera's story. She was with him the entire time until nearly eleven o'clock when he and his wife walked her to her car after the symphony. So unless we think she hired the most inept hit man in the history of the universe, she's cleared."

Molly opened her mouth to share Pete Daly's hunch that Victor held a secret over Gloria, but caught herself. While she loved collaborating with Andre, they weren't on the same team anymore. She worked for Gloria Rivera, and until she could learn if her secret was relevant to the case, Molly wouldn't share it with the police. Pete may have thought Gloria should be the prime suspect, but an airtight alibi was difficult to refute.

"You still here, Mol?" he asked.

"Yeah. What did you learn about Isabelle?"

"Isabelle grew up in foster care after her adoption went south. She had a sealed juvenile record, but I learned she did a short stint in jail for vandalizing a store, among other things."

"That's interesting."

"Her P.O. got her involved with Teen Town, the organization that turns troubled teens around."

"I've heard of it," Molly replied. "They do good work."

"Well, they changed her. She's an upstanding citizen, except maybe for that cage fighting thing," he added.

"It could be that Victor was holding her hostage at GRD, threatening to expose her to potential employers as well as pigeonholing her into the one position he wanted her to have— office manager."

"And never letting her use her degree," he added. "If you knew you were in a dead-end job, that might be enough to kill the person holding you back."

She peered at his list. "What else do we know?"

"I checked through all the names of the vandalized cubicles, and most of the victims worked closely with Victor. Not all," he emphasized, "but most."

"But if the shooter is internal, that could be because Victor isn't the only person she's angry with. Remember, Isabelle thinks everyone hates her."

"And they probably do," he agreed.

"Have you interviewed Christine Pierpont yet?"

"Not yet. She's in court the rest of the day. I'm going to get her tomorrow. I've interviewed thirty-four people. Most weren't thrilled to work with Victor, although they adore Gloria. Many were neutral and wouldn't say anything derogatory, but some were hateful. Almost all said they stayed on his good side because he had something on them. Fortunately, they can account for their whereabouts, and they have someone who can vouch for them."

"So, you're interviewing Christine tomorrow?" she clarified.

"Yes. Would you like to tag along?"

"Sure."

She shifted in her seat and kept her mouth shut. If she'd been leading the investigation, Christine would've been pulled out of court yesterday. "All of our evidence points to someone who works there, someone who could wander through the building and not be noticed. Plus she needs a badge to access the building, the elevators and the stairwell."

"Hold on," he interrupted. "We're not a hundred percent sure it's a woman."

"True," she admitted. "But do we have any viable male suspects?"

"No."

"We already know they hand out washroom keys like candy, and several people have lost their badges, including our victim. But just to play devil's advocate, what would it take for a non-employee to gain access, someone like Victor's ex? How would she know about the malfunctioning camera?"

He finished his coffee and dabbed his lips with a napkin. "If she'd hung around some afternoon, I don't think it would be noticed since there's a ton of traffic. The IRS customers wander everywhere, looking for restrooms and hunting down the vending machines. Anyone who's been in the building lately noticed the workmen dealing with the camera at the northeast exit. I think the killer could easily check out the exits and never be questioned." He leaned back and asked, "What did Pete Daly say?"

She recounted her conversation and he frowned. "He doesn't think any of Victor's clients should be suspects?"

"He might've liked Lonnie Wilkerson, but he's got an alibi."

"Not Mackenzie?" he pressed.

"No, but I'm inclined to keep her in the suspect pool." She explained her concern that things might be missing from the file. "I'm not sure where the rest of that file is, and it's possible Pete has it."

"Do I need to get a warrant?" he asked sharply.

"Not yet," she said. "Pete's playing ball with me and I want him to keep playing. I'll let you know."

"Then I'll run Mackenzie's background," he said, tapping on his iPad.

"Great. I'm going to visit Eden Venegas."

"Good luck with that one," he snorted. "She's a piece of work. It's not just a chip sitting on her shoulder. Try the whole iceberg. That woman is mad and she doesn't have any qualms about venting her hatred against Victor in front of their son Miguel."

They walked out to the parking lot, discussing the rumors about Pete Daly that circulated throughout the police department. His phone dinged and he read a text.

"Shit!"

"What?"

"It's Jean-Claude, the IT guy at GRD. Guess who left work early today, complaining she wasn't feeling well?"

She groaned and clenched her teeth. "Brittany Spring?" He offered a sad look and she snapped. "You need to get over to her place right now. She knows something, Andre. This investigation is about secrets," she stated. "We just don't know which one got Victor Guzman killed."

CHAPTER THIRTEEN

Andre had promised to call Molly after he visited Brittany's west-side apartment. She imagined Brittany was gone. She had suspected someone at GRD told Brittany the IT department was analyzing her emails and printing history, so she'd decided to run. Either she was guilty of murdering Victor and they just hadn't put the pieces together correctly, or she'd been a witness. In that case, the police wouldn't be the only ones searching for her. Such an angry killer wouldn't hesitate to eliminate her if she thought Brittany was a threat.

Molly resumed her planned agenda. Eden Venegas had been quite cordial on the phone and invited Molly to her home at the Cascades condo complex. She didn't sound like a grieving widow, nor did she sound angry, as Andre had reported.

The Cascades had once been apartments, but because they'd been built in the seventies, at a time when developers were still selling Phoenicians on the concept of apartment living, their square footage rivaled that of a small house. Since Millennial thinking suggested condos were always larger than apartments, the current owners had upgraded the units and sold them for quite a profit.

She entered a swank lobby with leather furniture and marble floors. A handsome young security guard sat behind a large counter that looked as if it was the command station for a spaceship. His name badge read *Ramon* and he greeted her with a smile. When she mentioned Eden's name, his face turned to putty, much like Pete Daly's had. Molly was quite curious to meet a woman whose name inspired such physical reactions from men.

He gushed when he called Eden. She must have asked him to do something unpleasant, because his goofy smile cracked slightly. But he still agreed. When he hung up, he looked surly when he buzzed her through. She took the elevator to the seventh floor, and as the doors opened, a child pushed inside. Molly quickly stepped to the left before the boy and the remote control plane he held smashed into her stomach.

"Miguel, wait!" a woman shouted.

He moved to the corner, holding the plane under his chin. She guessed he was about eleven. He didn't look thrilled to be sent outside, and she guessed the unhappy security guard would be babysitting him while she talked to Eden. He wore blue shorts and a white polo shirt, a standard school uniform. She noted a school emblem on the shirt, an atom embroidered in bright yellow thread. She remembered he went to school at the Phoenix Technical Science Academy, along with Brittany Spring's kid. She wondered why he wasn't in school, but she didn't think such a question would be the best opening for her conversation.

Eden stood against the open doors and smiled at Molly. Lovely and exotic, she had the fragile face of a doll, with large, dark eyes and flawless light brown skin. Her cream colored dress and matching hose suggested she'd be attending a fancy luncheon after their chat, but Molly sensed she dressed up when the plumber visited.

She said something to Miguel in Spanish before she turned to Molly. With a thick Mexican accent she said, "I apologize to you, Ms. Nelson. The last day has been quite hard for Miguel, and his manners are not good."

Molly glanced at Miguel, who seemed indifferent to his manners. He offered no apology to her and continued to stare at his mother.

"Please, go inside and I'll send him downstairs."

She motioned to the open door at the end of the hall. Molly heard her hiss at Miguel in Spanish until the doors closed. By the time she'd joined her in the apartment, she'd adopted the glowing demeanor of a debutante whose cotillion was about to start.

"Ms. Nelson, again, please accept my apology on behalf of my son. I'm Eden." She extended her hand gracefully, as if Molly should kiss it.

"Thank you for seeing me. I've been hired by Gloria Rivera to collaborate with the police and investigate your ex-husband's death."

"Of course. Please sit down." She gestured to a worn, brown leather couch. "May I get you anything to drink?"

"A glass of water would be great."

She drifted to the kitchen and Molly studied the layout of the space. A scratched and scuffed mission-style coffee table sat between the sofa and two claw foot chairs covered in a floral pattern. She recognized the small dining room table, a butcher-block top with white legs and matching chairs. She'd owned an identical set in her first apartment. It was obvious Victor got the furnishings in the divorce, and Eden got a trip to Goodwill. There was a picture of Miguel on a side table, but noticeably absent were any family memorabilia or decorative touches. Yet when Eden brought her water, Molly couldn't miss the gorgeous gold bracelet dangling from her extended hand as well as a lovely scent that could only be purchased in a high-end store; years of dating and one-night stands taught her the rules of perfumes and colognes. She knew from her background check that Eden didn't have a job and received two thousand dollars a month in alimony, as well as a thousand dollars in child support. Molly deduced she spent her money on *herself*, rather than her home, hoping her looks could land the next husband who would purchase much nicer digs.

When she'd settled into a chair, Molly said, "First, let me offer my condolences on the loss of Miguel's father and your ex-husband."

She nodded with hooded eyes. "Thank you. When I received the news yesterday morning late, it was difficult. Victor and I are divorced, but Miguel was still his son."

Molly noted that while her English was good, she still misplaced modifiers and switched tenses, a typical challenge for second language learners. "I understand there was a little confusion yesterday and Miguel's driver took him to the law firm."

"That stupid company," she hissed. "I left a message and they forgot to text the driver. Fortunately, Hannah called me right away. Victor was so lucky to have her."

She nodded but offered no comment. She didn't want the conversation to go off in another direction. "I might repeat some of the questions you've already answered, so I'll apologize before we start. Can you tell me where you were Tuesday night?"

"I was here. Home with Miguel. He went to bed about eight thirty and I watched television."

"What did you watch?"

She hesitated a moment before she said, "*Chicago Fire*. I already told Detective Williams all about the plot, but I could tell you, if you want?"

"No, that's okay. You must be aware that the police consider you to be a suspect in his murder because of your difficult divorce. How do you feel about that?"

"Well, it's not true!" She jerked forward on the chair as if she might pop off it. "Yes, he and I had problems. I didn't like him having girlfriends and not coming home. And he embarrassed me many times. One time a woman called from his office and told me Victor grabbed her breast and she was thinking of suing. I don't know what to say."

"When was that phone call?"

"Oh, this was over a year ago, I think. I'm not sure. He told me she made it up, but she didn't sound like it."

Molly offered a sympathetic look. "It sounds like you put up with a lot."

She took a deep breath. "You have no idea. When I met Victor, I was naïve."

"How did you meet?"

"My aunt worked the cleaning crew at his law firm. I used to pick her up after her shift. She and Victor were buddies because he stayed late. Sometimes they'd walk out together. She introduced us."

Molly glanced up from her notes. "Your aunt worked in the building? Does she still work there?"

"Uh-huh, but not in the law office anymore. The company moved her to a different floor."

Molly made a note and circled it. "Did you visit Victor's office much when you were married?"

She fiddled with her bracelet and wouldn't look at Molly. "Not often. I could see the way the other women looked at me. They talked behind my back and made fun of my accent. They thought I was stupid because my English wasn't very good."

Molly shifted on the sofa. "Unfortunately, that's a common error many white people make, when in fact, you should be commended for learning two languages."

She met her gaze and said softly, "Thank you, Ms. Nelson."

"Was anyone nice at Victor's office?"

The corners of her mouth turned up. "Isabelle was nice to me. She understood what it meant to be de clase baja."

"The lower class," Molly translated. "When did you get divorced?"

"Six months ago it was official. That's when he moved out."

"And how has your relationship been since then?"

"Up and down. I think Miguel realized his father didn't really want to be a father."

"What do you mean?"

"When we started the mediation, he made this huge show about wanting to spend more time with Miguel. He talked

about how much he'd miss his son if he didn't see him. I tried
to say that he spent very little time with him, but I didn't do a
good job. I sounded like a bitch and he looked like a superhero.
You know, he was a mediator."

Molly nodded, thinking of his last mediation assignment,
the Long family.

"He knows what they want to hear," Eden continued. "So
the court gave him every other weekend and every Wednesday.
But Miguel hated to go. Every time we fight about him spending
time there. On Wednesdays he had to sit in the office for hours,
waiting for Victor to be ready to leave. And on weekends he
works mostly and Miguel just plays video games." Her voice
strengthened, as if she were persuading Molly to take her side.
"Miguel just wants me," she said. She blinked to stop the tears
from smearing her makeup. "And now it is just me."

"How are you both dealing with his death?"

She crossed her legs and turned to the side. "It surprised me,
but Miguel's been very upset and he won't talk to me about it.
I guess he loved his father even though Victor didn't treat him
well."

"How so?"

"He picked at him. He called Miguel fatty when he was
overweight. Sometimes he told Miguel to quit acting gay. He
was always worried Miguel would be a homosexual."

"How did Miguel respond?"

"He just pouted." She threw up her hands. "I don't care if
he's gay but I don't think he knows either. He's only eleven."
Molly saw her flip the switch. Gone was the friendly debutante
voice, replaced by the sharp tone of a protective mother.

"And how are you coping with Victor's death?"

She chuckled. "I'm fine. He was just a son of a bitch and
got what he deserved," she spat. "He finally violated the wrong
woman."

"So you think the killer is a woman?"

She smiled. "Absolutely."

The answer sent a chill down her back. She thanked Eden,
who walked her to the elevator.

"Thank you for coming by, Ms. Nelson. Let me know if you have further questions." She smiled brightly and turned to leave as Molly stepped into the elevator. Eden belonged at the top of the suspect list. In the era of DVR she had no real alibi. She could've easily watched the TV show after fleeing the building. And she was certainly fit enough to chase after Victor in the stairs, even in heels. Andre would need to check out the aunt, since she could've easily slipped up to the tenth floor and stolen Hannah's key and then given Eden her own badge.

As Molly suspected, Ramon stood in the lobby watching Miguel fly his plane outside in the grass. His arms were crossed and his shoulders hunched. He clearly didn't like this assignment.

"Does she ask you to do this often?"

He sighed and nodded. "I feel bad for her because she's alone. I hope she gets a lot in the will."

He reminded her of her youngest brother, Brian, who was also a nice guy. She smiled and asked, "So when was the last time she asked you to do something like this?"

He thought for a moment and said, "About a week ago."

"Not last night?"

"No," he said adamantly. "I don't work nights. That's Sonny's shift." He looked at her seriously. "Who are you? I already told this to the cops and I gave them a copy of the parking garage footage, too."

She handed him a business card. "I've been hired by Mr. Guzman's firm to run a parallel investigation to help the police find his killer. I'd love to see that footage." He looked from Miguel to his desk, unsure of what to do. "You go pull it up," she said. "I'll keep an eye on him."

He nodded and went to his computer while she watched Miguel land the plane. He walked toward it and plopped down in the grass. His head was downcast, as if he was studying a bug. Sitting in the enormous swath of green, he looked completely alone. She wondered how many friends he had.

"Here it is," he called.

She glanced at Miguel once more before joining Ramon at the computer. The time stamp on the video read four forty-five p.m. "I told the police she phoned me at four fifty-eight, just two minutes before my shift ended. She asked if I would bring up a package. I was a little ticked because it was time to leave, but I took it up. She was in her condo at five p.m. Here you see her enter at four-forty." She watched Eden's Range Rover pull up to the parking gate and wait for it to open. "And if I fast forward, you'll see more cars enter, but only two other cars leave before ten thirty, and neither is a Range Rover."

"Do you know the drivers of those two cars that left?" she asked, pointing to a Chevy Cavalier and then a Toyota Prius.

"Yes, the Cavalier belongs to a tenant on the fourth floor and the Prius is owned by a gentlemen on the fifth."

"Is it possible she borrowed one of their cars?"

"I guess so, but why would she do that?" His puzzled expression told her he was as naive as he was upstanding. He couldn't imagine Eden killing anyone. He glanced through the front window and hurried to check on Miguel. The boy was spinning in the grass.

"Does Miguel have any friends in the building or do you see friends coming over to play?"

"No."

She saw a disturbed look on his face.

"Did the police get the information about the two cars that left?"

"Uh-huh," he said absently.

"Are there other pedestrian exits out of the building that aren't covered by cameras?"

"A few," he said grudgingly.

"So it's possible she could've walked out and the night guard never would've known."

"Highly doubtful," he argued. He looked at Molly like a protective lover. "She was here all night. I'd swear to it."

She knew to let it go. "Thank you, Ramon. I appreciate your assistance." He nodded but she could tell he was upset by the nature of her questions.

She glanced at Miguel again, quietly playing by himself. She always felt sorriest for children without siblings. She didn't know what she'd do without her brothers, and she felt a pang of hurt for Ari, who'd had a brother and then became an only child. Her phone buzzed. Andre. She had a bad feeling.

"What's up? Did you find Brittany?"

"Little hiccup in the investigation," he said.

She closed her eyes. His words downplayed the situation, but she heard the quiver of nervousness in his voice. "And?"

"She's gone, Mol. The building super saw her putting a suitcase in her car around noon."

She tried to control her response but she'd used up all of her restraint with Ari. "Damn it, Andre!"

CHAPTER FOURTEEN

"I knew it was too good to be true."

Jane was bemoaning the loss of her girlfriend Rory and the physical evidence that proved her unfaithfulness. Ari scanned the grainy eight-by-ten photos lying on the bar. She picked up one that showed Rory kissing another woman in a parking lot. It looked as if the pair were concluding an evening together and exchanging an amorous goodbye. Another shot clearly showed Rory copping a feel of the woman's right breast.

"I can't believe you hired a P.I. to follow her," Ari said, leaning close to Jane to be heard above the din.

"And it was a good thing I did," Jane replied, as she downed her fifth green Jell-O shot.

She and Ari were sitting in the Pocket, which was packed for a Thursday night. Ari imagined it had something to do with the free booze. Jane had defied Muriel, the health inspector, in a legal way, according to Jane's attorney. Since the Groove was private property, it was entirely acceptable to give away products, in this case, alcohol, and ask for a charitable donation.

Today all monies collected would benefit the Arizona Animal Welfare League, the AAWL, an animal rescue group. People were throwing in more cash than they would have had they paid for the drinks.

"Why did you suspect she was cheating?" Ari asked.

Jane wagged a finger. "Facebook. You never know when someone has a camera. One of my old friends from Laguna Beach had a b-day party at a gay bar. I'm innocently looking at the pics she's posted, wishing I could attend, when I notice Rory in the background. She's got her arm around this little thing," she said, stabbing at one of the pictures. "They look like they're having a fine time. So to be sure, I had my birthday friend find a good P.I. and tail her for a few days. I thought about hiring Molly, but I didn't think she'd take a case in California."

"Probably not." She took Jane's hand. "I'm sorry, sweetie. Have you called Rory and talked about this?"

"Oh, we talked about it," Jane replied, licking the rest of the Jell-O from the inside of the glass. "She wanted us to go on a cruise, and since I didn't sound enthusiastic, she asked what was wrong. I told her. I told her I had proof, too."

Jane grabbed another shot and threw her head back as she drank. She started to keel over, but Ari grabbed her arm and righted her on the stool. "Don't you think you've had enough?" Ari gestured to the empty shot glasses that stood in a line between them.

"Nope."

"So what did Rory say? Did she deny it?"

"No. She said she didn't want to be exclusive, and she thought I felt the same. Said she thought we had..."

Ari couldn't understand the rest of Jane's sentence, but she got the gist. "Did you have an agreement to date other people?"

Jane's mouth struggled to form words. She finally blurted, "Probably."

"But you want to be exclusive with Rory now. Is that it?"

"Probably. But that's not what she wants."

Ari bit her lip and held her tongue. She'd watched Jane turn away so many women who longed to have a relationship with her. Some of her angst was payback and a bit of karma, but Ari wouldn't say that to her best friend. "So what's next?" she asked.

"Nothing. We're done. She's called me five times and I've blocked her number, unfriended her on Facebook and deleted her from my Instagram, Snapchat, LinkedIn, Google Plus, Tumblr, YouTube channel and Twitter feed. She is persona non gratitude."

Ari almost corrected her but decided to leave it alone. She rubbed Jane's back and said instead, "Honey, it'll be okay. I know you're not used to feeling this way, but you and Rory will figure it out. If you're meant to be together you will be. If not, you won't."

"I won't. I decide and I decided."

She looked into Jane's blurry eyes and offered a sympathetic smile. "Tell that to your heart."

Tears streamed down her face and Ari held her. Several patrons turned and offered her comfort. She stopped crying when two young model-types sidled up and simultaneously pecked her on each cheek, leaving two lipstick kiss outlines on her face. One woman was a blonde and the other a brunette. Jane wrapped an arm around each one, and Ari could tell she'd found a way, at least for the short-term, to deal with her hurt heart.

"What is going on here?" a voice bellowed.

All the revelers turned to the front door and faced Muriel, the health inspector. She had her hands on her hips and her eyes were slits of hatred. Her red and white polyester pantsuit of the day was unfortunately pinstripes, and she looked like a candy cane. Standing behind her was Officer Joe, the beat cop who regularly patrolled Grand Avenue. He glanced at Ari and rolled his eyes. Jorge the bartender muted the music and the bar went silent—except for Jane. She flirted with the two women, whispering to one and then the other, making both of them laugh and blush. Ari could only imagine what she told them, or what she told them she wanted to *do* with them. Muriel glared at Jane. She either hadn't seen Muriel arrive or she'd chosen to ignore her.

"Ms. Frank, I ordered you to shut down this establishment."

Jane's face had disappeared underneath the brunette's flowing locks as she kissed her neck, so Ari stepped in front of the show and faced Muriel. "There is no alcohol being sold on these premises. It's free, and as the owner of this private property, I'm allowed to have a party, am I not?"

Muriel scowled. "What do you mean it's *free*? Nobody gives away alcohol!"

"She does," Ari said, pointing at the AAWL sign and the five-gallon water jug they were using to collect donations.

Muriel swerved and faced Office Joe. "Can she do this?"

He nodded and Ari could tell he wanted to laugh.

"I am recommending to the unit chief that this bar be permanently closed!" she bellowed.

That got Jane's attention. "Now, hold on," she slurred. The models helped her off the barstool and remained at her side. She smiled seductively at Muriel. "These are my new friends. What are your names, ladies?"

"I'm Kendall," the blonde said.

"And I'm Raven," the brunette replied.

"Ladies, this is Muriel. She's completely stressed out. Can you tell?"

They nodded and floated out of Jane's arms and toward Muriel. She seemed completely dumbfounded as each gave her a kiss on a cheek. The crowd roared its approval, awaking her from the spell cast by the beautiful women. She spewed incomprehensible sounds and ran out the door, wiping her cheeks with her palms.

"Ari, we good?" Officer Joe asked with a thumbs up.

"We're good, Joe. Thanks."

He left and the women floated back to Jane. She offered a chaste kiss to each one, and the threesome headed to the other side of the bar. Ari motioned to Jorge and he bounded over to her. "Don't let her drive. Call me, if necessary."

He nodded and gave an okay sign before he returned to shaking three martinis.

She glanced at her watch. It was six thirty, and she still had half an hour before her monthly date with Molly. Dr. Yee had insisted they have one night a month where they left their jobs and problems behind and did something together that was fun, exciting or romantic. They took turns planning the activities and reveled in surprising each other. Last month they had spent the evening at Flip/Dunk, an indoor trampoline facility. Ari had reserved a trampoline for them, and they'd spent two hours bouncing and laughing hysterically at the tricks they tried to perform. This month it was Molly's turn to choose an activity, and she'd already told Ari to bring a sweater and dress casually. They'd decided to meet at the Groove, but Ari could tell Molly had not yet arrived. The lights were off at Nelson Security and her truck wasn't in the lot.

She threw a twenty into the AAWL money jar and got a glass of merlot from Jorge before using her own key to enter Molly's office. She'd brought three more of Glenn's movies from a different box. She threaded the first one and saw the familiar sunrise over Murphy Park. Glenn was nothing if not consistent. He was also becoming quite proficient with focus. Within a few seconds it morphed to Blythe eating cereal. She flipped Glenn the bird and was apparently chastised by someone off camera because she mouthed *Sorry* before returning to her breakfast. The camera moved to the left, and for the first time in twenty-four years, Ari saw Henrietta Long, or what was left of her after the cancer ravaged her body.

She looked nothing like the photos Ari had perused in the garage. The disease and its cruel treatment had stolen her beauty. Her skin was pasty, nearly transparent. The black circles outlining her eyes had swallowed her pupils. Still, she attempted a smile for Glenn, who had the decency to pan the camera to Scott after her feeble effort.

The film skipped to a car ride on the freeway. Glenn held the camera out the window as they sailed past other cars. Some drivers and passengers offered a friendly wave when they saw the camera. Suddenly a goat stared into the camera and Ari realized they were at the zoo. Glenn panned to Scott, Richie and finally Ari.

"Oh, gosh," she exclaimed, flinging her hand over her mouth. She'd completely forgotten the visit to the zoo. She stopped the projector to allow her own memories to surface. She laughed when she remembered that same goat had stuck its head in a woman's open purse and emerged with her wallet in its mouth.

There had been other excursions, too. Blythe and Carlin were far too old for most of the outings, and Junior allowed Scott to invite his friends. Other memories came to mind, like eating pizza at Organ Stop Pizza and singing along with the giant pipe organ. There was also a trip to the TV studio for the local *Wallace and Ladmo* show. She and Scott had won Ladmo bags, something every kid in Phoenix wanted. She remembered she gave hers to Richie since he'd been so disappointed that he hadn't won one. They'd gone to Legend City and ridden the Zipper and braved the ice at the Metro ice rink. She closed her eyes and savored the memories. She'd forgotten how kind Junior Long could be. He always invited them and he always paid. She blinked and started the film again.

They came to the lion paddock, which was one of the best in the nation. Modeled after the savannas of Africa, the African Veldt was hugely popular. Glenn captured their enamored faces and panned over the veldt itself and the lions that played with their cubs. He kept the lens on the cubs for only a second and continued to turn counter-clockwise, past the spellbound crowd and over the walking path. He'd almost made a complete three hundred and sixty degree circle, and suddenly the camera jerked backward to the path. She struggled to find what Glenn was studying amid the clusters of zoo patrons walking in and out of the frame. Then she saw them. Junior Long stood very close to a redhead, who she immediately recognized as Millicent Farriday Long. She stood in profile talking to Junior, continuously stroking her flat belly. At one point she grabbed his hand and placed it on her stomach.

Ari stopped the film. She searched her memory of that day at the zoo, but all she remembered was how much fun they'd had. She couldn't recall a redhead distracting him. She re-watched the footage five times. There was only one way to interpret that moment. Although she wasn't showing yet, Millicent was pregnant and Junior Long was the father.

It wasn't proof but it was motive. If Henrietta died just a few weeks after the zoo video was made, and they were married a month later, they could announce the pregnancy almost immediately. Anyone with a calendar and a shrewd eye might figure it out, but most people weren't that observant when it came to other peoples' lives.

She rewound the film once more and watched Junior's body language. Was she breaking the news to him? This time Ari didn't stop the film. After Millicent grabbed his hand and placed it on her stomach, she looked at him longingly, watching him.

Suddenly the screen went white and the film's tail flipped in circles. "Damn!" she cried, just as the door opened.

"Are you okay?" Molly asked.

"I just found something incredibly important on one of Glenn's videos, but he ran out of film before it captured the final moment."

She dropped her messenger bag on a chair and joined Ari on the couch. "What was it?"

She told her about the trip to the zoo and the appearance of Millicent. "This had to have been shortly before Henrietta died. She looked awful at the beginning of the reel."

"Why would Millicent tell him at the zoo?" Molly asked. "I thought they used the Gaslight Inn as their love shack. Why not wait until they had an afternoon together?"

Ari shrugged. "Maybe Henrietta was getting too sick and Junior didn't have time for a tryst. Maybe Millicent didn't want to wait. Maybe she wanted to know his level of commitment immediately."

"Did everyone know the child was conceived out of wedlock?"

"Some people knew but Millicent wanted everyone to think Barry was a result of her and Junior's wedding night. The fact that they were having an affair was old news by then."

"So Henrietta had to have been dead before Millicent started showing," she concluded.

"Exactly. Millicent was desperate." She looked at her watch and grinned. "So where are we going?"

"You'll see," Molly said mysteriously. Then she looked stern. "Before our date officially starts you need to show me that threatening message."

She sighed and pulled the photo from her purse. "It's nothing, except it means I'm onto something."

Molly flipped back and forth between the three words "Let it go" scribbled on the back and the photo of Henrietta. Ari could tell she was controlling her anger, trying not to explode. Eventually she gave the picture back and said in a reasonably calm tone, "Please be careful and let me know how I can help."

"I will," she said.

She pulled Molly against her for a long kiss. They fit together so perfectly, and she was disappointed when Molly's phone rang. Their rule was no cell phones on date night, but technically they hadn't left yet. She groaned and they both looked at the display.

"Andre," Molly said. "If I don't take this, I might regret it, but if I answer it, I *know* I'll regret it. What should I do?"

"You have to take it," she said. "You're in the middle of an investigation with your newest and biggest client." She pecked Molly on the cheek and went to the film projector.

"Hey," she answered. Ari could hear him talking really loud and fast. "Slow down," Molly said. "Okay, okay. We'll be there as soon as we can."

She hung up and dropped the phone on the table. "I knew I'd regret answering it."

"What happened?"

"I think he's a little tense. He's having a lot of trouble narrowing his suspect list. He got a call from Phoenix Fireball."

"Who?"

"She's an MMA fighter like Isabelle. She wants to meet him down at the Panther Club. She says she has evidence that *proves* Isabelle Medina killed Victor Guzman."

"I'm sorry, babe," Molly said for the fourth time as they headed east on McDowell Road. "I know we're not supposed to screw with date night. I feel really bad."

She caressed Molly's shoulder and imagined her naked body on top of—no, under—her own. She leaned closer and whispered, "Date night's still on. But I believe we'll need a change of venue and time."

"Absolutely," Molly agreed. "I'll just defer my plans."

"Which were?"

"Oh, no," she chuckled. "I'm saving that surprise."

The Panther Club was located in the industrial section of downtown Phoenix. In a past life it had been a machine shop, but like many of the other buildings in the area, it was repurposed as the hip downtown area expanded its reach. As they crawled through the parking lot in Molly's truck, she grew uncomfortable. On the surface, the idea of women fighting and sweating had a rough appeal until she glanced at bumper stickers that proudly waved confederate flags, advertised Skoal chew, and supported Donald Trump. She hoped they could find Ms. Fireball and conclude their business quickly. Maybe there would still be time for Molly's date night plan.

Andre had provided directions to the back entrance, and as they opened the door, the rank smell of sweat slapped them in the face. She doubted a hundred women sweating together could make that stench, but as they passed a tunnel that provided a view of the stage and a fight, she saw one guy punch another squarely on the nose. Blood and sweat went everywhere. It wasn't the women stinking up the place. It was the men.

They found Andre in a dressing room talking to a female fighter Ari assumed was the Phoenix Fireball. She wore neon orange briefs that cupped her ass cheeks and a matching sports bra. Ari marveled at her washboard abs and bulging biceps. She scratched her nose and an entire muscle group flexed to attention. She was the living definition of rock-hard. Although she was Hispanic in coloring, her short hair was bleached blond and slicked back with gel. When she turned to meet them, Ari saw an enormous black eye on the right side of her face.

Andre introduced her as Shauna. She quickly shook hands with Molly, but her eyes slowly traveled up Ari's body. "Nice to meet you."

"You too," she offered in a clipped tone. She cleared her throat and looked at Andre, hoping Molly recognized she was using one of Dr. Yee's suggestions for extinguishing unwanted advances.

Through her stiffening body language, Molly's jealousy radiated in the room, but instead of acting on it, she asked Andre, "What have we got?"

"We were waiting for you. She says she has proof that Isabelle is the killer." He looked at Shauna. "Like the lady asked, what have you got?"

"I got this," she said, pulling out an eight-by-ten black and white photo.

Seven female fighters stood on the main stage surrounding a chunky man in his late twenties. He held up a certificate and they all smiled for the camera. Isabelle was not in the picture, and Ari guessed that was the point.

"How does this prove Isabelle killed Victor Guzman?" he asked.

"Tuesday night is Fan Appreciation night. We've got to be here at eight thirty or we could lose our jobs. That's when this was taken. I heard Isabelle said she was here all Tuesday night and that's bullshit. If she'd been here, she would've been in this picture. Whatever she was doing could've cost her job. She didn't show up until nearly ten o'clock when our fight was scheduled to start."

"She fought you Tuesday night?" he clarified.

"Yeah, but weigh-in is supposed to happen thirty minutes before the fight. Let me show you my other evidence," she said, reaching for a folder on the table behind her. "I borrowed this from CC, the manager. This is the weigh-in sheet for Tuesday. Take a look at the time he wrote for Isabelle."

"It says nine-fifty."

"I rest my case," she said smugly. "Isabelle didn't get here until nearly ten. I don't know where she was, but it wasn't here."

"I'll need to keep these," he said.

"Be my guest," she said, her gaze drifting back to Ari. "Now, sweet thing, would you like to join me for a drink?"

She shook her head. "No thanks. But I do have a question for you." Shauna puckered her lips as if she was about to give her a kiss. "Who gave you that nasty black eye? Did Isabelle do that?"

Shauna frowned and huffed out of the room. Molly giggled and pulled her into a hug. "You crack me up."

"It was just a question," she said mildly.

Andre's phone rang and he waved goodbye as he answered it.

"Maybe we could still have date night?" Ari suggested on their way back to Molly's truck.

Molly's cell phone rang. It was Gloria Rivera. "Or not," she groaned. She tapped the screen. "Nelson."

Ari watched Molly who remained stoic through the call. She said, "I'll be there in ten," before she disconnected. She frowned at Ari. "Someone broke into Victor Guzman's condo about an hour ago. Gloria wants me to get over there and see what happened."

"I'll bet that's what Andre's phone call was about."

"Probably." She exhaled. "I'm sorry about date night."

"Let's go. Hopefully we can slip in with Andre."

Molly nodded and called him with the phone on speaker. "I just heard about the break-in at Guzman's condo."

"How'd you hear about that?"

"Little bird. Mind if we join you?" she asked in a friendly voice.

He sighed. "No, it's fine. Just—"

"I promise I'll be under the radar. I won't order you around."

He chuckled. "Okay."

"How did the perp get in? I thought PD had it cordoned off."

"They do. But a neighbor who was going out for the evening saw someone in jeans and a baseball cap come out of the condo. He called to the person but she ran away and headed down the stairs."

"She?"

"The man said the intruder ran like a girl."

CHAPTER FIFTEEN

The Chateaux on Central was by far the gaudiest and most ostentatious condo building in all of Phoenix. Built to resemble an English castle, the exterior included turrets, elongated windows, dark colors and parapets. It reminded Ari of Hogwarts in the Harry Potter series. From what she'd learned about Victor Guzman, she imagined the place appealed to his narcissistic heart. She'd only been inside once with a fickle buyer who eventually dumped her for an agent who'd sleep with him.

Molly had insisted they stop so she could get a Coke at QT. Ari knew she wanted Andre to arrive first and direct the investigation without her present because her law enforcement connections ran so deep. In fact, they rode up to the eighth floor with some of her former crime scene cronies.

Victor's unit was easy to find. Each condo boasted over two thousand square feet of living space, which meant only three condos could fit on a floor. His was the open door around the corner from the staircase, Eight C.

His place had been ransacked. Overturned furniture, slashed cushions and a trail of a yellow substance across the engineered hardwood greeted them.

Andre came around the corner and threw up his hands. "I don't get it. What's with this perp?" They laughed at his bootied feet and rolled up trousers. "Yeah, you keep laughing," he snapped.

"What do we know?" Molly asked.

He took a deep breath and opened his iPad. "Mr. Jackson, the neighbor in Eight B, called the front desk at six fifty-four. He was on his way out for dinner. As he locked his door, he looked up in time to see someone exiting this unit. He called to her but she ran off. He said it was definitely a woman wearing dark stretch pants, a sweatshirt and a baseball cap. Unfortunately she turned away so he didn't get a look at her face."

Molly bent over to see the yellow trail. "Is this mustard?"

"It is."

"What color was the ball cap?" Ari asked.

"Red. I asked if he'd noticed a logo, but he said no. So the front desk called us. Our people had left about three thirty, so the perp came in some time after that. There aren't any cameras up here, but we'll get the footage from the lobby." He pointed at their shoes. "You'll want to take those off, unless you'd like to buy new ones."

They took off their shoes and socks and donned police-issue booties and gloves. The hallway had turned into a lake and was wending into the living room. An empty bookcase greeted them, the books scattered on the floor. A few were soaked from tendrils of water that had escaped the hallway. Ari read titles like *Good to Great*, *Blink* and *Who Moved my Cheese?* She glanced at the empty shelves and looked for the rest of the books.

"What are you doing?" Molly asked.

"Give me a second," she replied.

She wandered further into the living room and realized several books had been dropped onto an overstuffed chair. She noted a leather-bound copy of *Don Quixote*. Opening the cover with a pen from a nearby table, she searched for the publication date. *1927.* She glanced at the spines of the other books that shared the chair. All belonged in a rare book collection.

"This is weird," she said. "The perp shoves most of the books onto the floor, not caring if any of them get soaked. But she takes the time to move these over to this chair."

"To save them," Molly concluded.

"Yes."

"They need to be fingerprinted," Andre said. He motioned to a technician and pointed to the chair.

They followed him down the hall. Three pictures of Miguel bobbed on top of the water, which was deepest in the bathroom. Decorative black and white tile lined the floors and walls. A claw foot bathtub with an oversized showerhead merged the vintage look with modern accessories. A tech dusted the sink fixtures for prints, and the blade of a man's striped tie hung over its edge like a tongue.

"She stuffed a tie in the sink, just like at the law firm," Andre observed. "Whoever did this has some serious anger issues."

"I'm guessing she came in right after your people left," Molly surmised. "Maybe she was waiting for them to go."

They slogged to the bedroom. Feathers covered every surface and two mangled pillowcases lay in a heap on the floor. Nightstand drawers had been tossed on the bed, and Ari chuckled at the dozens of colorful rainbow condoms lying on the white comforter. Dresser drawers were strewn across the carpet, and the mirror had been smashed and sat askew on the wall. Only an original oil painting by someone named Lamilo had been spared, but it hung crooked. Its bold colors formed various rectangular shapes. It reminded her of Mark Rothko's work, and she liked it very much. Victor may have been an asshole, but he had good taste. She studied the painting's brushstrokes and ascertained it was an original. She tapped on her phone while Molly and Andre ventured into the expansive walk-in closet.

"Babe, you have to see this," Molly called.

"Give me one sec." She skimmed a Wikipedia article on Pia Lamilo, a Mexican artist. The picture on the wall had sold in 2015 for twenty thousand dollars.

She headed to the closet and was met by an enormous pile of clothes as high as their heads. Every hanging rod and drawer was empty and his entire wardrobe lay in the center.

"I've never seen a man who owned this much clothing," Molly commented. "I have three brothers and I don't think they have this many clothes *combined*."

"Well, I don't think it's that much," Andre countered.

She snorted and crossed her arms. "Said the man who has a different suit for every day of the month."

"Hey, now," he warned.

In the back of the closet was a pine armoire. Ari admired the hand-carved decorative top piece. Both doors were open and she wasn't surprised to see it had also been cleared out. Drawers lined the left side while the right side was a suit cabinet with a hanging rod.

Dejectedly, Andre scratched his head. "We need a break on this case. I got a missing suspect, a vandalized crime scene and a computer password that can't be cracked." His phone rang. "And now the chief's calling me." He continued to mumble as he headed back toward the kitchen to answer the call.

"This isn't the same perpetrator," she announced to Molly.

"What? You don't think Victor's killer did this?"

"No. Let's say Isabelle is the killer. Do you really picture her taking time to move rare books out of harm's way?"

"You're right," Molly said, nodding. "In fact, if you hated him enough to kill him, you'd probably stick those rare books in the sink after you stuffed the tie in the drain."

"Yes," she said. "I think this was staged to look like what happened in the office, but it's not the same person." She pointed back at the bedroom. "There's a piece of art in his bedroom that's worth twenty grand. It's not damaged."

"Whoever did this has an appreciation for art and fine things," Molly suggested. She cocked her head to the side. "Why do this at all? Was she looking for something?"

Ari grinned. "I think she was. Notice everything that was on the walls is either tossed to the floor or slightly askew, even his bedroom mirror. She smashed the glass, like the copy machine. Why look behind the mirror?"

Molly clapped her hands. "A safe. She was looking for all of the stuff he has on everyone." She grinned and stared at Ari with great admiration. "You are so hot right now. I love the way your mind works."

She winked. "Well, get ready for the big finale." She reached into the pile of clothes and withdrew a suit hanger. She hung it on the clothing rod in the armoire's suit cabinet. It stuck out beyond the edge. "This side isn't as deep. There's no way you could hang anything on this rod and close the door."

"Because there's something back there," Molly said.

They both carefully searched for a release button. Then her finger ran over a bump in the bottom drawer. She tapped the flashlight app on her phone and illuminated a small white button. "Wait, I think I got it," she said. She pressed the button several times but nothing happened. "This is it, but I can't get it to work."

"Hold on," Molly said. "There's a light up here at the top. Let me turn it on." She twisted the knob of a small dome light and a bright glow splashed the right side of the armoire.

Ari pressed the button and the back panel slid to the left, exposing the door to a safe and a keypad entry.

"Well, I'll be damned," Molly said. "It's like a crazy *Get Smart* episode. We're gonna need a safecracker."

"I don't think so," Ari countered. "I know he used a complicated password for his computer, but this setup was complicated enough that he wouldn't be that concerned about the safe itself."

"So he made the combination easy to remember."

"Just a guess. When was his birthday?"

Molly shook her head. "Let me find it. I have the file in my email."

She pulled it up and gave a long look toward the bedroom. Ari raised an eyebrow. "Aren't you going to tell him?"

"Sure, after we see if you're right." Ari cocked her head to the side with a questioning look. Molly leaned closer and whispered, "I have to keep reminding myself that I'm not on his team anymore. I work for GRD, and if there's something inside that hurts my client, I need to know before the police take it and hand it to the D.A."

"That makes sense…but it doesn't," she replied honestly.

"I know."

They entered Victor's birthday on the keypad in various number and letter combinations. When none of those worked, Ari said, "Let's try Miguel's birthday."

Molly scrolled through the file on her phone. "Ironically, it's the fourth of July."

Ari entered in the standard two-digits for month and day and four-digits for year. The door popped open. Molly looked over her shoulder, but no one had joined them. She looked at Ari with a panicked look. She didn't know what to do. Ari made the choice for her.

"I'm going to get Andre."

She squeezed Molly's arm and left the closet. She proceeded slowly, cautiously, looking for him in each room. She didn't like keeping things from him, but she understood Molly's thinking. Victor Guzman had leveraged many secrets. He controlled the people around him, stalled their careers and forced them to kowtow to his will.

He reminded her of Millicent, an equally controlling person. She couldn't wait until Henrietta's debilitating disease naturally removed her from the earth. Ari reminded herself that Junior also benefited from Henrietta's death. She wondered how much he knew.

Eventually she wound up back in the kitchen. She saw an old friend of her father's, Officer Nunez, who offered a wave. "Where did Detective Williams go?"

He pointed toward the hallway, and Ari slid outside with a sense of urgency in her step and a serious expression on her face. Andre was concluding his conversation with the chief. When he saw her, his eyes widened.

She nodded and his answers became short and agreeable. Another thirty seconds and the chief let him go.

"What'd you find?"

"You're not going to believe it."

He followed her back to the closet where Molly waited. She gestured toward a treasure trove of envelopes, boxes, DVDs, and micro-cassette tapes stashed in the small safe. She held up a document and said, "Anyone want to see what Victor has on the governor?"

CHAPTER SIXTEEN

When Molly arrived at the office tower, she had to remind herself to press the fifth-floor button instead of the tenth. She was meeting Andre to interview Christine Pierpont, Victor's former lover and the attorney Gloria Rivera favored to replace her. She yawned, wishing they could've avoided a seven thirty a.m. interview, but Christine was due in court at nine.

They hadn't left Victor's apartment until midnight, perusing the entire contents of the safe—minus the two items Molly had removed before Ari ushered Andre into the room. She smiled when she thought about Ari's trust in her judgment. Pete Daly had said he and Victor were a great team, but Molly knew she and Ari were a better team.

They had unearthed many secrets when the safe door opened including a sex tape of Victor and Christine and a picture of the law firm's third partner, Richard Dorn, snorting cocaine. In addition, Victor had acquired a police report from Kansas that detailed a serious domestic violence call involving Arizona's sitting governor and his first wife, a woman with mental illness.

Molly wondered how much he'd paid to keep that out of the press.

Very disturbing was the amount of info Victor had collected on his ex-wife Eden. He'd had her tailed, and he'd bugged her condominium. They found pictures showing her getting into a Dodge Charger and an audio recording of her having sex with someone in her condo, but it was too muffled to recognize her partner's voice. All of the time stamps were post-divorce, implying he couldn't let go of his wife and had resorted to stalker-like behavior. Most chilling was a hand-written list of ways he'd like to kill her. Perhaps Eden had learned of his murderous plans and struck first.

Andre promised to follow up and report back. They hoped the D.A. would suppress all of the secrets except those involving ongoing illegal activities—illegal activities within the statute of limitations—or secrets germane to the eventual case against Victor's murderer. Most items in the collection were personal and embarrassing. Several were innocuous; they involved people who were dead or probably far too old to care anymore.

The elevator doors opened to the fashionable GRD lobby. While she waited for the receptionist to finish a telephone call, she watched a promo video about the firm on an overhead TV. A narrator talked about the courageous cases GRD tackled, noting their victory over CPS. She almost laughed out loud when Victor called the GRD employees his family. Gloria Rivera eloquently spoke about fighting for the underdogs. Even the late Richard Dorn was featured, discussing the pro bono work done by GRD. Photos of employees working in a soup kitchen, building houses and playing softball gave credence to his narrative, although the shot of the softball team in their red shirts, matching hats and jeans seemed almost comically antithetical to the sea of expensive suits she'd seen two days ago in the courtyard.

"I'm sorry to keep you waiting," the receptionist said. "Detective Williams is already here."

She led Molly to a conference room where Christine Pierpont and Andre sat across from each other, chatting. Molly could tell he'd turned on the charm with his flirty smile. They both looked to the doorway when Molly appeared. She nodded at Andre, whose smile vanished.

Christine rose and stuck out her hand. "Christine," she said.

She wore a smart charcoal grey suit, and her blond hair was pulled away from her face by a barrette that sat at the crown of her head. Molly knew she was in her late thirties and had spent her entire career at GRD.

"Would you like some water?" she offered.

Molly declined and took a seat next to Andre. Christine sat at the head of the table with her hands folded in front of her. She clearly wanted to start on time, and Molly couldn't blame her. She remembered what court days were like when she was a detective. She prepared extensively for cross-examinations by the defense and had gained a reputation as one of the most difficult detectives to trip up during a cross. Juries believed her because she was credible, but it all started with her routine on court day.

"Thanks for meeting us today, Christine," Andre said. "We know you have to get to court, so we'll go as quickly as we can." She nodded and Andre glanced at his iPad. "Can you please retrace your steps on Tuesday night for me?"

"Certainly." She pulled two documents from her notepad and handed them each a copy. "I've taken the liberty of preparing a written statement. It includes my whereabouts on Tuesday night and the names and phone numbers of the attorneys who were with me. You'll notice in the first paragraph that I was with a group of friends from law school. We had a seven o'clock dinner reservation at the St. Francis restaurant on Camelback Road. At approximately eight thirty we decided to go to the Sky View Lounge downtown. We were there until about ten thirty."

"Did you carpool with anyone to dinner or the club?" Molly asked.

"No," she said. "Unfortunately, I drove alone."

Andre cleared his throat. "Ms. Pierpont, we've heard some of the office scuttlebutt and I'm hoping you can address a few things—"

"Yes," she said plainly. "I had an affair with Victor Guzman. He was separated from his wife at the time, at least that's what he told me. It lasted a few short weeks and I tried to put it behind me." She paused and took a breath as if to recover from her utterance of the bald-faced truth. "Then, when Ms. Rivera announced her retirement and wanted me to be the one to replace her as a name partner, I knew the affair would surface." She looked up with dismay. "I was an idiot," she summarized. "I jeopardized my entire career and now I'm a suspect in the murder investigation of my former lover."

Andre glanced at Molly and asked, "Ms. Pierpont, it sounds like you've done a lot of personal reflection about your behavior, but we've heard from other employees that you were still angry with Mr. Guzman as well. In fact, you were overheard saying recently, 'I'll kill him.' Do you remember saying that?"

She looked momentarily stunned until she remembered when she'd made the comment. She adopted a look of resignation. "I said that on the phone to my best friend, Sheridan Upchurch, who also happened to be with me Tuesday night. During the phone conversation you're referencing, Detective, I was angry, but I certainly didn't mean it literally."

Molly watched her carefully but noticed no change in her body language. "We also know that another attorney, Brantley Dalton, is being considered for partner. Until Mr. Guzman's death, he likely would've been chosen. Had you heard that?"

Her face fell and she shook her head. "Brantley and I have a healthy competitive relationship. Honestly, he's like the brother I never had. If I'm not named partner, I'd be disappointed, but if I'm going to lose, I'd be happy for him. He's a good attorney."

Andre leaned on the table and clasped his hands. He was getting his flirty self together. "Aw, c'mon, now, Ms. Pierpont. I think you'd be more than disappointed. You've worked here twice as long and three other guys leap-frogged over you to make senior associate. I heard headhunters have courted you, but you turned them down. Isn't it true that Mr. Guzman cuckolded you and threatened to sabotage any plans you might have for leaving?"

Christine stiffened as he laid out the crass history of her tenure at GRD. "Yes," she admitted. "When I ended it with Victor, he was furious. He told me he'd never give me a good recommendation."

"When was this?" Molly asked.

"About a year ago."

Molly held up a hand. "Hold on. I need some clarity. You broke up with him and he told you that you'd destroyed your chance for advancement?"

"Correct."

"And did he further imply that if you resumed the affair those opportunities might reappear?"

She paused and nodded.

"That's illegal. Why didn't you report him?"

She gazed at Molly with a pathetic look. "Ms. Nelson, do I really need to explain that to you?"

Andre looked puzzled. "What about Gloria Rivera? Certainly her recommendation would carry weight with law firms in the valley."

"Victor said she couldn't help me, but he wouldn't say why. I assumed he had something on her as well. And she knew I was stuck, so she recommended me for partner."

"Now that Victor's gone, you have a chance and a choice," he concluded.

"I suppose that's true," she said, her voice a mixture of sadness and hope. She glanced at her watch. "I really need to get to court. Is there anything else?"

Andre glanced at Molly who shook her head. "No," he said. "Thank you."

She hurried out without a formal goodbye. Molly could tell her confidence had eroded as a result of the interview. She hoped she had enough time to rebuild it before court.

Molly glanced at Andre, who seemed to be reading the statement Christine had left. She felt the tension in the room and saw it in his shoulders.

He looked up at her and asked, "So what do you think?"

"I think she's telling the truth about her relationship with Victor."

"Do you like her for the killer?"

"Maybe," she said. "Do any of our suspects have a firearm registered to them?"

He shook his head. "None of the women owns a gun. But that doesn't mean anything."

It was true. Purchasing a gun in Arizona was easier than getting a fishing license. She stared at the statement Christine had provided. She pulled a sheet of paper from her notepad and made a drawing. "She had dinner at the St. Francis, which is one mile from this building. She didn't carpool, so I'm wondering if she stopped here on her way downtown to the bar."

"Why?"

"Maybe she forgot something she needed for court the next day? Remember, we couldn't interview her because she was in court."

"So you're thinking she might've been here. But why would she be on the tenth floor? Her desk is on five."

"What if she needed something from her paralegal? What if she wanted thirty minutes to practice in one of the tenth floor conference rooms?" He smirked. "What's wrong?"

"We pulled the lobby tape from eight thirty to ten thirty, but if she came by earlier, we wouldn't have seen her on the footage."

"If she heard the shots while she was here and escaped, she might have decided to take the northeast exit where the camera was out. Then she could avoid being questioned."

"We know she received those emails from the property manager about the work being done on the northeast exit. Are you thinking Christine *and* Brittany were both here?"

"Could be. Once Brittany surfaces, it'll be a good question for her." Andre frowned at the mention of his missing witness. "Whoever it was," she continued, "Victor counted on that person to do the right thing and call for help, but she didn't."

Andre snorted. "Yeah, but after what we saw last night in that safe, I think there's a hell of a lot of people who would've made the same choice." He fiddled with his iPad but wouldn't look at her.

"What's wrong?" she asked.

"She said Victor had something on Gloria Rivera, but we didn't find anything in the safe."

She felt her stomach tighten. "Maybe he really didn't and Christine was incorrect," she lied.

"Maybe," he replied, his gaze locked on Molly.

She stared back at him and finally said, "What?"

"Look me in the eye and tell me that you didn't take anything from that safe before I got back there."

She wasn't expecting the question, and she only had a second to decide whether to tell her former partner a lie…or the truth. "I didn't take anything," she whispered.

He studied her as if she were a specimen under a microscope. Molly hadn't realized how much he'd improved at interrogation. Under different circumstances, she'd be proud.

He walked out and left her in the conference room. She exhaled and closed her eyes. She'd never lied to him—until now. And they both knew it.

She headed down to the café on the ground floor. Andre had disappeared and perhaps it was for the better. Her thoughts were spinning and she was sick to her stomach. Just a few days before, she'd looked at Pete Daly's BMW with scorn, proclaiming no one could ever buy her. Now she wondered if that was really true.

She got a coffee and perched on a stool that overlooked the courtyard. As she sipped a bold French roast, she comforted herself with the conversation she'd had with Ari the night before. After Molly explained what she took from the safe and why, Ari said it was for the greater good.

"It's nothing like Pete buying himself a BMW," Ari had argued. "There's no personal gain. If anything, you've jeopardized your career and your relationship with Andre to help someone and solve a murder."

Ari's words soothed her for a moment—until she remembered she'd committed a felony. And broken trust with her former partner. In her mind, that was worse.

She glanced toward the parking garage. Gloria Rivera strolled across the courtyard amid several professionals on their way to work in the tower.

Molly drained her coffee cup. "Let's see if it was worth it," she muttered as she hurried after her.

CHAPTER SEVENTEEN

Gloria and Molly stared at the old manila envelope between them. "RIVERA" was written in the upper left hand corner. Gloria wrung her hands, almost as if she were afraid to touch it.

"Why don't I tell you the part of the story you don't know?" Molly paused but Gloria said nothing. "When Ms. Adams and I arrived at Mr. Guzman's condo last night, she quickly deduced the intruder was not Victor's killer. This intruder was looking for his safe. She didn't find it, but we did."

Gloria closed her eyes. "I'm so ashamed," she whispered. She looked up and asked, "How did you know?"

"I didn't until this morning," she said honestly. "His condo number is Eight C, and I knew I'd heard it before. The witness said he saw a woman in a red ball cap. This morning, as I waited to interview Christine Pierpont, I saw the promotional video in your lobby, which includes a shot of your softball team in red shirts and red caps. Then it clicked. I remembered when we met you on Wednesday, you told Brittany Spring to have your assistant get your gray suit and to go up to Eight C and find a flash drive. I realized you and Mr. Guzman lived in the same condo complex. The intruder knew specifics about the vandalism on the tenth floor, such as the tie being stuffed in the drain. The only people who had that knowledge, other than Victor's killer, were you and Isabelle. But you had access and she didn't. Also the police would never find you on any camera footage entering or exiting the building, except as a tenant. And you obviously had a key to Victor's condo since you told someone to retrieve a flash drive from his apartment."

She offered a slight nod and pointed at the envelope. "What are you going to do with this?"

Molly shrugged. "I have no idea what it is."

"You haven't opened it?" she sputtered.

"No."

"Why?"

She leaned forward, resting her elbows on her knees. "Here's what I've learned from examining much of the contents of the safe. Most of what Victor kept as leverage was embarrassing and potentially damaging to careers or personal lives. Very little of it involved criminal enterprise." She pointed at the envelope and said, "I work for you. I trust you. I know how much good GRD has done for the community."

Gloria's eyes pooled with tears. "Thank you." She picked up the envelope and slowly worked the metal clasp. "Within six months after we formed our partnership, he came to my office one evening and closed the door. We'd had a fight over something petty. We had a lot of fights simply because we had different leadership styles. He pulled out a photo of what I assume is in this envelope to prove he had damning evidence of the truth of my past."

"Which is?"

"See for yourself," Gloria said. She turned the envelope to the side and three items slid onto the table: an old black and white class photo taken in an antiquated schoolroom, a birth certificate for Jimena Aguado, and a copy of a deportation form for Jimena Aguado, who'd been deported in 1960 at the age of ten—and who bore a striking resemblance to Gloria Rivera.

"You're an illegal immigrant," Molly concluded.

"Yes. I came over with my aunt the first time. We hired a corrupt coyote and were caught just a few days after crossing into Arizona. We were sent back, but in that short time we were there, I'd seen the schools and I knew what I wanted. Eight years later, when I turned eighteen, I was better prepared. I had help."

"Where were your parents?"

"My mother was dead and my father had crossed years before. I only had an address, but he helped me establish an identity, one that fooled everyone until I met Victor." She shook her head with a sad smile. "My father was a gangster in New Mexico, which accounted for his exceptional connections in acquiring fake papers." She held up a hand. "To be clear, I didn't abide by my father's unlawfulness. I just wanted a chance in America. He helped me start and I moved far away as soon as I could. I got through school, but no one would take a chance on me. It was the seventies. There weren't a lot of minorities doing anything but washing dishes and mowing yards. And I was a woman. To his credit, Victor gave me a chance."

"How did he find out about your immigration status?"

"Just a fluke. He defended someone who knew my father." She waved her hand. "It doesn't matter now." She gazed at Molly. "You said most of the secrets Victor kept weren't illegal. Clearly, mine is different."

"I don't see it that way," she disagreed. "You've spent your entire adult life helping families and those in need. You've given far more to this country than you've taken, at least in my opinion." She put everything back in the envelope and pushed it to her. "What you do with this information is your choice. Frankly, I'd suggest you help me solve Victor's murder, find some good attorneys to replace you both, and go enjoy your retirement."

She clasped her hands together and Molly could tell she was on the verge of crying. "I never thought the day would come when this would be my choice. Victor always held this over me. He never talked about it after he initially told me. I just always knew it was there." She paused and said, "There's also the little issue of my breaking and entering. Will Detective Williams be arriving with handcuffs?"

"He doesn't know."

"He doesn't? But—"

"I work for you. And sometimes the ends justify the means. We never would've found that safe if you hadn't given us a reason to search his condo again. That information might be the key to solving his murder, so I'm choosing to focus on that point. Now that I'm a private investigator and not a homicide detective, I can be more flexible with my understanding of justice."

Gloria drifted further away as she took it all in, and Molly imagined it would take time to process everything that had happened. But Molly needed her help now. "Gloria, I need your impressions of Christine Pierpont. Do you think she could kill Victor?"

Gloria struggled to switch gears and compose herself, but eventually she said, "Perhaps. He treated her so poorly, and she made such an enormous error in judgment by involving herself with him." She pressed her hand to her forehead. "I tried to talk with her after I heard about the affair, but she told me she would do whatever it took to make partner."

"Why?" Molly asked, clearly showing her disgust.

"Christine's one of those people who has her whole life planned out. Make partner by thirty-five, find a man, have a baby by forty, and so on. She gets tunnel vision. The fact that Victor favored Brantley Dalton for the partnership could have sent her over the edge, especially since she believes Victor promised it to her."

"She claims she didn't know Victor intended to choose Brantley. But if she did, then it would definitely move her into the prime suspect category. I'm almost positive she was here Tuesday night."

Gloria sighed. "That would make sense. One of her routines is to practice her opening or her questions in one of the conference rooms on the tenth floor." She sat up and said, "Right now I'm not speaking as Christine's attorney. I hope that's understood."

"It is," she said. "Also, Isabelle has no alibi. She says she was driving around before a late evening engagement."

Gloria cracked a smile. "You mean her cage fighting?"

She couldn't hide her surprise. "You knew?"

She shrugged. "Of course. When an employee continually arrives at work with bruises and black eyes you assume they're being threatened. I was ready to call the cops, so she had to tell me the truth. It's her life. I think her alter ego helps her deal with her anger."

"Could she have killed Victor?"

Gloria struggled to accept the idea but then her shoulders shrank. "I'd forgotten something important. Tuesday was the day Victor told her he wasn't going to give her the cyber security position we created. She wanted that job badly. She stormed out of his office. She was very angry. And you know she has quite a temper."

"Yeah," she said. "That's quite a combination." Molly stood and prepared to leave. "That's all I need right now."

Gloria rose and moved toward the door. "Thank you seems insufficient." She paused and searched for words. "I hope that helping me has not put you in any jeopardy or disfavor with Detective Williams."

Molly shrugged as an answer.

Gloria put a hand on her shoulder. "If there's anything I can do, let me know. *Anything*."

Molly knew she meant it. She would hand over the folder to Andre, if Molly asked.

Molly nodded and left. She struggled to understand her behavior. She'd lied to Andre, her former partner and someone she trusted with her life. Yet she'd told the truth to Gloria Rivera, a woman she hardly knew.

Why?

Was it a woman thing? Was she standing up for an underdog? Was it loyalty to her employer? Was it just because she thought it was the right thing to do?

She didn't have an answer. But she'd polarized her relationship with Andre, and that would most likely come with a heavy price.

CHAPTER EIGHTEEN

Ari had felt slightly guilty when Molly had rolled out of bed at six to make her seven thirty a.m. interview with Christine Pierpont. She'd thought about getting up and making her breakfast, but when she woke up again, it was nearly eight.

She padded downstairs to the kitchen for a cup of cold coffee. Her phone rang while she was checking her calendar.

Her father. She'd been dodging his calls since Vada Michaels' bombshell about his re-entry into Lucia's life before she died. As the phone continued to ring, she realized she needed his help, and she wasn't ready to overturn the rock that covered his secret.

She smiled and answered. "Hey Dad."

"Hey. Andre said you helped find Victor Guzman's secret safe. Are you helping Molly with the case?"

"Not really," she fudged. "A little. We're just supporting each other."

"Do you have something going?"

He was trying to be nonchalant and casual, but she knew he hated it when she inherited a puzzle to solve. "Actually, it's a mystery involving Long Manor. Do you remember the Longs in Glendale?"

"Oh yeah. You played with the youngest son, right?"

"Yes, Scott. He's the one who asked me to help."

There was a pause before he asked, "Didn't the mother die that same summer?"

He didn't need to state what else specifically had happened that summer, as they rarely talked about Richie's death.

"Yes, that's what I'm investigating. There's evidence to suggest his mother might have been murdered."

"Really? That would be quite surprising."

"Are you free for lunch today? I have some questions for you, and I was hoping you could do me a favor."

"Sure. What do you need?"

"Do you remember the Beaton family? They lived in that little yellow house across the street from the Longs?"

It took Jack a second but he said, "Uh, yeah. It was really just the dad, though, wasn't it? There was a rumor about the mother and child leaving. What I remember most was his old beat-up truck."

"I was hoping you could run some financials for me. Garrett Beaton, Ned's son, told me he inherited a lot of money. I've seen his fancy truck, his Ducati motorcycle and a boat, so he's either wealthy or swimming in debt. He told me he got an inheritance, but it doesn't jive with the father's lifestyle. You remember the dad drove a dented truck, and I remember the yard always looked horrible. Where did he get money for Garrett to inherit?"

"Could a different relative have bequeathed the money to him?"

"He said it came from his father. Somehow, Ned Beaton had a windfall and Garrett inherited at least a portion of it."

"I don't think it would be possible to dig up Ned's financials, sweetie. And if he banked at the First Federal on the south side of Murphy Park, I guarantee you those records disappeared when the bank dissolved. Do you think this is tied to the murder? Are you thinking he was paid hush money?"

She grinned. He would always think like a cop. "It's possibly connected. Any ideas on how I could get the information?"

"What's the spelling on Beaton?"

She spelled it out and he said, "I'll take a look and see what I can find on Garrett. We may not be able to get at Ned Beaton's financials, but we can look at the son's history."

"That would be great. So what about lunch? I'll be near Murphy Park around eleven thirty."

"Then I'll see you at Piazza al Forno."

Ari got ready for the day, pushing her father's secret away every time it tried to invade her mind. That's what Molly had told her to do. "You can't change the past. It happened a long time ago," she'd said.

She knew Molly was right, and if she were honest, it wasn't her father's actions that infuriated her—it was her mother's. Ari had thought it was she and Lucia battling the cancer together. Her father was gone—out of the picture. They hated him equally. But apparently not. It felt as though her parents conspired against her. She felt foolish and angry. She sighed. She needed to close that door—at least for now.

Instead she thought about the previous night at Victor's condo. It had been such a rush. When the armoire's back panel had slid away and revealed the safe, she'd wanted to cheer. She'd helped Molly and Andre find key information, and Molly had been quite grateful. She warmed thinking about how date night had ended in bed.

She showered and headed out, taking care of real estate business first. She delivered the contract on the Willo house to the seller's agent. Then she drove to Grand Avenue and checked in with her office. Her partner, Lorraine, was relaxing on a ten-day cruise with her beau, Karim Hamada, their third business partner. The office seemed to self-propel since good employees rarely needed a boss acting like a boss. She looked across the street at the Groove. Traffic at Scrabble was heavy as everyone loved Chynna's coffee in the early morning, but Ari frowned when her gaze settled on the Pocket. They needed to do something about the health inspector issue, and Jane's refusal to handle the problem meant Ari would need to step in.

She sighed. "But not now."

She drove out to the Glendale Historical Society, located on the edge of the Catlin Court Historic District. Volunteers staffed the converted home, and as such, the hours proved inconsistent. Ari had left several messages before Mary Bellows had called her back. She assured Ari she would be in the office on Friday morning at nine. True to her word, the sign on the front door had been flipped to *Open* when Ari pulled up next to an ancient Dodge Dart.

A bell rang when she entered, but there was no one in the main room. Photos of the original buildings told the story of Glendale's beginnings, which, like many towns, owed its birth to the railroads. Glendale hugged the Santa Fe line, and Ari remembered being awakened by a train horn numerous times during her youth. Two large models sat prominently in the center of the room, Saguaro Ranch and Manistee Ranch. Both were colonial style plantation homes built in the early 1800's by two of Glendale's founding families.

A diminutive woman with white hair appeared from the back room. "Good morning, I'm Mary," she said in a willowy voice, extending her hand.

"Good morning, I'm Ari Adams. We spoke on the phone." Ari found herself matching Mary's quiet tone.

"Of course. It's a pleasure to meet you." She made a sweeping gesture and said, "Please look around. You said you grew up in Glendale?"

"Yes, but more recently than what you've captured in the displays. My family lived here during the seventies and early eighties."

"Then you saw the downtown at one of its worst times," she said sadly.

"That's true. I remember some of the buildings around Murphy Park were shuttered. There was a lot of crime, too."

"Yes, for a while the area was filled with gangs and drug users. That finally changed in the early nineties when the area was declared historic and the new City Hall was built." She narrowed her eyes and rubbed her forehead. "I apologize, but I can't remember specifically what it was you asked about on the phone. My old memory is just that, old." Her laugh was a soft cloud that floated away.

"I wanted to ask you about the Long family and what you remember about Henrietta Long's death. You said on the phone that you knew her?"

She offered a sad smile. "Yes, I was her friend. She used to be a part of the Rose Society. Let me show you."

Ari followed her to a display of pictures that showed the original location of the club a few blocks away.

"I didn't realize the club was still active."

"Oh, yes. In fact, we have a Rose Society meeting tomorrow."

Ari thought of Henrietta's rosebushes along the brick walkway and how she'd insisted they be planted when she moved to the sunroom.

"Here are some group photos of the membership." Mary pointed to one of the color photos in the display. "That's her on the top row. Third from the left."

Ari leaned closer and stared at the tall, proud woman. "I suppose this was taken before she got sick."

"Yes, this was in 1991. We were quite the bunch. The next year she and I were elected club rosarians."

"Would that be someone who's an expert at cultivating roses?"

Mary beamed at Ari's use of the word expert. "We both had won the annual contest." Her face suddenly crumpled. "But Hennie never finished her term. She felt so bad she had to resign. Poor thing. She became a shut-in, refusing to see anyone."

Ari raised an eyebrow. "You tried to see her?"

Mary looked aghast that she would ask the question. "Of course, dear. Even though I was ten years younger, I was one of her best friends. I stopped by several times and dropped off flowers. I called. I sent notes. Every time I was told by her husband or their hired lady that she was too weak for visitors, but they would be sure she got whatever I'd brought. We all came to her funeral, too." She held up a finger, as if she'd remembered something. "I have a photo."

She went to the back room and Ari heard her rummaging through some drawers. Scott had said no one bothered to visit his mother, so if Mary was turned away, then it was Junior making the decision. Perhaps he thought he was saving Henrietta from a pity visit, or perhaps it happened that Mary's visits fell on days when Henrietta felt poorly. But then wouldn't Junior have encouraged visitors on her good days?

Mary returned with a five-by-seven photo of a grand wreath made entirely of different colored roses. "Every member of the Rose Society contributed their best roses. They displayed the wreath at her funeral and it was buried on top of her casket."

"It's beautiful." Ari was touched. "You all must have been very close."

"We were." Mary sighed and shook her head. "It was a different time. Before cell phones and the Internet. You had to really work to be a good friend. You had to make an effort, not just push a button and automatically become friends." She covered her mouth in embarrassment. "I'm sorry. Just an old lady going on a rant." She chuckled and said, "I learned that word from Dennis Miller."

They both laughed and Ari's gaze strayed to the 1993 club photo. Standing in the back row on the end was a woman with fiery red hair—Millicent. "Mary, how well did you know Millicent Farriday?"

Mary closed her eyes and sighed. "Millicent. What I just said about working to be a good friend? Millicent had no interest in that. She tried to be a social climber. Wasn't very successful." Mary's voice turned raspy and she coughed. "I think I need some water. Would you mind grabbing me a bottle out of the fridge in the back, dear? I need to sit down."

Ari helped Mary to a chair and went into the back, which served as a work area and storeroom. The fridge was against the wall, beyond several stacks of tables and chairs that were probably used for events. Like any good amateur detective, she took a few extra seconds to notice the labels on the filing cabinet drawers and the pictures on the opposite wall. The club's organizational skills were commendable, and everything seemed to have a place. She saw the drawer labeled Members. "Mary, may I please use your restroom?" she called.

"Sure, dear. Bring my water back with you when you're done."

"Thank you!"

Ari quietly opened the drawer. Each member had a file. Inside Hennie Long's were several photos of flowers she'd grown, her application to be a rosarian, dated November 1991, and a record of her membership and dues payments. She'd joined in 1969 and faithfully paid her dues every January. The amount, which increased as the years progressed, was noted alongside the initials of the sitting treasurer. The last time Henrietta had paid dues was 1992. For the 1993 entry, which would've been the year after she died, RIP was written in red pen and underlined. Ari noted the treasurer's initials were MFL, Millicent Farriday Long. Perhaps Ari was reading too much into it, but the bold way RIP appeared on the card suggested the writer, presumably MFL, took joy in making the pronouncement.

She replaced the file and returned to Mary with the water. "Here you go."

"Thank you, dear. Now what were we talking about?"

"I'd asked you about Millicent Farriday Long, and you didn't seem too pleased to hear her name."

Mary drank greedily from the bottle. She licked her lips and said, "That would be an understatement. She blew in here about three months after Hennie died as the new Mrs. Long. Most of us had heard the rumors about her and Junior, but we tried to set that aside. It seemed the Christian thing to do. She wanted to be an officer in the club, and our treasurer was moving, so we voted her into the position." Mary slapped her thigh. "Dumbest thing we could've done. Soon there was money missing and the books didn't balance. She couldn't explain it and we took pity on her and told her to be more careful. Some of us also noticed she made regular appointments at the beauty parlor and carried a new purse every week."

"She spent the club's dues on herself," Ari summarized.

"Yes. Because we also knew the Fizz plant was laying off workers. So if the plant was struggling, how was it Millicent could afford so many new handbags?"

"Did you all confront her?"

"Of course not," she said bitterly. "We should have." She placed a hand on Ari's arm and said, "Honey, if getting older has taught me anything it's the importance of confrontation. Don't piddle around problems. Deal with them directly. No, we let it go and just elected a new treasurer, Ned Beaton."

Ari blinked. "Ned Beaton? He was in the Rose Society?"

"Oh, yes. A gruff, pain in the behind but at least an honest one. Never had a penny go missing after he took over. He couldn't grow a rose to save his life, especially considering the condition of his yard, but he was an excellent treasurer."

"Mary, did you ever hear a rumor that Millicent may have murdered Henrietta to have Junior for herself?"

Mary took a drink from the bottle and looked away. "I did but nobody could prove anything."

"Who told you?"

"Ned."

"What did he tell you?"

"He was doing a tile job at the Gaslight Inn one day. He overheard Millicent on the phone with her father. She said something like, 'Daddy, this can't continue. I won't have my baby be born a bastard.' A week later Henrietta was dead. Ned was certain she'd done it."

"But he didn't *see* her do it, as far as you know?"

She shook her head. "No, if he'd seen her do it, he would've called the police."

"So did it get around that she was already pregnant when they got married?"

"Oh, yes, but nobody said anything, at least not to her face." She paused and seemed to struggle about whether to say more. Finally she blurted, "Truth be told, Ned was half in love with Henrietta, always was. If he knew someone had hurt her, he would've killed that person himself. No, he didn't have concrete proof, so he did the one thing he could do."

"What was that?"

"He told Junior Long."

CHAPTER NINETEEN

Ari strolled through Murphy Park on her way to La Piazza al Forno, a brick oven pizza place in the middle of old town Glendale. She and Jack had made a pact to have lunch together at least once a month. In addition to trying new places, they continually returned to their favorite haunts like this small pizza parlor at the edge of Catlin Court.

She'd enjoyed her conversation with Mary Bellows, and she'd promised to attend a Rose Society meeting in the future. Mary's information about Ned Beaton fit with the other clues she'd discovered. When Henrietta died, Ned assumed Millicent had acted on the conversation he'd overheard. He saw Blythe and told her, but what Blythe didn't know was that he'd also talked to her father. And most likely, Junior Long paid Ned to make it all go away so he could start his new life. And Ned had squirreled away the money. That would certainly explain Garrett's truck, motorcycle and boat.

She glanced up at the ancient trees that shaded most of the park pathways. Since March weather was so pleasant, many people who worked in the nearby government offices enjoyed lunch on the benches. Two groups of picnickers had settled on the lawn in front of the bandstand where music concerts occurred on a regular basis.

Glendale had become a destination city with events like the Glitter and Glow celebration and the Ceretta Chocolate Festival. Shops and eateries framed the park, and since it was still snowbird season, all of the public parking spaces were full. During events, those same stores and restaurants were packed with customers and ensured the businesses stayed afloat through the boiling summers when no one went outside for long.

After her meeting with Mary, she'd spent a few hours perusing more photos and some of the documents. She'd kept the gate locked and her gun close, but she doubted the windshield basher would return. A pattern had emerged from her analysis of Fizz. Whereas Wilfred Sr. was an excellent businessman, Junior was too mild-mannered and couldn't make the hard decisions, like laying off part of a division when it was time to automate the plant. He continued to employ those people at the expense of the entire company. That was one of many mistakes he'd made, but they all stemmed from the same cause: his good nature.

She breathed in the spring air. She was glad she'd decided to walk the three blocks from Long Manor to the restaurant. When she arrived at La Piazza al Forno, she didn't see her father so she elected to wander down the sidewalk, staring into the enormous glass storefronts that defined Glendale Avenue. Collectibles, antiques and handmade products enticed potential customers to venture inside. The picture windows were throwbacks to the mid-forties, when most of the buildings were constructed to accommodate the post-World War II boom. Barbers, drugstores and a telegraph office were the first tenants of what would become downtown Glendale.

By the time she'd reached the end of the block and turned back, she saw her father hustling across the street. Jack Adams was difficult to miss. A tall, good-looking man, he towered over the rest of the pedestrians and hardly looked as though he was approaching sixty. He waved to her and she quickened her step.

The lunch rush was on, and they wanted to get a table before there was a wait.

"Hi honey," he said, kissing her cheek. "How are you?"

She saw the look of concern in his eyes. Visiting Glendale was hard for both of them.

"I'm good, Dad. Thanks for meeting me."

Once they were situated and had placed their lunch order, Ari eyed the folder he'd brought with him. "Is that something for me?"

"Yes," he said, handing it to her.

She glanced at the single sheet of paper inside. It was a recent bank statement for Garrett Beaton. Between his savings and checking account he had thirty-four thousand dollars in the bank.

"That's a lot of cash on hand," she commented. "Anything else?"

He smiled slyly. "There's always something else." He pulled out his notebook. "On a much less official level, I made a few phone calls. I spoke with Cecil Oaks. He managed the First Federal bank across the park back in the eighties. I had no idea he was still alive, but he is, and his memory is still sharp."

"What did he say?"

"At first, not much. Then he said he didn't like to gossip, but he'd make an exception because he always appreciated how nice my wife was when she came to the bank and how well-mannered my children were."

"Mom was insistent about good manners," she mused.

"Cecil remembered that entire year, not just the summer, as the worst year for him as a banker. Said it drove him to retirement by the end of winter."

"Why?"

"A lot of things happened. One large headache was Junior Long pressuring him to do some shady things. Fizz was going under, and Junior wanted a loan, but First Federal wouldn't give it to him, even though Cecil vouched for him with the Board of Directors."

"Did he say why Junior wanted the loan?"

"Wanted to retrofit the factory, but the price tag was too high. Junior wanted Cecil to fudge some numbers so the board members would change their minds. He refused."

"Well, shame on Junior for asking him to do something illegal," she retorted.

"Agreed. But then the bank also refused to give Junior a personal loan."

"Why did he want that?"

"The application said it was for medical bills and care at a facility, but Cecil knew Henrietta had refused to go anywhere. He wouldn't lie to the board, so Junior went to a Phoenix bank, one that didn't know him personally, and got the loan. Cecil said the whole thing caused a huge rift between them and they never spoke again."

The pizza arrived and they dove in, sidelining the conversation to enjoy one of the best pies in Phoenix. When she picked up her second slice, she resumed her questions. "Did he remember how much the loan request was for?"

"Two hundred thousand dollars."

"Wow."

"Not long after Junior got the loan, Ned Beaton opened a money market account and deposited one hundred and twenty-five thousand dollars."

She cocked her head to the side. "Not two hundred thou?"

"No. But also making a big deposit around that time was Morris Michaels, the owner of the Gaslight Inn. How much do you think he deposited?"

"Seventy-five grand?"

He smiled. "That would be correct. Cecil said a third of the money left the account quickly, but he couldn't remember why."

"I think I know why," she said. "Morris bought a mint condition '66 Mustang. It's sitting in front of the Gaslight Inn right now."

He looked at her inquisitively. "Why would Junior pay hush money to Ned and Morris?"

"The Reader's Digest version of the story is that when Henrietta got sick, Junior took a mistress who would later become his wife. A woman named Millicent. Do you remember her?" Jack nodded and she continued. "Millicent got pregnant before Henrietta died, and Ned Beaton and Morris Michaels knew about the whole thing. He bought their silence, possibly to cover up the fact that Millicent murdered Henrietta. And on top of it, Beaton was an abuser. That's why Garret and his mom left."

"Bastard. I mean, I get that I'm not going to win a father of the year award, so I probably shouldn't be bad mouthing the guy, but still…"

He sucked on his iced tea and she remained silent. The conversation was moving dangerously close to the one topic she'd asked they never discuss again—the time he disowned her because of her sexual orientation.

She rested her chin on her upturned palm. "What do you remember about that time, Dad? I know Mom was friends with Henrietta, but do you remember any neighborhood gossip?"

He sat back in the chair and seemed to retreat inside himself. When he looked up he said, "I remember Junior. Nice man who always said hello or waved if you passed his car. Even though I was Phoenix PD, once in awhile I'd talk with some Glendale PD folks around the neighborhood. They always called him a stand-up guy, even when Fizz started to struggle. He was still on good terms with the police."

Ari pulled a notebook from her purse. "Were there other problems, other than financial ones?"

"There was some vandalism. They caught a couple of hoodlums who claimed they were hired to stop production, but they wouldn't give up the name of whoever hired them." He paused and then added, "One of them admitted the end game was supposed to be a fire that destroyed the whole place. Of course, that never happened because they got caught."

"But who hired them? Junior Long? Maybe he was trying to get insurance money to move the business to a more updated facility?"

He shrugged. "That could be, but nobody ever found out. A year later they moved to a warehouse way out in the west valley where real estate was cheap. Junior hated leaving the building his father designed, but there was no other way."

"Going back to the guys hired to sabotage production; do you think I could get their names?"

He shook his head. "I don't know, honey. That was before technology was fully integrated. And if they were under eighteen, that record is probably gone."

She nodded, doubting she'd learn much about Henrietta's murder from those past incidents. "There's just a couple more things and then we'll talk about the Suns, the Diamondbacks, whatever."

A smile tugged at the corners of his mouth. "It's okay, honey. What else do you want to know?"

"I remember hearing a discussion between you and Mom once about the new stepmom, Millicent. I got the feeling Mom didn't like her."

He nodded slowly. "Your mother was the best judge of character I've ever met. That's where you get it."

"Oh, I think you're a good judge of character too," she assured him.

He laughed but then his eyes narrowed. She could tell he was reaching as far back as he could go. There was something else tickling his brain.

"You'll think of it," she offered.

"I will. Give me a little longer to noodle on it."

"What else do you remember about Mr. Beaton? You said he was a tile setter?"

"Yes, there was a sign on the side of his truck, an old, beat up Chevy. Beaton's Tile. I drove by that truck a few thousand times over the years. I remember your mother went over to his house one Saturday to get a quote. She wanted to retile the bathroom." He laughed. "She came back as angry as a hornet's nest. He asked why her husband wasn't making the inquiry."

"Oh, I'll bet that got Mom fired up."

"Then he wanted to charge her some ridiculous price. She knew he'd quoted such an outrageous amount because she was a woman, and he didn't think she'd know any better."

It was a perfect opening to ask her father if he'd renewed a relationship with her mother before she died. But instead, she opted to finish her iced tea and change the subject. "Molly hoped to join us today because she wanted to ask you about Pete Daly."

His smile became a hard line. "A disgrace to the uniform."

"What did he do?"

He glanced at his watch and after a permissive nod from her, grabbed the last slice of pizza. "Technically, nothing. He was never charged with a crime. That's the union's line." She waited him out, and he finally said quietly, "We all get caught in questionable situations. It happens. We're not dealing with society's model citizens. We make judgment calls. Sometimes we might step over the line, but we're doing it for justice or the victim. In Pete's case, he was doing it for himself. There was talk of kickbacks and bribes, but Sol didn't do anything about it." He wiped his hands on his napkin. "That probably doesn't surprise you, now that you know what Sol was capable of."

Ari nodded. Sol Gardner, the corrupt former police chief, had been her godfather. "Pete gave Molly the impression he was shown the door. What happened?"

"He went too far. My understanding is fifty grand from a high profile bust disappeared. Sol got in trouble with the feds. It's not a good idea to make your chief look bad. Pete had been the lead detective and the one in charge of the evidence. Sol threw him under the bus and he took early retirement. They never found the money, though. I've always thought he took it and gave Sol a cut so he wouldn't investigate diligently."

"So no one had any proof that he took it."

"Right. I heard a rumor there was a video but I never saw it. Then after he retired, he opened his own P.I. business, but he only had one client, Victor Guzman."

Ari wondered if somehow Victor had obtained that video and Molly now had it in her possession.

"Hey," he said. "How about those Suns?"

She blinked and set aside her notebook. They talked about the local sports teams for another twenty minutes until they paid the check. As they left, he asked, "When can we get together so you can meet Dylan?"

She opened her mouth to make an excuse, but she realized she'd used them all up. "I just don't know if I'm ready," she admitted. "I want you to be happy. I really do."

He pulled her into a hug. "Hey, it's okay. Let's think of something low-stress, like a movie and coffee afterward. That way if the entire conversation dies, we can talk about the movie. Would that work?"

She looked into his pleading eyes. This was important to him. "Okay, but not a police movie. Those aren't any fun when I'm with you and Molly. You two pick them apart. I can't imagine what it would be like having *three* cops critique it."

He laughed. "Well, you were a cop, too. You could join us."

"I was a cop for less than a year," she reminded him.

"No police movies," he acquiesced. Then his eyes widened. "I remember now. You asked about your mom's relationship with Henrietta. The day after Richie died, Junior Long came by the house. He threw his arms around us. He cried and gave us hugs. Then he left quickly. We were in a state and didn't think anything of it, but later when we could finally talk about those early days, Junior's visit seemed really odd."

"I don't know," she said. "You'd lost someone. He'd lost someone. You and Mom were probably the only people who knew what he was going through."

He considered her point. "Yeah, that might explain it."

He gave her a kiss and turned to go, but she said, "Hey, Dad. One more question." She leaned closer so she wasn't shouting over the revving engines on Glendale Avenue. "You said sometimes you did what you had to do. What did you mean, exactly?"

He shrugged. "It means what you think it means, honey. I'm not going to lie to you. I made some tough choices, particularly when I was younger, and especially regarding your brother's case. I don't regret any of them. We should've had Richie's killer by now."

He squeezed her arm and hurried across the street before the light changed. His last sentence punched her in the stomach. *We should've had Richie's killer by now.* Was he still working the case? Did he have a suspect? She followed the back of his head as he made his way further down Glendale. He turned right on Fifty-Seventh Avenue and disappeared. She wanted to run to him and demand he explain himself. She suddenly felt terribly betrayed. If he'd initiated his own investigation for Richie's killer, why hadn't he included her?

CHAPTER TWENTY

Molly had one more delivery to make—to Pete Daly. She hoped it would result in an exchange, and her sixty-mile round trip drive would be worth the effort. She spent the time thinking about her interview with Gloria Rivera. She'd meant what she said: GRD, despite its internal shortcomings, had saved many families and victims of domestic violence. But she realized she couldn't judge Victor or Pete about their flexible ethics when she'd done the same thing for Gloria. She knew the recently departed sheriff of Maricopa County, a man who would personally build a wall between Arizona and Mexico if given the chance, would love to make an example of Gloria and deport her if he ever learned her true citizenship status. And although the sheriff was gone, the anti-immigrant sentiment was still strong throughout the state.

She found Pete in the same lawn chair and wearing the same shorts, but he'd replenished his beer cooler and had guzzled a six-pack already. He greeted her with a smile and pulled out another beer for her.

"Pete, to be honest with you, I'm a recovering alcoholic. You left the department just as I was arriving, so you probably don't know that I also exited Phoenix PD under a black cloud. I made my own problems and I've had to live with the consequences." She threw a glance at the empty beer cans. "Alcohol was the biggest reason I'm no longer a cop."

He looked at her warily. "Is that a sermon, Ms. Nelson?"

She shook her head. "Nope. I don't tell anyone else how to live, but I wanted you to know I wasn't accepting your offer of a beer for a reason."

He gave an understanding nod. "Thank you for your honesty." He pulled out a cigar and offered it to her.

She laughed. "I gave that up, too."

He laughed with her. "Wish I could," he said out of the side of his mouth as he lit the stogie. After a good puff, he asked, "And what brings you out here to visit me again?"

"I have something for you," she said, reaching into her messenger bag. She pulled out a bulging manila envelope and handed it to him.

He looked at it quizzically until he saw DALY written in the upper left-hand corner. His face fell. He set aside the cigar and fumbled with the clasp. A few beads of sweat dripped off his forehead but he appeared not to notice. He ripped open the envelope and withdrew a VHS tape. The label read, "Property of Phoenix Police Department" and included the official city seal. Written in black ink was the date "7-15-2004." He seemed too stunned to say anything.

After a generous swig of beer he asked, "Where did you find this?"

"In Victor's condo."

He took a deep breath and examined the tape. "I would be lying if I said I hadn't already searched his place several times over the years. Please tell me it was well concealed and a two-bit P.I. who spends most of his days pleasantly trashed would never have found it."

She met his sardonic grin with one of her own. "Truth is, it was one of my associates who has a real eye for detail and fashion. She realized his armoire looked funny and found a secret panel."

His mind started to turn. "So, you found the other stuff too," he deduced. "I hope my name wasn't attached to anything."

"No," she said. "We've involved Phoenix PD and I imagine much will be destroyed."

"But they don't have a copy of this?" he asked, waving the VHS.

"No."

He took a breath and then his face grew dark. "What about Gloria Rivera? What did you learn about her?"

Molly smiled and pointed at the tape. "One secret per customer." He laughed and poked the stogie back in his mouth. She waited until his gaze met hers again. "There's something I need from you, Pete."

"Ah," he said. "Tit for tat. That's your game, Ms. Nelson. I see."

"No, it's not," she said firmly. "I'm not Victor Guzman. I'm not going to hold that video over your head. I gave it to you and it's yours. But I do need the rest of the Dearborn file so I can do my job."

He offered a puzzled expression. "What do you mean?"

"C'mon, Pete. There are crucial pieces missing—like witness statements and Victor's notes and strategies. All the stuff he included in his other case files."

He eyed her shrewdly between puffs. "And what makes you think I have it?"

"It's not in his office, and since it wasn't in his secret safe, I'm certain he didn't have it. You're the person he trusted."

He looked away and smoked. His brow furrowed and she could tell there were more secrets attached to the Dearborn file than she knew. He was deciding how many to share. He finally looked at her and said, "Suppose there was a second half to the file, but you never found it. Perhaps the file had been modified in the name of justice. What would be the worst thing that could happen if it never turned up?"

She knew better than to say the worst thing would be never learning the true identify of Victor's killer. Even she had some ambivalence about finding justice for someone so cruel and heartless. But there were other ramifications. She faced him and said, "The worst thing that could happen is the wrong person might go to jail. At this point the best evidence points to Christine Pierpont." His face twitched slightly, and she knew she'd struck a nerve. "If she killed him, then murder solved. Great. If she didn't, and she winds up in jail, that would be horrible. She's clearly going places with her career. I imagine Gloria Rivera sees her as the future of GRD."

He stared blankly ahead and suddenly jumped up from the chair. He disappeared inside and when he returned, he held a bulging accordion file. He handed it to her and said, "You didn't get this from me. Now we're even."

"Are you going to tell me why all of this was removed from the case file?"

He smiled. "Oh no. You figure that out for yourself."

As Molly pulled up to a red light, she peeked inside the file, irresistibly curious to see what Victor had pulled out. It would be good light reading tonight when she and Ari went on a little stakeout. She chuckled, wondering if there was a way they could hook up the projector in the car to watch more movies by Cousin Glenn.

Her phone rang and Gloria's name appeared. "Molly Nelson."

"Ms. Nelson, I've just learned the whereabouts of Brittany Spring. I've spoken with her. She's very nervous about talking with the police. Can you meet with her before Detective Williams arrives? My understanding is that he's on his way."

"Certainly. Give me the address."

Fortunately, Brittany was hiding out in Tempe at a house that belonged to a friend's grandmother, and Molly was only ten minutes away. Assuming Andre was at the precinct, she would arrive before he did.

As she sat in traffic, she wiped a hand across her face. She needed to have another conversation with him. Maybe he would be more understanding if he knew why she took the two envelopes from the safe. She certainly didn't want to destroy the best link to Phoenix PD that she had. She needed him—probably much more than he needed her. He was definitely picking up the skills to be a good detective. And she'd taught him many things, including one of her cardinal rules: never get burned twice. Even if she could get him to understand, she'd spend a long time regaining his trust.

She exited the freeway and headed for the Tomlinson Estates Historic District, just off McClintock Drive. The house was a modest white ranch-style, typical of the forties and fifties in Phoenix. She pulled into the driveway behind a Ford Focus. She noticed a car house, a predecessor to the modern garage, further down the driveway. Sitting in front of the car house was a pristine Chevy Nova from the seventies.

"That probably belongs to the friend's grandmother," she muttered. "Why isn't it in the car house?"

She saw a curtain move in the car house window. The building had been converted to a living space, accounting for the Nova's outside location. She headed for the car house and knocked on the door. "Brittany, it's me, Molly. Gloria sent me over."

The door slowly open and Brittany's wide eyes greeted her. Her face was red as if she'd been crying, and her hair was a stringy mess. She wore an old T-shirt and cargo shorts. Molly thought of her conversation with Pete about proper dress. Victor would definitely not approve.

"Am I getting arrested?" she asked meekly.

"No," Molly said reassuringly. "The police know you didn't kill Victor, but you need to tell them the whole truth. May I come in?"

She nodded and Molly followed her into the small living quarters. It had a bed and a TV, but there wasn't a sink or a bathroom. She dropped into an old metal patio chair while Molly perched on a periwinkle blue loveseat. She picked up a framed school photo of a boy who couldn't have been more than seven. "Is this your son?"

Brittany melted and tears streaked her cheeks. "Yeah, that's Ben. He's with my mom. I hate being away from him."

"Why did you run?"

"When Jean-Claude from IT told me you were looking at the security tape and my printer history, I knew I was in trouble." She wrung her hands, distraught. "I needed time to think. I figured you thought I killed Victor, but I didn't. Then I wondered if the real killer thought I'd seen something, and she'd come after me, too."

"She?"

Brittany shrugged. "I just assumed."

Molly shifted on the loveseat. "Why don't we start at the beginning? It's after work on Tuesday and most everyone's left. What are you doing?"

She swallowed and then said, "Well, I pulled up the PTSA website and the Google doc I share with the vice president. We're getting ready for the big spring fundraiser. We're going to have a huge basket raffle and it's going to be awesome. Since no one was around, I decided to print the brochures to start soliciting donations." She reached behind her and handed one to Molly.

She scanned it and noticed the logo for the school, the atom. She kept seeing the logo and hearing about this school. She made a note. "What else happened?"

She looked puzzled. "I left?"

"You didn't hear or see anyone suspicious?"

"No. I finished my copying and I took the elevator to the nineteenth floor—"

"What time was that?" Molly interjected.

"Just before nine. My friend Ruth was working late. She works for the IRS. She buzzed me in, we talked while she finished her work, and then we went down the elevator with two of her other co-workers around nine twenty or so. I can't remember the exact time."

"You were on the nineteenth floor at nine o'clock?" she reiterated.

"Uh-huh. I was. I remember because when I arrived, my friend made a comment about how it sucked to be working at nine p.m."

Molly realized Brittany had missed everything by a few minutes. If she'd stayed on the tenth floor five minutes longer, she probably would've been shot. By heading up nine floors, she escaped injury, and she wouldn't have heard anything.

Brittany still looked terrified so Molly said, "Brittany, I believe you. I know you didn't kill Mr. Guzman. But I wish you'd told me the truth before."

She nodded and started crying again.

"I'm not going to tell anyone about the copying," she continued, "so you can stop worrying. What I need to know is if you saw anyone or anything else that might be helpful. Was anyone on the tenth floor with you? Did you see anyone when you were leaving? Did you notice anything?"

She wrapped her hands over her head and closed her eyes. "I remember I was worried Isabelle would find my computer still switched on the next morning. I forgot to shut down. Then I remembered I'd left the original copy of the flyer on the copy machine. I didn't realize that until I was getting ready for bed." She groaned. "And it was gone when we were finally allowed to go upstairs. I'm guessing Isabelle has it, and she'll probably use it as evidence to fire me."

"What else do you remember about that night?" Molly pressed. "What about when you left? Visualize leaving the building with your friends. Think about what you're seeing."

She closed her eyes. Her head bobbed slightly before her eyes suddenly flew open. "I do remember something! We walked to the parking garage and got on the elevator together. As we waited for the doors to close, I noticed a bright red Porsche parked next to the FedEx pickup box. I remember thinking that the Porsche looked like Christine's car."

"Anything else?"

"No," she said, shaking her head.

Molly stared at her for an extra beat. After years of interviewing suspects and witnesses, she'd learned how to gauge when someone had told her everything. Brittany was at that point.

"Okay," she said, rising from the loveseat. "In a few minutes Detective Williams is going to arrive and ask you the same questions. Just be honest with him. Got it?"

She nodded. "I will."

Before she left, she gave Brittany her card. "If you have any other questions or concerns, you call me."

"I will," she said with a little smile. "Thank you."

"Go home to your son. It's okay."

She nodded fiercely and tears streamed down her face. She waved and shut the door quickly.

Molly headed for her car just as Andre pulled up to the curb. "No getting out of this," she muttered.

He approached with a frown. "So is that how we're doin' it?" he asked.

"What do you mean?"

"I thought we were in this together."

She knew his statement had a double meaning. She took a breath and said in a calm voice, "We are, Andre. But Gloria—"

"You couldn't wait for me?"

She took another breath and ordered herself to stay calm, despite the fact that he now stood a foot from her face. "Gloria specifically asked me to talk with Brittany before you arrived. She was too nervous for her own good. You and I both know she didn't have anything to do with Victor's murder. It's not like I was coaching a viable suspect to lie to you."

"No, you wouldn't do that," he said sarcastically. "You just steal evidence."

The words slapped her in the face but she said nothing in response. He needed to get it out of his system and she needed to let him. She doubted she would ever forget the look of betrayal on his face.

"Do you know how many procedures and rules I've *relaxed* for you since you left the force?" he growled. "How many times I've shared information with you that could fry my ass?"

He paused and she looked at him sympathetically. Then she nodded.

"And look how you reciprocate!"

He suddenly realized he'd raised his voice. He stuffed his hands in his pocket and hunched his shoulders, physically and emotionally deflating.

He turned to go and she said, "Believe me when I say that I've done nothing to undermine this case, but I know I've lost your trust, at least for now."

Without looking back at her he blurted, "You got that right."

CHAPTER TWENTY-ONE

"This is the most romantic date we've had in a long time," Ari declared sarcastically.

"I agree," Molly said, her right hand caressing the back of Ari's neck. She purred with pleasure and Molly gazed longingly at the curve of her breast. She sighed deeply and pulled away, resting her forehead on the steering wheel of her truck.

It was five thirty p.m. and they were outside Eden Venegas' condo complex. They had a great view of the parking garage, and Molly's expensive telephoto lens would easily capture the faces of those who entered or exited for Friday night fun, including Eden's alleged lover, should he make an appearance. Between her and Ari was the brown accordion file, the second half of the Dearborn case notes. She'd been excited to see the rest of Victor's case file, but after her confrontation with Andre, that excitement had fizzled.

Ari rested her hand on Molly's shoulder. "It's going to be okay, babe. Not for a while, but eventually. You and Andre have way too much history for this to destroy your relationship. He knows what he owes you."

"Yeah, but I lied to his face." She turned and stared at Ari. "I committed a felony."

"For a good reason," Ari replied. "Even though you didn't tell me the details, I'm sure it was for the greater good."

Molly chuckled. "It was. But that's not how a judge would see it."

"I know. And I know that's not the part that's bothering you the most. You're worried about losing Andre's trust."

"Yeah."

"So is Eden at the top of the suspect list?"

"Pretty close. We learned that her aunt worked for the cleaning company contracted by the tower, but the aunt left months ago. So we're still not sure how Eden would've gotten a badge or key. And Andre interviewed the night guard at her condo complex, who says he didn't see her Tuesday night, but she could've snuck out one of the pedestrian exits that aren't covered by a camera after Miguel went to sleep."

She sat up as a car approached the garage gate. "And here comes someone now," she murmured. She hiked up the camera as an old Ford Fairlane approached. She held down the shutter button as the driver tapped on the keypad.

"Does it look promising?" Ari inquired.

"Not unless Eden is dating someone in the AARP. This guy is about seventy and wearing a porkpie hat. He looks like Jimmy Durante. I'll just practice," she said. She viewed the photos and smiled. The new lens was so powerful it captured the wart on the end of Mr. Durante's nose. She glanced at the file. "What have we got?"

"Okay," Ari said, reading the tabs of the first four files. "Witness statements, medical reports, financials and... PTSA school information? What?"

"It's Phoenix Technical Science Academy. There's something about that school. Victor's son Miguel goes there. Brittany Spring's kid goes there. Mackenzie Dearborn's kid goes there."

"That doesn't necessarily mean anything," Ari said, nonplussed. "A lot of times when parents are unhappy with a school, they'll ask their neighbors for recommendations. That's how charters get their enrollment."

"True," she conceded. "What's in the school folder?"

"A map, a newsletters and a school directory."

Her gaze focused on the slowly rising parking garage gate. Her heartbeat quickened when she saw Eden's Range Rover, only Eden wasn't behind the wheel. "This is it, babe," she said. She held down the shutter button and followed the car as it turned left and drove past them. She thrust the camera at Ari and pulled away from the curb.

She stayed two car lengths behind the Rover, trying to get a glimpse of the driver while Ari thumbed through the pictures. "Any of his face?"

"No," she said. "They're wearing baseball caps and he's turned toward her the entire time." She looked at the windshield and noted the cross streets. "I think they're headed to the west side, maybe to a spring training game."

"Ugh," she groaned. "Baseball." She merged onto Grand Avenue, heading for Surprise. "I think you're right, babe. They're going to the ball game."

"Here's something," Ari said, holding up a file. "The school nurse's name and office phone number is circled in blue, and there's a comment in purple that says, 'Talk to her.'"

She nodded. "Victor called those purple postulations. Look in the witness statements and see if she gave one."

Ari rummaged through the file. "Yes, there's a statement from the school nurse, Phyllis Johnson, as well as a statement from a Dr. Ross Bernard."

"Bernard. The same doctor from the Wilkerson case," she observed. "And Victor thought he may have falsified his report on that case. Are there any purple postulations on his statement?"

"Not on the first page… whoa."

Ari held up the page and Molly glanced up long enough to see purple lines and circles covered most of it. "I guess Victor had a lot upon which to postulate."

"Do you want me to read it to you?"

"Just the highlights."

"Okay, give me a second."

"Good 'cause I need to concentrate. Our driver thinks he's Mario Andretti."

The Rover weaved in and out of traffic. At first she thought she'd been made, but she realized Eden's beau was just impatient, unwilling to lag behind the snowbirds who clogged Grand Avenue, the major artery connecting Sun City to Phoenix. They were notoriously slow and changed lanes without looking.

"Let me summarize," Ari said. "Dr. Ross Bernard's statement indicates that Gabrielle, the daughter, broke her arm while in the care of her father, Carlos Pino. He states, 'Bruises found along the radius and ulna conducive to an arm literally being twisted until it broke.' Gabrielle confirmed Dr. Bernard's findings, stating that her father had become very angry with her when she attempted to pick up a hot cookie sheet from the kitchen counter and dropped it, ruining the cookies they'd been making. That set the father off."

She set it to the side and picked up a different document. "But apparently something didn't ring true to Victor or Pete, because they did some additional investigation. They talked to a few neighbors who said Mackenzie was the one who constantly grabbed Gabby to discipline her. A clerk at a neighborhood market, who had seen Gabby with both parents on separate occasions, said Carlos is the calm, even-keeled parent. Mackenzie is the one with the short fuse. Gabby is prone to temper tantrums when she doesn't get her way—"

"I could see that," she said, thinking back to the way the little girl marched up to her at GRD and boldly asked for a drink of water.

"The neighbors say Carlos is the one who uses a soft voice but firm answers, while Mackenzie screams as loud as Gabby."

"Wait, wait," she said. "Mackenzie is Victor's client. Why is he digging up all this stuff against his client, or have I got this backward? Did he and Pete dig this up or was it presented to them by the dad's lawyer?"

"No," Ari said, shaking her head. "They figured this out. And the school nurse at PTSA told Pete that Mackenzie often got defensive when she, the nurse, questioned her about some of Gabrielle's injuries, like deep bruises on her shoulders. She said one day the teacher sent Gabrielle to her office because she had a black eye."

"Sounds like they interviewed the nurse to confirm their suspicion that Mackenzie was the abuser, not Carlos."

"Or maybe they're both abusive."

"Happens all the time," she agreed.

Ari dug inside the file. "Oh," she said with a sweet voice. "I'm not the only one who's going to watch movies tonight."

She glanced at the DVD sleeve Ari waved. "Is that video footage?"

"Yup. This is footage from the market near their house." She read the sticky note attached to the cover. "They wrote a time stamp of three minutes and twelve seconds."

"Something significant must have happened in the store. Maybe Mackenzie lost her cool."

"Probably."

The answers were close. Maybe it was Isabelle. Maybe it was Mackenzie. Perhaps it was Eden. Her money was still on Christine. She groaned. Surveillance had been her least favorite part of police work. She needed to be at her office going through evidence, trying to cobble together the truth, not playing automotive leapfrog on the west side.

The Rover moved to the center lane, and only one car separated them. "New idea," she announced.

"Shoot."

"Exactly," she replied and Ari looked puzzled. "We've got four intersections ahead. I'm going to pull up on the Rover's left. Hopefully you can get a shot of the driver's face and maybe a few shots of them playing kissy face."

"They'll probably notice us."

"Yes, and I think that would play to our advantage. I'm beginning to believe the way to reveal Victor's killer is by unearthing all of the secrets."

"That sounds like a plan."

"Okay, I'm making my move. Get ready, babe. I don't know how long you'll have."

She quickly jerked into the left lane and they heard a horn honk behind them. Ari lowered the window and was poised for the shot. They sailed through the first light as she pulled up next to the Rover. She heard the shutter whirr repeatedly. They approached the second light and she willed it to go yellow. When it finally did, she knew the impetuous driver would floor it, but she was ready and sailed through next to him. The third light was only two blocks away and not timed with the rest of the lights. They cruised to a stop and Ari held down the shutter while they waited for the light to change.

"She's practically sitting in his lap," Ari reported. "Turn around, buddy. Got it!" she said. She pulled the camera away from her face and turned to Molly with an amused look on her face. "Babe, he's not a he and we've been made."

She leaned forward and stared at the shocked couple—Eden Venegas and Isabelle Medina.

They laughed all the way back to Nelson Security. Molly's gaydar had completely missed Eden.

"So if Eden and Isabelle are lovers, perhaps Isabelle went to Eden's condo Tuesday night after Victor squashed her promotion?" Molly suggested.

"Could be," Ari said. "Or maybe Isabelle was so angry, that she went over the edge all by herself."

"Maybe Victor told Isabelle he knew about the two of them and wasn't promoting her because of it."

They looked at each other, recognizing that would definitely give hotheaded Isabelle enough reason to kill him. And Molly still wanted to hear Isabelle's reaction to Phoenix Fireball's claim that she didn't arrive at the Panther Club until nearly ten p.m.

Back inside the blue cabin, Molly downloaded photos while Ari threaded another cinematic masterpiece by Cousin Glenn. Many of the pictures were blurry because of the moving vehicles, but the ones at the stoplight were crystal clear. Eden caressed Isabelle's cheek while she kissed her ear. Then there was a great shot of them looking toward the truck. Their mouths hung open in surprise.

She glanced at the accordion file. She was tired and it seemed ominous, but she wanted to play the DVD snippet mentioned on the sticky note. The drive whirred to life and the drawer popped open. While she waited for it to slowly load, she glanced at the whiteboard. Ari had started a new reel. The sun rose and Glenn panned across the yard.

"Huh, that's different," she commented.

Ari looked up from the file she was reading. "What?"

"The beginning. It's different."

They stared at the screen and watched Carlin shovel eggs into his mouth. "How?" Ari asked.

"Not that part, the very beginning." She got up and rewound the film.

Ari sighed and dropped the file. "I've definitely seen too many of these. They're blending together. Okay, you have my full attention."

The film began again, and instead of watching sunrise over Murphy Park as they had for the last twenty-plus films, they were treated to a shot of Scott sleeping. Ari chuckled at his mouth hanging open. "I'd love to show this to him," she laughed. Then came the eggs and an angry Carlin who looked as if he was ready to fling them at the camera. The film cut to a car ride. It pulled into a parking lot. The glass front reflected off the camera's lens. Molly glanced at Ari, who seemed so completely mesmerized that if she fired a gun, she wasn't sure Ari would react. A sign in the front advertised blue raspberry Slurpees. A 7-Eleven. Molly knew there had been two stores in the neighborhood, but she wasn't sure if this was the one where Richie had been murdered. The camera remained focused on the door, and soon Scott and Blythe appeared in the frame, heading inside. Eventually they emerged, each holding two Slurpees. Molly guessed one was for Glenn and the other for Carlin, the car's driver. Blythe and Scott stopped and looked to their left, greeting someone who hadn't yet entered the frame. Glenn turned the camera slightly to the right. Richie showed Scott a new trading card he'd acquired. They laughed and Blythe coaxed Scott back to the car. Richie shouted something to Scott as he left. Then he clearly mouthed,

 red. The camera jumped and Glenn's right
rner of the frame as he furiously waved back.
Ari's pained expression. She wrung her
p. As much as she needed to look away, she
ended and Ari stared at her lap.

"Are you okay, babe?"

"I don't know," Ari said in a tiny voice. "I don't know if I can keep watching these movies. He's so…alive." Her voice cracked as a flood of emotions poured out. "I've coped all these years by burying the memories that made him a person. That made me feel guilty that I wasn't properly honoring his memory, but it was the only way I could move forward." She picked up another reel, and pulled at the tail. "For the last week, I've been digging him up bit by bit. I just don't think I can do this anymore," she said, her voice a broken whisper.

Molly rushed to the couch. "Okay, I've not said anything, but now I am. I obviously will support whatever you want to do, but I think you need to step away from this. Maybe Henrietta Long was murdered and maybe she wasn't. We don't know. And even if she was, it's highly unlikely you're going to find evidence to prove it twenty-five years later."

Ari nodded and fell against her. "You're probably right. I have one more angle I want to investigate, and if nothing comes of it, I'll stop."

"Good idea," she agreed, tenderly kissing her on the top of her head. She retrieved the laptop and brought it back to the couch. "Let's take a look at this," she said, starting the video from the time suggested on the sticky note.

The front of the store filled the screen. The camera was mounted high on the wall, close to the ceiling, affording a view of all four aisles and the cashiers. It appeared management was equally concerned about employee theft as they were about shoplifting. Mackenzie and Gabrielle weren't readily visible.

"Do you see them?" Ari asked.

"Uh, yes. There."

She pointed to the third aisle where mother and daughter looked at cereal. Gabrielle pulled a box off the shelf and tried

to put it into the little basket Mackenzie carried on her
She jerked the basket away and leaned down. She pointed at ι
box's side panel and spoke with Gabrielle.

"She's explaining the sugar content and why it's junk food,"
Molly said.

"That would be typical of a teacher," Ari agreed.

Gabrielle crossed her arms and shook her head vigorously.
Mackenzie stood up and returned the cereal to the shelf. When
she turned to look at a different choice, the stubborn little girl
pulled the same box off the shelf and attempted to throw it into
the basket. Instead, it hit Mackenzie in the back and fell on the
floor. It looked as though Gabrielle laughed at the sight.

"Uh-oh," Molly said.

Mackenzie whirled around. She grabbed Gabrielle's arm
viciously with her free hand. Gabby tried to pull away, but she
yanked her back so forcefully, her feet flew off the ground before
she practically landed on top of Mackenzie.

"Ow!" Ari exclaimed. "That had to hurt."

Mackenzie kept a tight grip on Gabrielle as she lectured her.
At first Gabrielle shook her head, but then she glanced at her
arm and her knees buckled.

"She's squeezing her arm so tightly, Gabrielle's ready to
drop," Molly observed.

"I'll bet if she squeezed much harder, she'd break her arm."

Mackenzie whispered to her, removed her arm and stepped
away. The little girl shuffled to the box, picked it up with two
hands and put it back on the shelf. As soon as she completed the
task, she stuck her right thumb in her mouth and hugged her
body with her left arm. Mackenzie continued down the aisle.
When she noticed Gabrielle was still standing in front of the
cereal, she called for her and Gabrielle immediately darted to
her mother, her thumb still in her mouth.

"I've seen enough," Molly spat. She slapped the space key to
pause the DVD. "I'm not sure what the hell the father is doing
to that little girl, but this mother is a monster. She's disciplining
her into submission." When Ari said nothing, she asked, "Babe,
what do you make of this?"

Ari got up and went to the desk. "There was something else in that envelope." She looked at the DVD cover and the yellow sticky note with the time stamp. She picked up the thick accordion file and located the manila folder that had held the DVD. Inside she found two receipts: one from AV Reproductions and the other from Lightning Delivery. She smiled grimly as she presented them to Molly.

"Take a look at these. First, someone named Jake Gittes had a DVD made, just of the section we watched. Then," she said, looking at the second receipt, "Mr. Gittes had the copy delivered to Mr. Kenneth Perryman, Esquire, Parks & Perryman, Attorneys at Law. The message attached simply read, 'Mackenzie Dearborn.'"

"Ken Perryman is the attorney for Gabrielle's father, Carlos Pino." Molly scratched her head. "I'm lost. Who's Jake Gittes? How's he involved?"

Ari wrapped an arm around her. "Oh, honey, we need to watch more old movies. Jake Gittes isn't real. He's Jack Nicholson's character in *Chinatown*. I think your friend Pete Daly was being cute. He made this video at Victor's request and sent it to opposing counsel."

"This is like the CPS case," she realized. "He's done this before. He wants Carlos to have custody."

Ari nodded and raised her hand. "There's one really important question here."

She looked at the screen and the frozen image of Mackenzie gesturing at Gabrielle, who was so afraid she was sucking her thumb. "Yeah, I know what you're going to say. Was it possible Mackenzie knew Victor was setting her up?"

Ari returned the invoices to the envelope. "That would definitely give her a motive to kill him."

CHAPTER TWENTY-TWO

Christine Pierpont and Gloria Rivera faced Andre in the conference room. Molly had chosen to sit at the other end, distancing herself from everyone. Gloria had called her last night and told her Detective Williams wanted to speak with Christine again on Saturday morning.

"It's at eight in our fifth-floor conference room. Can you attend?" Gloria asked.

"Of course." She took a breath. "There's one other thing you should know, Gloria. Detective Williams and I are somewhat at odds currently." She didn't explain why and Gloria didn't ask. Perhaps she could guess that it involved the envelope found in the safe that had her name on it.

"I understand. These things are complicated. Do you have any idea why Detective Williams has asked for the meeting?"

"I do. Christine's red Porsche, or a car that looks like hers, was seen at nine p.m. in the parking garage on the night of Victor's murder."

There was silence on the line and Molly thought she heard Gloria tapping on her keyboard. Eventually, she said, "Thank you for the information. I'll see you tomorrow."

Molly had avoided phone contact with Andre. She'd sent him the market footage of Mackenzie and Gabrielle via Dropbox. He'd pinged her back, thanking her and agreeing that Mackenzie would be a prime suspect, if in fact she'd learned Victor had shared evidence with opposing counsel. What he had not done was invite her to the Saturday morning interview with Christine, and he'd been rather cool about her presence until Gloria mentioned she'd asked Molly to attend.

"Ms. Rivera, thank you for joining us on this Saturday morning," Andre began. "However, the police are not formally charging Ms. Pierpont with anything at this time. This is a follow up interview based on some new information I've received, information that calls into question some of the statements Ms. Pierpont made to myself and Ms. Nelson previously."

"I understand," Gloria said.

He opened the folder he'd brought and withdrew a photograph of her entering the building. The time stamp at the bottom read eight twenty-seven. "Ms. Pierpont, you told us you went straight from dinner at the St. Francis to the Sky View Lounge for drinks. Yet, this photo shows you entering the office tower. Did you stop here on the way downtown?"

She looked at the photo and then glanced at Gloria, who gave a slight nod. When she locked eyes with him she said, "I dropped by at eight twenty-seven to pick up a file for court the next day, and I was gone by eight thirty. I didn't mention it previously because I knew I'd left prior to any of the unpleasantness that occurred later."

"Unpleasantness," he repeated. "I see. Well, we have a witness who says she saw your red Porsche in the parking garage at nine twenty-five."

"She's mistaken," she said flatly. "I was gone by that time."

"If I may interject," Gloria said. They all gazed at her as she reached for a file folder and withdrew a short list. "I took the liberty of asking building management for a list of red Porsche owners that are registered with the garage. You'll see Christine is one of four."

"We'll definitely check this out," he said. He offered Molly a sharp gaze. The only way Gloria could've known about the Porsche sighting was if Molly had told her.

"And there's something else you should know about that parking garage, Detective," Christine interjected. "After-hours visitors often park on the lower levels and go across the street to take the light rail downtown for events or dinner. When they return for their car, the gate goes up automatically since there's no one there to take their ticket. I don't know why that happens, but it does," she said with a shrug and a smile.

"So you're saying that even if the other red Porsche owners deny being here Tuesday night, it could be a random visitor."

"Exactly."

He shifted in his chair. "So, to summarize, you admit being in the building just before Victor Guzman was murdered."

"Yes."

"But you deny killing him."

"Yes."

"And you deny having knowledge of his murder while it was in progress."

"Yes."

Molly noticed she'd blinked at the last question. But she wasn't going to admit what she'd done.

He looked at Molly. She could tell his frustration was growing. She knew what question to ask next, but Andre had shoved her onto the other side of the fence and aligned her with Christine and Gloria. Perhaps that was where she should've been all along.

He looked at his notes and asked, "If you only stayed a few minutes, why doesn't the security footage capture you leaving?"

"I didn't leave through the main door. While the main door is the only entrance, there are other exits. I went out the northeast door because I'd pulled up into a loading zone facing Indian School Road. I knew it would be faster than parking in the garage." She offered a sheepish look. "A lot of people park in the loading zone for a few minutes, even though we're not supposed to."

"You just happened to use the exit that doesn't have a camera," he said. "Did you know it was being repaired this week?"

"I had no idea until I went out the door and saw some of the equipment. Frankly, I don't pay attention to those emails from maintenance. As you know, I've been in court all week."

He tapped his stylus on the table and scrolled to his next question. "I interviewed two of the lawyers who joined you at the Sky View, and they don't recall seeing you before ten p.m. Your friend Sheridan looked for you and couldn't find you."

She glanced at Gloria who gave another nod. She pulled out her phone. "What she neglected to tell you was that she sent a text and I replied."

She opened her messages and showed him the exchange between herself and Sheridan. Andre passed the phone to Molly. Sheridan had inquired about Christine's location. Christine mentioned a long line at the ladies' room.

Molly handed the phone to Christine, who continued. "Tuesday was the first day of my period. I have horrific first days with heavy flow. I actually wound up in *two* very long lines, one at the St. Francis and then the other at the Sky View. I debated about going home, and then I decided to make a quick appearance. That's what took so long."

He looked away. Molly knew he hated discussing things like feminine hygiene. Then he took a deep breath and leaned forward. "Christine, we think one of two scenarios occurred." He waited until Christine's eyes met his before he said, "First scenario: you came back here between dinner and drinks and killed Victor Guzman. We know you entered the building soon before he died, and after you killed him, you could've left through the northeast exit. Second scenario: you stopped here to practice in a conference room for a little while, which I understand is part of your ritual. Perhaps you were on the tenth floor because you needed to pick up a file, and you just used one of those rooms because it was convenient. You heard the shots and when you thought it was safe, you headed down the west staircase and went out the northeast exit. You went back to the garage and drove downtown to meet your friends. What you didn't do was call the police to report a felony in progress. If this scenario really occurred, we believe Victor Guzman heard you leave. He was hiding on the tenth floor, and when you left, he figured you'd call the police. That's why he decided to lock himself in the washroom, rather than try to follow you down the west staircase. That decision cost him his life and potentially saved yours. Had he followed you, and the shooter followed him, you both might be dead."

The blank expression cracked for a second but quickly returned. "Well, I'm happy to be alive and I'm truly sorry about Victor's murder, but it didn't happen the way you suggest, Detective Williams." She glanced at Molly before her gaze returned to Andre. "Do you have any further questions? I'd like to get on with my Saturday plans."

He shook his head and she rose slowly from the chair. Molly guessed her knees were wobbly from the intense questioning. She whispered a thank you to Gloria Rivera, grabbed her purse and left. Once the door had shut behind her, he asked Gloria, "Are you okay with Victor's murderer going free?"

She ignored his question and asked one of her own. "Since the footage clearly shows Christine entering the building, what about the woman in the hoodie who enters later?"

"That could be a tenant who's cold," Andre suggested.

"Ah, I see," she replied. Her gaze moved from Andre to Molly. "I don't think Christine killed anyone."

"Are you sure about that?" he asked, drawing Gloria's attention back to him.

She paused before she said, "Yes. As for the rest of her story, she's the only one who knows what happened. She'll have to live with her conscience." She stood and picked up her purse. "Do you need anything else from me?"

They shook their heads and she left.

Andre leaned back in the chair and chewed his thumbnail. He remained silent but eventually looked at her. "She's lying," he spat. "I know it. She was here. She probably killed him."

"I don't know about that," she countered. At least he was speaking to her. "We can't discount the figure in the hoodie, but either way, she's somewhat responsible for his murder. Even if she just stumbled upon the crime, she didn't call it in. She knows she could lose her license, but she probably sees this as justice so it makes her lie okay. After what Victor did to her, she wasn't going to lift a finger to help him."

He leveled his gaze at her. "Lies that are okay. Is lying really okay?"

"Sometimes," she said in a hard voice. She was growing angry. She wasn't good at groveling for very long. She reached into her backpack and withdrew the accordion file Pete had given to her. She shoved it toward him, but he ignored it.

He tented his fingers and looked up at the ceiling. "You know, after I watched that tape you sent me of Mackenzie and Gabrielle in the store, I wondered what you had to give Pete to get the rest of that file. I imagine Victor was smart enough to keep a file on his P.I. How else could he keep him in line? Yet, there was nothing in the safe on Pete—not even that legendary videotape that's rumored to show him stealing fifty thou."

His gaze drifted back to Molly and they stared at each other. When she said nothing, he grabbed his iPad and stormed out.

She waited long enough for him to get on an elevator before she departed. She thought about Christine's actions. If she heard the shots and came out of the conference room long enough to see Victor run onto the tenth floor, then she knew what was happening. Of course, her first reaction would be to save herself, which was understandable. But once she was safely down the stairs, she had a responsibility. Molly knew they could never prove she was present, and unfortunately for Victor, he treated her like shit. In her mind, Victor got what he deserved.

As she strolled to her truck, tires squealed a level above. She turned to see a Dodge Charger make the turn and barrel toward her. She ran to a nearby staircase as the Charger suddenly stopped. She gulped air as Isabelle Medina leaned out the driver's window, a sneer on her face.

"Now you know what it's like to be followed." Molly glared at her. "And for the record, I was with Eden when Victor was murdered. I picked her up outside her condo complex and we had sex in an empty lot. I went down on her and she went down on me."

"So is that why you missed Fan Appreciation Night?" Isabelle blinked in surprise and recoiled in her seat. She squatted and leaned on the door. "The police know you didn't arrive at the Panther Club until nearly ten. So you can expect Detective Williams is going to ask you and Eden for some proof of your whereabouts. You're both suspects."

"We didn't kill Victor," she spat. "But when you catch the woman who did, let us know. We want to buy her a drink." She threw her chin toward Molly. "Get the hell off my car."

Molly obliged and Isabelle peeled out, tires screeching. When her knees stopped shaking, she trudged over to her truck. She was certain Isabelle would've run her over had that staircase not been nearby. And as she predicted, Eden was Isabelle's alibi and she was hers. Her hands were still shaking as she reached in the glove box for a cigarette and her lighter. Just the act calmed her. She didn't need to light it. She tossed them both back and drove to a QT for a Coke. She called Pete Daly but got his voice mail. She needed to talk to him ASAP.

She'd found more bio on Mackenzie Dearborn in the missing file. Pete had tailed her a few times to establish her routine. His notes said she and Gabrielle frequented Encanto Park on the weekends. She would read a book while the little girl played on the equipment. It was a beautiful March day, so Molly imagined Mackenzie and Gabrielle might be there.

Encanto Park included a golf course, band shell, lagoon, and every child's favorite, Kiddieland. She had fond memories of birthday celebrations there, a mini-amusement park for the under-seven crowd. As she pulled into the full parking lot, she wondered if she'd get a space. Every Phoenician knew mild temperatures in the desert were like a good wine, highly enjoyable, but fleeting. Fate was on her side and a sedan pulled out at the end of the row.

The last time she'd been to the park was on a terrible date. The woman had insisted they go canoeing. She laughed, remembering how she barked at Molly incessantly every time they rammed into the bank because Molly couldn't steer. She tried to think of the bad date's name but couldn't remember. Most of the women she'd met during that decade were forgettable, and the amount of alcohol she'd consumed ensured even the memorable dates faded into the distilled fog.

She trekked across the spacious grassy areas, avoiding Frisbees, picnics, touch football games and romantic interludes occurring every five feet. As she circumvented a hetero couple quickly moving from second to third base, she rolled her eyes. She was all for romance—but not with an audience.

She heard children laughing and screaming before she saw the play structure. Dozens of kids climbed, crawled and hung on it. She scanned the benches of adults who formed a circle around the children. On the shadiest bench that had the luxury of a tree overhead, she saw Mackenzie Dearborn reading a book. She wore purple sweatpants and a T-shirt with the atom and PTSA logo on the front. Her hair was still pulled back in a ponytail, and Molly couldn't see much difference between her casual clothes and school wardrobe. She plastered a warm smile on her face, hoping Mackenzie would react differently to meeting her for the second time.

She looked up quizzically when Molly stopped in front of her bench. "Hi, Mackenzie, I'm Molly Nelson. We met briefly at GRD. I was hired to replace Pete Daly, the previous private investigator."

"I remember."

She said nothing further so Molly forged ahead. "I imagine you're concerned about Victor's death since your court date is coming up."

She set the book aside. "I am. I don't have any idea who'll inherit the case, and I want this over. I want my abusive ex-husband out of our lives."

Molly thought of the video footage from the market, but she nodded in agreement. "I'll do whatever I can to get you the information you need." She glanced at the play structure and saw Gabrielle sitting on the swing, making swirls in the sand with her toe.

"Poor kid," Mackenzie lamented. "There's not much else she can do right now." Tears pooled in her eyes and Molly saw she was physically affected by her daughter's plight.

"Do you mind telling me how she broke her arm?"

Mackenzie pulled her gaze from Gabrielle and dabbed at her eyes. "I'm sorry. She's all I have so I get a little emotional." She took a breath and said, "I'd dropped her off for her weekend visit with her dad. This was about a month ago. They were making cookies. She dropped a pan and Carlos got angry and grabbed her arm. The doctor said he squeezed it until it broke. At least, that's what he reported."

"That was Dr. Bernard, wasn't it?" she asked casually.

"Yes, he's a very caring person."

"How long have you been divorced?"

"About three years. Gabby was eight."

"So he took her for a visit, and she came back with a broken arm?"

"Well, sorta," she backpedaled. "She came home and said her arm hurt. She told me about how he grabbed her so we put some ice on it and I gave her ibuprofen. She went to bed and I fell asleep on the couch. She must have had a bad dream, because she tried to come down the stairs on her own. I woke up to her wailing and found her at the bottom. We went to the ER. According to the doc, she now had a true fracture, but he agreed with me that Carlos had originally caused a hairline fracture. I'd already spoken with Mr. Guzman since this wasn't the first time she'd come home with a physical injury. Several times she'd come home with bruises." She looked out at Gabrielle who'd found a friend. They were laughing and she was showing off her cast. "Such a great kid."

"Has the firm told you who will take over your case?"

She scratched her head. "Christine? We're going in to meet her next week." She leaned back and crossed her arms. "It'll be so different without Victor there. I can't imagine they'll replace him."

"Do you know his paralegal, Brittany?"

She laughed and gave Molly a sideways glance, as if she was telling a secret. "You mean the paralegal of the month?"

"Oh, you know about that?"

She nodded with self-importance. "I know the firm doesn't advertise that fact, but Hannah and I are friends, so we've made this rule about the dome of silence. I let her vent, but I promise it goes nowhere. She was a teacher in a previous life, so she knows I understand confidentiality."

"Well, I'm new to the firm, so I'll admit I don't know much of the gossip."

"There's some pretty juicy stuff, for sure." She looked inquisitively at her and she continued. "For example, Isabelle, the office manager, has a second career as a cage fighter."

She feigned surprise. "I had no idea."

"Nobody does. But can you imagine how difficult Isabelle the Hell would be to work with if she didn't have fighting as an outlet? All that hostility would come to the firm, at least that's what Hannah says."

"I imagine Isabelle wouldn't want that to get out," she replied.

"No way. But it won't come from me. I promised Hannah." She licked her lips in preparation for another divulgence. "And I know a little something about Victor, too. Well, not Victor," she corrected. "It's more about his ex-wife. She's dating a woman. Hannah's not sure who it is, but she's been dating her for some time. In fact, Victor found out and was going to cut off the alimony."

"How could he do that?"

"The divorce decree said if her behavior was deemed scandalous and detrimental to the image of a family law firm as determined by the GRD Board of Directors, she'd lose her claim to alimony. And since she's in a homosexual relationship, I can guarantee a few board members would call that scandalous."

"So if Victor hadn't died, the wife could've found herself in serious financial trouble."

"Absolutely," Mackenzie said smugly. "And that woman is such a bitch."

"You really know a lot about the place," she commented.

"I've had to go there enough. But hopefully it'll all be over soon, with or without Victor."

Molly leaned forward and rested her elbows on her knees. "I don't know if you're aware, but the firm asked me to work with anyone who might be questioned by the police regarding Victor's murder. Have the police questioned you yet?"

"No, why would they?"

"Because Victor was looking at your file when he died. I'm certain a detective named Andre Williams is going to question you. Can you tell me where you were last Tuesday night when Victor was killed?"

She grew nervous. "I, uh, well, I was home with Gabby, of course. It was a school night. We had dinner, she took a bath and we read stories until she fell asleep. Then I stayed up doing lesson plans until eleven thirty. I'm not sure you're aware how many hours teachers put in of their own time, but it's significant."

"I'm very aware it's not an eight-to-five job. Was anyone else with you, other than Gabby? Did anyone come to the door? Did you see a neighbor after she went to bed?"

She shook her head. "No. Is that bad?"

"Well, it just means no one can corroborate your alibi."

Mackenzie tapped her foot and chewed a nail. Either she was genuinely frightened, which tended to happen when honest people were accused of a crime, or she was worried about being discovered. She threw up her hands and shrugged. "Well, that's all I've got. It's the truth, so I hope it's enough."

"One more thing," Molly said gently. "When I talked with Gabby the other day while you were in the office, she mentioned you were going to see Mr. Guzman. Does she know he's dead?"

She shook her head adamantly. "No, I'm not telling her that until I absolutely have to. When we've gone to the office for an appointment, Gabby stays up on the tenth floor with Hannah. That's kind of how we've become friends. I'm not sure Victor ever saw Gabby, and she's never seen him. We hadn't started to prep her as a witness yet, so I'm hoping I can keep his death from her for a while."

"I understand. Just tell Detective Williams everything and answer his questions as best you can." She reached into her pocket and pulled out a card. "In the event you think of something else, please don't hesitate to call me."

She read the card and said, "Thank you." Her eyes welled with tears. "I just don't understand why this has happened to us." She sniffled and wiped her tears away. "Thank you, Ms. Nelson. Thank you."

Molly decided to stroll a little further into the park and clear her head. She waved at Gabrielle, who recognized her and waved back. She couldn't let go of the interview with Christine or the video footage of Mackenzie in the market. Then there was Isabelle and Eden. She returned to the three aspects of crime: means, motive and opportunity. Isabelle and Christine clearly had the means since they were office employees. Victor had damaged their careers, and either one could've been the woman in the hoodie. Mackenzie and Eden were outsiders. They would've had a harder time gaining the means since neither possessed a key card or badge. She doubted Mackenzie would attempt to steal those things in the middle of the busy office, and Eden wouldn't have a reason to be in the office. However she may have used Isabelle's. Molly circled back to the idea of a partnership. When she'd sent Andre the video of the market, she'd included some of the Range Rover photos of Isabelle and Eden. Normally he would've replied, but he'd said nothing.

Her phone rang as she crossed to the parking lot. *Pete.* "Good morning, Pete."

"Good morning, Ms. Nelson. How may I assist you on this fine Sunday?"

"I reviewed the file you gave me. I need you to confirm or deny some inferences I've made."

"Like what?" he said, his voice gravelly. She wondered if he'd just woken up.

"Can I assume that Victor sent a copy of the security footage from the market to the opposing attorney—the one who represents Mackenzie's ex-husband, Carlos Pino?"

There was a pause before he replied, "Yes, but let me explain." He coughed and she heard water running. "We saw that footage and I went to question the doctor, Ross Bernard. Same doctor on Wilkerson. The guy's an idiot. He's on his third probation for his residency. He totally bought everything Mackenzie told him just because she's a teacher. When I investigated him further, he admitted he hadn't been very thorough. And he hadn't bothered to involve CPS. Mackenzie told him Dad broke Gabrielle's arm and then she *fell* down the stairs. Yeah, right. More than likely that stubborn child wouldn't go to bed and got pushed."

Molly closed her eyes, hoping he was wrong. "Here's my other question, Pete. Did Mackenzie suspect Victor sold her out?"

"I don't think so," he retorted.

"Did anyone else know about that footage besides you, Victor and the guy who made the copy?" she pressed.

He didn't answer and she heard his labored breathing. He obviously wasn't sitting in his lawn chair. Then he groaned. "Hannah."

CHAPTER TWENTY-THREE

Ari stared at the abandoned factory in the distance. She'd told Scott there was plenty of circumstantial evidence to suggest Henrietta was murdered, but she wasn't sure she'd find the proof that would give him, Carlin, and Blythe's children equal footing with the award kids. Before she officially dropped the investigation, she wanted to see the place at the center of the fight—the place Wilfred Sr. had built and where Junior met Millicent.

She'd spent the morning giving a cursory review of the boxes of documents. The wills were straightforward. She'd carefully read Millicent's, which was created the week after Junior died. While Millicent couldn't override Junior's wishes regarding Long Manor, since he'd left the factory to her when he died, she'd cut out Carlin, Blythe and Scott completely upon her own death.

Ari also discovered all of Junior and Henrietta's personal papers had been destroyed. There were no bank statements, bills or mortgage payments to peruse. And there certainly wasn't a paper trail leading to Morris Michaels or Ned Beaton. Millicent had expunged everything except the photos.

She walked the five blocks south until she came to the fence that surrounded the immense red brick structure. She'd reviewed the interior and exterior photos online. While the building was condemned, others had visited, and in fact, several news stories had been filmed inside. She was walking a fine line between justice and trespassing, but a key and Scott's blessing would keep her out of jail.

"I just hope he'll give me his blessing after the fact," she mumbled to herself.

A single-story entrance opened into a three-story, ten thousand square foot rectangle. Two additional stories grew from the center, and Ari imagined Wilfred Sr.'s, office sat on the top floor, providing him an expansive view of growing Glendale. Symmetrical windows on each floor wrapped around the whole building. The ground floor windows were boarded up, but the upper ones were still intact or broken.

She followed the fence, noticing the graffiti tags on some of the boarded windows. None of the red brick had been vandalized, suggesting even taggers had a little respect for historic buildings. At the front, she discovered the plaque provided by the Registry of Historical Places. She yearned to see inside and wondered if the taggers had found a breach in the fence. She pulled out the large ring of keys Scott had given to her. Since they still owned the property, she hoped the key might be on the ring. She found a match and smiled when the lock popped open.

She looked around and went in. She debated whether to lock the padlock, but if there were a squatter inside, she would prefer to make a hasty exit. As she approached the front door, she took her gun out of her purse and tucked it into her waistband. She walked the perimeter of the south end, admiring the detail in the masonry and imagining the factory in its heyday. When she arrived at the loading dock, she looked at the faded Fizz sign that still hung over the archway.

She ascended the ramp to a door marked, "Deliveries". She sorted through the keys and found three that looked as though they belonged to a commercial building. The second one slid in and opened the door. She suddenly froze, wondering if there was an alarm. She hadn't seen any signs and she couldn't imagine the Longs paying for security on a condemned building.

"We'll just see if the police show up," she muttered.

She found herself on a long platform that extended into the main guts of the building. Light poured in from the upper banks of windows, highlighting the decades-old dust particles caught in a flurry of activity from air currents. Huge portions of the ceiling were gone, allowing her a view of the sky and making it impossible to visit any of the upper floors. A row of steel beam pairs divided the floor in half, like soldiers in formation, each pair held together by rivets that ran the length of the beams in what was known as flat-iron construction. It had been prominent in the early twentieth-century when buildings like the aptly named Flat Iron Building and Empire State Building had been constructed.

She watched where she stepped. Only the cement floor provided clues to the factory's previous life. While the machinery had been removed long ago, the bases that held the equipment remained. Steel plates and inch-thick screws and bolts jutted up from the concrete in various configurations. It would be easy to trip and fall.

She came upon an immense steel staircase that led to the second floor. It was steep, and if the building were ever reopened, a landing would need to be added for the building to comply with current codes. She debated whether to ascend. The ceiling at the top of the staircase was intact, and her curiosity overwhelmed her good sense. She went up three steps, and when nothing rocked or wobbled, she went up three more. The staircase seemed quite sturdy. Slowly she climbed until her head peeked into the second story. So much of the floor was missing that it was impossible to visualize what important functions it had served. She gazed at the ancient window casements and imagined what it would've been like to stare out at the sorghum fields that surrounded the building in the early twentieth-century.

A door slammed shut. She jumped and almost lost her balance. She wasn't alone. Someone had entered through the delivery door, and she guessed it was the same person who had smashed her windshield. There wasn't any time to run down the staircase. He'd be across the platform in a few seconds. She quietly ascended the few remaining steps. The floorboards at the top of the stairs seemed durable. She hoped they could withstand her weight for a few minutes, or she'd plunge to her death, most likely impaling herself on one of the long bolts extending from the foundation. She took a deep breath and moved off the ladder, grabbing onto a horizontal beam behind her. If in fact the floor collapsed, perhaps she could dangle from the beam.

She remained perfectly still on her little island of floorboards. She peered to the left where a gaping hole existed, hoping to catch a glimpse of the intruder should he walk underneath her. Heavy footsteps drew nearer. Definitely a man. A high-pitched scraping noise. Silence. She guessed he'd stopped at the stairs. Her gun pressed against her spine and she hoped she didn't need to use it. A moment of déjà vu struck her as she remembered the scene in the garage with Garrett Beaton. *And he might be at the bottom of this staircase, too.*

The footsteps drew closer. She watched from her vantage point as a figure in black and wearing a ski mask passed underneath the missing second story floorboards. He carried something in a plastic shopping bag at his side. He walked past her, but he was still close enough that she could hear his footfalls.

The plastic bag rustled. He was removing whatever he'd brought with him. She was a literal sitting duck at the top of the staircase, but she also had an advantageous position, if she needed to defend herself. She looked at the four square feet of real estate protecting her and decided she needed to get down those stairs. She withdrew her gun—just as the intruder stepped into view. He held up something that looked like a newspaper. She held out her gun, ready to fire. He also held something in his left hand as well. When the paper caught fire, she knew it was a lighter. He bolted away and she began her descent. She stopped suddenly when she saw what waited for her at the bottom of the stairs: an old wooden pallet, starting to burn from the flames of the paper. It was growing quickly and she wondered if he'd doused the pallet with lighter fluid.

She descended until the flames were just out of reach and the heat was unbearable. She lowered herself over the side of the stairs. She glanced down and guessed she would drop about five feet, but fortunately the area beneath her was free of protruding bolts and other hazards. She dropped and tumbled to the floor. When she stood, she felt pain in her hip from her landing. She started to cough and hobbled toward the exit. She turned the knob but the door wouldn't open.

"Shit."

She pulled out her phone and dialed 911. She explained where she was and that she was okay. The operator dispatched the fire and police departments and she went in search of some fresh air. In the far corner she found a restroom. A more modern window had been installed, and the glass was protected on the outside by wrought iron bars. She opened the window and suddenly felt better.

She needed to call Molly, but she decided to wait until after the fire department arrived and she was unequivocally safe. Otherwise, Molly would have half of the Phoenix PD outside the factory in ten minutes. She might have relinquished her shield, but she still had many friends who owed her favors.

Ari heard the approaching sirens, took another few gulps of air and left the bathroom. The burning pallet was quite a spectacle, but since it was the only flammable item in the concrete and steel structure, she didn't consider it dangerous or life threatening. The man in the mask wanted to make a point. She kept visualizing Garrett Beaton standing in his kitchen and staring at the garage. He'd been friendly, but she wondered if that was an act. Did he know what happened to Henrietta? Was there a reason he didn't want her to uncover the truth?

The firemen told her to stand back from the door. At the count of three, and in an impressive display of force, the metal door flew off its hinges and smacked to the ground. A foxy firewoman immediately led Ari out while two other firefighters doused the pallet. She inhaled some oxygen and was examined by the firewoman, who proclaimed her okay. Then her phone rang.

"Why is my dispatcher friend calling me about you?" Molly barked. "What's going on?"

"Nothing, babe. I'm fine."

"Ari!"

"Uh-uh. You don't get to do that. Dr. Yee said—"

"Dr. Yee can kiss my ass! Why are you wandering around a condemned building?"

"I had a key, but I think someone followed me."

"That's it. I want you out of that house," she declared.

A Glendale police officer approached her to take a statement. "I need to speak with the nice police officer now. We can talk about this later. I promise you, babe, I wasn't in any real danger. This person is trying to spook me. I want to talk about it with you, but I need you pissed off at him, not me."

Molly sighed deeply. Ari had used all of the words Dr. Yee had told her to use. One of the facts Molly had learned to accept was Ari's curiosity would, at times, put her in dangerous situations, just as Molly's new occupation would put her in life-threatening situations.

"Fine," she said. "We will talk later. And I am *definitely* pissed."

Talking with Officer G. Quigley of the Glendale Police Department proved to be far more pleasant. When she produced the keys that opened the gate and stated she had permission from the Longs to be on the property, his focus shifted to the man in the mask. She gave him a description and they called Scott, who had to be pulled away from his son's soccer match to save Ari from jail. He had no idea who the man in the mask was but he was on his way.

Officer Quigley studied her business card and asked, "Are you Jack Adams' daughter?"

"I am," she said.

His face fell, and she steeled herself for what she guessed would come next. "I was one of the first officers on the scene at your brother's shooting. I was a rookie back then. I've never stopped praying we'd find the bastard who did it."

He sounded so sincere that there was nothing she could do when a tear wormed its way down her cheek. She thanked him and hurried back to Long Manor. She wanted to get away from Glendale.

She texted Jane to see if she could go to a movie. Ari needed to escape and forget the past, which seemed to be permanently parked on her shoulder. She intended to continue the investigation—ten miles away at her home.

She packed the rest of the movies and photos she'd not yet seen in her 4Runner. She dismantled her family tree and gathered all of her notes. Finally, she toured the house, snapping pictures with her phone. She found a portable screen in the basement and took it out with her.

She'd just slammed the 4Runner's hatch shut when Scott's Corvette arrived. Behind him was a convertible BMW. The driver emerged and the first thing she noticed was his thick patch of red hair.

Scott rushed up to her. "Ari, I'm so sorry." He pulled her into a hug and she felt his heart pounding.

"It's okay, Scott. I'm all right. Thanks for covering for me," she whispered.

"No problem."

The redheaded man joined them. He didn't smile but waited patiently for an introduction. Ari could tell he was much younger, and she doubted he'd reached his thirtieth birthday.

Scott stepped away and said, "Ari Adams, this is my stepbrother, Barry Long."

Barry offered a cordial handshake but immediately started asking questions. "What are you doing here exactly?"

Ari looked at Scott. He faced his brother and crossed his arms. "I told you, Barry. Ari's looking into Mom's death."

Barry's gaze returned to her. "You don't think it was an accident? The coroner said it was."

"I know. And frankly, I was ready to quit this morning." Scott looked stunned but she continued. "I *was* ready to quit until someone tried to roast me at the factory. Of course, this was after that same person took a bat to my windshield," she explained for Barry's benefit.

Scott shook his head. "I never expected anything like this to happen. I totally understand if you want to quit."

"And I don't understand why you started in the first place," Barry retorted.

"I'm not quitting, unless you're telling me I have to. The fire and the damage to my windshield prove there's something to this. I plan to uncover whatever I can."

"Who would do all this?" Barry wondered, shaking his head.

She started to mention Garrett Beaton but decided against it. "Right now, I don't know. I'm relocating for the time being, but I'll be in touch."

Scott smiled his gratitude. They said goodbye and left. She heard the revving of a motorcycle and saw Garrett Beaton pulling out of his driveway. He slowed and offered Ari a wave before he sped off.

Her anger was still simmering when her phone pinged. Jane said she'd love to go to a movie. She groaned as she composed a reply.

Sorry. Something just came up. Soon! Right now I have work to do.

She definitely had work to do. Meeting Barry Long made her want to try harder for Scott—and Carlin and Blythe. *Poor Blythe.* Ski-mask man thought he could scare her off. "Bad move," she muttered. "Now you've really pissed me off. Even worse, you've pissed off Molly."

CHAPTER TWENTY-FOUR

Molly stopped at a QT for her second large Coke with extra ice. She'd discovered a cold soda with crushed ice was the best remedy when she craved a drink. And after Ari's phone call, she wanted a whiskey. When Ari had told her she was looking into a mystery that was a quarter of a century old, Molly had thought nothing of it. For once, it seemed as if Ari had stumbled upon a benign puzzle. She should've known better.

She got in her truck and thought about what Ari could be feeling after learning her father might be privately investigating Richie's murder, and that somehow her parents had reconciled before her mother died. Ari had always thought of herself as her mother's caretaker and closest support in her final weeks. For Lucia not to mention that Jack was back in the picture... Molly shook her head. She wouldn't try to fix this. She'd just listen to Ari as she processed.

She chewed the ice furiously and refocused on her case. Hannah was now the key. She'd admitted confidentiality was her growth area, and she'd thought she could share everything with Mackenzie. She probably told her about the video footage to be a good friend. Had she also given Mackenzie her badge and key? Had they conspired to kill him? Yes, Hannah had a solid alibi since she was "auditioning" Colby, but Mackenzie's alibi was flimsy.

She had a hard time believing Hannah was a conspirator, but she needed to ask her. She called and Hannah picked up on the first ring.

"Ms. Nelson, it's wonderful to hear from you," she gushed in a flirtatious voice.

Molly chose to ignore her tone. "Hannah, could I stop by today? I have some follow-up questions. Would you be available in thirty minutes?"

"For you, of course. You have my address, don't you?"

"I do. I'll see you soon."

She hung up before Hannah could say anything else. She just hoped when Hannah opened the front door she was clothed.

She lived in a ranch house at Maryland Avenue and Fifteenth Drive. The entire area had once been horse property before the city gobbled up many of the homes in the sixties and built the Palo Verde Golf Course. A handful of those spacious ranch-style homes still remained, and a few actually kept horses and other livestock. Although Hannah's red brick house was small, the plot of land was huge. The properties now sold for nearly half a million, so she imagined Hannah had either inherited her house or the adult film industry paid her incredibly well.

After she rang the bell she heard, "Hi! I'm out back!"

She opened the wooden gate and entered a tropical jungle. Her eyes couldn't decide where to land, so she glanced at the colorful pots and decorations, still unsure of Hannah's location.

"I'm over here in the hot tub," she called.

"Crap."

She navigated past the standing planters and ferns that hung at forehead level and arrived at the hot tub without giving herself a concussion. Hannah's long, gray hair spread over the foam, and her large breasts sat on the surface. When she silenced the jets and the water stilled, it was obvious she was completely naked.

"Join me," she coaxed.

"I'm sorry, but I'm on the job, and my girlfriend and I have an exclusivity agreement about hot tubs," she said with a nervous laugh.

She seemed surprised and her gaze landed on Molly's left hand. "I'm sorry. You don't wear a ring. How was I to know you were taken?"

Good point, she thought. She'd have to talk to Ari about that. She'd bought Ari the ring for Christmas since she was the jealous one. Ari trusted her implicitly.

"We're still working on the jewelry," she said. "Hannah, I have to ask you a couple of really important questions, and I need honest answers."

"Okay," she replied hesitantly.

"Did you tell Mackenzie Dearborn that Victor gave some evidence to the opposing counsel?"

"No," she said mildly. "I had no idea he'd done that."

"That's not what Pete Daly told me. He said you and he discussed it, and you were very upset. Is that true?"

She looked away, her lip in a pout. She obviously envisioned a different afternoon.

"Okay, yes, I knew about it."

"And did you tell Mackenzie?"

Her gaze dropped and Molly had her answer. "What did she say when you told her?"

"It was so sad. She started bawling. She felt completely betrayed. We both did. We didn't understand how he could do such a thing, an unethical thing."

"Did she become angry?"

"Not that I saw."

"When was this?"

She searched her memory. "I guess about three weeks ago? Maybe a month?"

"Did you ever speak about it again? Did she bring it up?"

"No." Her voice grew quiet and she stared at the water.

When she finally met her gaze, Molly asked, "Is it possible that Mackenzie took your key and badge last week?"

She frowned. It was clear Hannah had not willingly given either item to Mackenzie. "I don't think so," she said slowly.

"But you're not sure?"

"No, I am," she said with conviction. "You met her on Wednesday, and that was the first time she'd been by since last month. I'm certain of it."

"How can you be certain?"

She looked embarrassed. "Well, it's not a nice thing to say, but every time she and Gabby come by, they raid my stash of candy and take all of the chocolate. It pisses me off but I haven't said anything to her because she's my friend, and I shouldn't mind that she eats it, right?" Molly nodded and she continued. "I mean, Miguel sometimes eats it too, but once in a while Mr. Guzman would bring a bag of chocolate as a replacement. Anyway, I haven't had to stop by Costco for chocolate in nearly three weeks. That's how I know. The day of her last visit was the day I told her about the videotape going to Carlos's attorney."

In an odd way it made sense to Molly. She suddenly had another thought. "But you know your badge and key went missing last Thursday or Friday, right?"

"Yes, absolutely. If somebody had picked it up by accident, they would've returned it to me by now. I hate to think somebody stole it, but I guess I'll have to tell Isabelle on Monday." She groaned. "I'm dreading that conversation."

"Just one more question, Hannah. Who took care of Miguel last week?"

"I did, as usual. A few weeks ago Isabelle got smart and restructured her meeting schedule so she no longer has time to take care of him on Wednesday afternoons. That falls to me." She paused and said, "Well, at least it used to."

"One more thing, Hannah. If you speak to Mackenzie, you can't tell her about our conversation. If you do, I imagine you'll be arrested for obstructing an investigation. Am I clear?"

Her eyes widened and she nodded. "Yes."

"Thank you," she said, turning to leave.

"Sure you won't join me?"

"No thanks," she called over her shoulder.

Once she was safely in her truck and out of Hannah's driveway, she checked her phone. Eden had left two messages. She put the phone on speaker and headed south.

"Ms. Nelson, it's Eden. Please come to my condo as soon as you can. The police are here. Hurry!"

When Molly arrived at the Cascades, she saw Andre's car and three black and whites parked in the circular driveway. Ramon wasn't at his normal post at reception. Instead an older African-American gentleman greeted her. When she explained her connection to the police, he waved her toward the elevators. She found Eden's front door open and the officers in the midst of a search. Eden and Miguel sat on the couch. He held his phone and seemed engrossed in a game, while she held a protective arm around him and watched the officers. They were being respectful, but thorough. One had removed the entire contents of her refrigerator and was checking inside the jars, while another searched kitchen cabinets. She imagined the majority of the team was down the hall in the bedrooms and bathrooms.

When Eden saw Molly, she rushed to her. "Why are they doing this?"

"Did they present you with a warrant?"

"Yes," she said, handing her a copy. Molly glanced over the page. It gave them permission to search her house and car.

"Did they say what they're looking for specifically?"

"No. They wouldn't tell me."

Molly saw the fear in her eyes. She wasn't sure if it was fear of being caught or fear of being accused of something she didn't do. "Just stay with Miguel for now, and I'll see what I can find out."

Eden returned to the couch while Miguel continued to stare at his phone. Andre emerged from one of the bedrooms, holding a square box. "We found this in her closet." He removed the lid and showed her a .38 caliber pistol.

"Are you sure this is the murder weapon?"

"No, but after you mentioned to me that the young security guard delivered a package, we ran a check on him. We've got him downstairs in the building office. This gun belongs to him. He gave it to her the night Victor was killed."

She recalled Ramon telling her that he'd delivered a package to Eden just as his shift ended. He'd forgotten to mention that the package was from him and that it was a gun.

She massaged the back of her neck. "Did he say why he gave her a gun?"

"For protection. She asked for it. It's obvious he's got it bad for her. I'll bet it's a match to the slugs we retrieved in the office building. We're looking for the badge and key, but I doubt we'll find them. She probably dumped those."

"Did she ever confess to Ramon that she killed Victor?"

"No. He was completely rattled when I mentioned that. I thought he was going to pee his pants. Said they talked about how difficult Victor had made life for her and Miguel, but she never mentioned shooting him."

"And you believe him?"

Andre weighed the question. "I'm inclined to. I don't think he knew what she was planning."

"Did she say how she got the badge and key? Did he see them?"

"No, but I'm thinking Isabelle's her partner or she's had them all along. How easy would it have been for her to waltz past Hannah's desk and take them? She could've stolen them months ago, or maybe Victor gave her a set while they were married."

She made a face. "I doubt that happened."

He shrugged. "I don't know, but I'm not going to worry about that part now. I'm more concerned about this gun. Let's confirm this part of the puzzle, and maybe she'll tell us the rest."

He went back and checked in with the officers. No one had found the key or badge. The officers departed, leaving Molly and Andre in the condo with Eden and Miguel. He confronted Eden and showed her the gun sealed in its plastic evidence bag. "I'll be confiscating this weapon. Have you fired it?"

"No," she said casually. "Ramon gave it to me because he was worried about me being alone." She suddenly understood. "Do you think I killed Victor with that gun?"

"I don't think anything, Ms. Venegas, but I know a thirty-eight caliber weapon killed your ex-husband."

"But I didn't do it," she cried, her voice becoming a raspy tear. "You need to believe me!"

Molly glanced at Miguel. He wasn't playing his game anymore. He watched the exchange between his mother and Andre intently. His brow furrowed and he looked down at his shoes.

"We're also looking for a missing badge and key. Do you know anything about those items?"

"No, I don't know what you're talking about!"

While Andre attempted to calm Eden, Molly joined Miguel on the couch. "I think you know something about all of this, Miguel. Is there something you need to tell us?"

He glanced at her and then looked away. When Eden began to cry, he jumped up and ran to her. He threw his arms around her waist and said, "Don't cry, Mommy. Please! I'm sorry! I'm sorry!"

CHAPTER TWENTY-FIVE

With renewed energy, Ari combed through the remaining boxes of photos. Jane agreed to help, and while Ari sifted through Scott's boxes, Jane perused Carlin's boxes. Ari had brought everything home, as it was too crowded at Nelson Security. Now the Long family history covered the floor of her solarium.

"Are we looking for something specific, like a photograph of Millicent holding a knife behind Henrietta?" she grumbled.

"That would be great," Ari chuckled, "but I doubt we'll find that. Ski Mask Man knows there's something here, and that's why he's tried to dissuade me from continuing the search."

"Speaking of searches," Jane said, "What are we going to do about Muriel and her quest to kill the Pocket?"

"That doesn't have anything to do with searches," Ari commented.

"I know, but I'm stumped. What do I do?" she whined.

Ari looked at her. "I have an idea, but let's get through this, and I'm on it. Okay?"

Jane kissed her cheek. "You're the best."

They worked in silence, scrutinizing each moment the Long family was captured with a photo—and there were many. Ari came to a set of pictures in an envelope. The first four pictures showed Scott in his bedroom, grinning broadly. Next to him was a five-story house of cards. Ari closed her eyes. She remembered this. She'd never seen it but she'd heard about it. Each of the four photos showed a different side. It was truly impressive, which was why the last three photos were so sad. As Scott had prepared another shot, Glenn barged in. The fifth picture showed his arm swiping at the house, and the sixth photo showed the result: a pile of cards from various decks.

Then she remembered. Glenn had moved into Scott's bedroom, a fact that was confirmed when she saw two twin beds in the first picture. Junior had forced him to welcome Glenn into his room, and the card house destruction happened during the first week. Ari remembered Scott retelling her the story. He'd said something like, "Glenn is not a good bunkie!"

"Hey, Ari! What are you doing?" Jane asked. "You look like you're a frozen statue."

"I'm remembering something, possibly something important."

"What?"

Instead of answering Jane, she grabbed her phone and called Scott. "Hi, Ari. Are you feeling okay after this morning?" he asked immediately.

"I am. Sorry to bother you, but I have a question. I was looking at the pictures you took of the huge card house you built. Do you remember that? The one Glenn knocked over?"

He laughed. "Oh, God yes, I remember that. I'd worked on that all day, and then he came along and deliberately knocked it over. I was so mad."

"Had he moved into your room?"

"Yeah, that's right. He didn't like sleeping alone. My dad told me I didn't have a choice. Glenn would get scared and go down the hall and climb into his bed. That's when Dad dismantled the bunk beds and made two twin beds. Then Glenn woke *me* up with his damn camera instead of my dad. He'd have that thing going when I first opened my eyes. Scared the shit out of me every morning."

"So he was in your room, using the video camera, early in the morning."

"Yeah, that's right." He took a deep breath. "Ari, are you thinking—"

"I'll call you back," she said and hung up.

She looked at Jane, who'd already opened the projector. She held up a reel of film. "I have no idea what to do next," she announced.

Ari took over and threaded the film through the projector. As soon as she saw Murphy Park at sunrise, she turned it off.

Jane gasped. "Well, that was a little harsh. Looked like a nice sunrise to me. We're lucky you're not on the Oscar committee."

She laughed and pulled the reel off. "We're only looking for reels that start on the south side of the house. The park was on the north side. If the movie starts in the park, it means that it was filmed earlier in the summer, before Glenn moved in with Scott."

"You're thinking he filmed Henrietta's death!" she cried.

"It's possible," she said. "He was always up before sunrise. And the day Henrietta died, Scott said Glenn was inconsolable when they discovered her body. He babbled endlessly and didn't make any sense. What if he saw her fall, and then when he saw her dead body, he was trying to connect those two things?"

"That makes sense," Jane agreed. "That poor boy must have been terribly traumatized. How's he doing now, twenty-five years later?"

Ari shook her head. "Scott doesn't know. He'd heard Glenn was in a group home in Cali, but that was several years ago."

Jane offered a sympathetic look. "Well, I hope he's okay."

The next reel began facing the garage. They watched the sunrise and breakfast, but then they were suddenly outside the Glenfair Cinema. Scott and Richie both held large brown grocery bags. Next to them was Ari.

"My God, you were gorgeous even then," Jane exclaimed. "And that's Richie."

"Yes," she whispered.

"Where are you?"

"It was the summer movies. We went once a week. They showed old G-rated movies like *The Love Bug*, the original *Nutty Professor*, stuff like that." The film shifted to a game of marbles before it finished. She changed out the reels and they watched the beginning of the next one, which started at Murphy Park.

"Not to be a pessimist," Jane said, "but even if Glenn saw Millicent, he might've missed recording it. He seems pretty focused on capturing the sunrise."

"That's true," Ari conceded as the next one started with sunrise and the garage. They watched another few minutes, which included Scott's birthday party and another cameo appearance by Richie and Ari.

"I just can't get over how cute you were," Jane gushed. "I would've had to seduce you."

"I had no idea at the time. Remember, I thought Scott was my boyfriend."

Jane snorted. "We would've had to set him straight. Although that sister of his was a looker."

"Yeah, she was," Ari agreed.

"You had a crush on her!" Jane exclaimed.

"I did, but I just didn't know to call it that."

They continued to watch the beginning of every movie, and as they approached the last three reels, Ari's hope of finding Henrietta's killer on film dwindled. Once they were down to the last one, she sighed. It began with sunrise over the garage, moved to breakfast and then Vacation Bible School at First United Methodist Church.

"Well, that was a bust," Jane said. "I'm sorry, honey. I've got to go to a client meeting." She grabbed her purse and kissed Ari on the head. "Forgetting about the Long family for a moment, and thinking about the Adams family, do you think you'll want to collect all the parts with Richie and maybe show them to your dad?"

"Maybe," she admitted. She wanted to ask Dr. Yee what she thought would be the best way to deal with the ninety reels of film.

Jane left and Ari closed her eyes. She felt defeated. She hated unresolved puzzles, and there was a lot of circumstantial evidence to suggest Henrietta was murdered. But she hadn't been able to find anything concrete. She packed up the reels and looked at her list. She'd stuck a piece of masking tape on each one, so she knew how many she'd actually watched. She'd numbered each reel as she watched it, and she'd noted which films included Richie.

She frowned. "Seventy-seven? That's not right."

She re-opened the boxes and checked her numbering. It was correct. She was missing part of the summer. Glenn had captured summer movies, Vacation Bible School and Scott's birthday. All of those events occurred in June and July. Where was August? If Ari remembered correctly, Glenn's mother didn't reappear until Labor Day. He would've been making movies the entire time, and if he'd taped over previous footage, the later dates would be the ones she'd watched.

Her heart rate quickened. She wondered if she was missing a box. That had to be it. It could've been shoved aside when she loaded or unloaded the 4Runner. She was certainly frazzled about the fire. Maybe she left one in the garage? Also, she never opened the boxes she'd categorized as miscellaneous. Maybe one box was mislabeled. Regardless, she was returning to Long Manor.

She thought of Richie as she headed west again for the second time that day. Each of Glenn's movies was a pinprick, drawing out a memory, like blood seeping from a wound. Even the happiest of occasions, like Scott's birthday, led to depression. Richie never got another birthday. He didn't get to have children who would attend Vacation Bible School. She herself had often bemoaned the fact that she never got to be an aunt to his children. She loved Molly's family. They had adopted her completely, and all of the kids called her Aunt Ari. Yet, the nagging feeling of loss never left her, and at times it ruled her heart with jealousy as its sister. Sometimes, when she was most depressed, if she saw siblings fighting, she'd be infuriated. They didn't know what they had or how much it would hurt if…

She was once again crying as she crossed into Catlin Court and pulled into the driveway. She unlocked the wrought iron gate and trotted to the garage. This would be fast. She had no intention of doing anything except picking up boxes. No memories, no stopping, no crying.

"Really, no crying," she chided herself.

She glanced around the garage and found another banker's box that had scooted behind a stack of chairs. Inside were at least twenty reels of film. She pushed the box close to the door, and seeing no other stragglers, she climbed the steep steps to the sunroom. It might be just the one box, but she wanted to make sure she took every reel on this trip.

The two-dozen boxes labeled miscellaneous were in a corner. She methodically started at one end and worked her way to the other. Miscellaneous was an appropriate word for what she found, including Henrietta's rosarian pin and badge. She broke her rule about stopping and pulled them out. She was certain Scott would let her give them to Mary Bellows, Henrietta's Rose Society friend. She quickly burrowed through box after box. No movie reels.

The last box was labeled DAD. It was very old and a layer of dust had permanently embedded itself onto the cardboard top. It had sat closed on a shelf for a few decades before the other boxes joined it. Inside was a large pine box Junior had made in shop class or Boy Scouts. The corners didn't quite align and a few of the nails were bent sideways. It contained trinkets, toys, keys, pins—all of his important memories from his childhood and some from his teenage years, including his first Zippo lighter. The bottom was lined with felt that had disintegrated over time, revealing some bald spots where the pine showed through. She pulled the wood box out of its cardboard home and inspected it. At the bottom of the front was a keyhole.

"That's odd."

She pulled out her knife and mentally apologized to Junior for what she was about to do. She jimmied the lock and the drawer popped open. Inside were memories of an adult, a few of which Junior certainly wouldn't have wanted his children to see. Ari picked up two Polaroid pictures of a naked Millicent. She was lying on a bed that Ari assumed was in room four at the Gaslight Inn. Junior had to have hovered over her to get the shots. In the first photo she cupped her breasts and blew him a kiss. The second photo was even steamier. She'd parted her legs, thrown her head back, and while her left hand caressed her left breast, her right hand spread over her bright red bush, approaching her clitoris.

Also in the secret drawer was a movie ticket to *L.A. Story*, for a showing on February 15, 1991. Ari imagined Junior's romance with Millicent had blossomed as Henrietta's illness grew worse. They had gone to the Scottsdale Drive-In, a location as far away from Glendale as possible, one that would allow them to quench their horny libidos, if the movie got boring. She found other trinkets that would be meaningless to anyone but them—a cork from a bottle of champagne, a bubble gum wrapper, an old dime and a dollar bill with a phone number on it. Ari imagined this could have been the way Millicent introduced herself to Junior at the Gaslight Inn's bar.

On the left side was a square handkerchief box with an embossed Hermes label. Ari guessed it was an expensive gift from Millicent, so she was quite surprised when she opened it and found another film reel. She closed her eyes and a sense of dread overtook her.

"I'll take that, please," a voice said.

She turned slowly toward the staircase. Barry Long stood on the stairs, half of his body above the floor and the other half below. In his right hand was a gun.

"Do you know what's on this reel?" she asked.

"No," he said, completely uninterested. "I don't know, and I don't want to know because nothing good will come of it, at least not for me, Nobel and Cal."

Ari looked at him with disdain. "Don't you want to know if your mother was a murderer?"

"Why would I ever want to know that? Why would anybody want to know that about their mom? The woman's dead! Leave her alone!" he shouted. "Now give me the damn reel so I can get out of here. I hate this dump."

"You're going to shoot me?"

"Only if you force me to. I'm a Millenial. We're lovers, not fighters. I wanted to scare you off, but that wasn't happening. When the film disappears, so will the idea that Henrietta was murdered. Life goes on. No one will believe you or Scott without any…" He swallowed the rest of his sentence and a horrible look of pain crossed his face. "Aaaagh!" He dropped the gun and disappeared from her view, falling down the stairs.

Still holding the reel, she pulled her gun and ran to the staircase. Barry lay in a crumpled heap at the bottom of the steps, screaming and cradling his knee. Standing over him was Garrett, wielding a bat.

He looked up and smiled at Ari. "Hi, neighbor!" He poked the end of the bat against Barry's head. "Shut the fuck up or I'll do the other one! I'm trying to have a neighborly conversation." Barry's cries turned to whimpers and Garrett faced Ari again. "I kicked his gun over there." He looked at the bat and said, "This asshole even had the decency to leave this for me in the backseat of his fancy car. I'm guessing this is what he used on your SUV."

"I imagine so," Ari said. "Thanks for coming around. You're a great neighbor."

"Thank you," Garrett replied sunnily. "Just tryin' to do my part."

"Is somebody going to call an ambulance?" Barry cried. "I'm in a lot of pain."

"Yeah," Garrett retorted. "I'm guessin' it hurts like nobody's business. At least you're alive!" He bent over and put his face close to Barry's. "A lot of people who tumble down a flight of stairs don't make it. You've probably got a shattered kneecap. No big deal. You'll walk again in a few months."

Barry's cries turned to yelps and Garrett stepped away. Ari retrieved his gun while Garrett called 911. When he hung up, he bent over and stared at Barry.

"And just so we're clear, that was for Henrietta."

CHAPTER TWENTY-SIX

It took twenty minutes to calm Miguel. Molly thought Eden's mothering actually made it worse. Once she'd retrieved a glass of milk and his favorite cookies, he settled on the couch with his snack. When Eden learned Molly wanted to question him without her, she insisted Gloria Rivera be present. While Gloria drove to her condo, Molly conferred with Andre.

"It's her?" he asked.

"Possibly," she said. "But I have a hunch."

"Which is?"

"I think Miguel took the badge and key from Hannah."

"That's how she got in," he said. "It makes sense."

"If we can get him to admit it, then our focus shifts from Christine and Mackenzie to Eden."

"Great. I got it," he said.

She held up her hand. "I know we're not in a great place right now, but I think we should do it together. How often are you around kids? You don't have nieces or nephews. Do you know how to get kids to trust you?" His look told her she'd offended him. "I'm sorry, but we're only going to get one shot at this. If he clams up and he's the one who took the badge and key, we'll probably never make a case that would hold up in court, not for first-degree murder. There are too many missing badges and keys."

His jaw set and he couldn't look at her. "You know, you talk about trust…"

She sighed and touched his arm. "I'm sorry. And we can talk more about this later."

She stared at him until he nodded. "Okay. We'll do it together."

When Gloria arrived, she explained why they wanted to speak to Miguel. Gloria was horrified but she agreed her theory made sense. They went to Eden's bedroom instead of Miguel's, so his toys wouldn't distract him.

Gloria put a gentle hand on his shoulder. "Miguel, Detective Williams and Ms. Nelson need to ask you some questions, and I want you to tell her the truth, yes?" His brown eyes moved about the room, but he didn't answer. "Miguel, mírame."

"Okay," he said.

Molly offered a warm smile and waited until the corners of his mouth turned up. "You're not in trouble," she said.

"Is my mom in trouble?" he asked immediately.

She took a breath and said, "I don't know for sure. And that's the honest answer." He nodded and his shoulders relaxed. "I need to ask you a couple of questions, that's all. Did you take somebody's badge and key at your dad's law office?"

Worry filled his face and he looked at Gloria. "It's fine, Niño," she said soothingly. "It's okay to answer the question honestly."

"Yes," he replied. He said the word like a tire expelling air. "I'm sorry. I shouldn't have done it. I know it was wrong, but she asked me to do it."

"Whose key and badge did you take?" Molly asked.

"Hannah's. They were on her desk." He looked up nervously. "Am I going to jail for stealing?"

"No," Molly reassured him. She glanced at Gloria before she asked the most important question. "Miguel, who asked you to take them?"

"Gabrielle."

She took a breath. It was one of two possible scenarios she'd predicted. "When did she ask you to take them?"

"At school. She's in my class."

"Why did she ask you to do that?" Gloria asked.

"She said her mom was really upset and wanted to talk to my dad alone about her case after everyone else had gone home. During the day was too busy. She said if her mom lost her case, she'd have to go away. I didn't want that to happen." His cheeks reddened and he said, "I like her." He added, "I said no at first. I know I'm not supposed to take things that don't belong to me."

Molly and Andre exchanged a glance before Molly asked, "When did you take the badge and key off Hannah's desk?"

"Last Wednesday. Not the Wednesday we just had, but the one before it."

"And when did you give them to Gabrielle?"

"The next day at school. She said she'd give them back to me after her mom talked to my dad, and then I could give them back to Hannah. But then my dad died, so I don't think Gabrielle's mom ever got to talk to him."

Molly bit her lip to control her anger. Mackenzie had horribly manipulated both Miguel and Gabrielle to gain access to the office tower. At least Miguel had not connected his actions with his father's death. When she glanced at Gloria's dark eyes, she could tell they were thinking the same thing.

She took a deep breath and said, "Miguel, I just have one more question. Did you talk to your mother at all about this?"

"No," he said with a scowl. "I didn't want to worry her. This was just stupid school stuff."

CHAPTER TWENTY-SEVEN

The Glendale police arrested Barry and took Ari and Garrett's statements. Garrett had been sitting outside enjoying the March weather when Ari drove up and unlocked the Long Manor gate. He saw Barry pull up to the curb after she'd gone inside. When he got out, he stuck a gun in his waistband. After Barry followed her into the garage, Garrett hurried across the street. He saw the baseball bat in the backseat and walked in on Barry's little rant. Barry had parked himself on a stair step that was just the right height for Garrett's swing.

Ari had texted Molly and Scott while they waited for the cops and the ambulance. Molly hadn't replied yet but Scott came over immediately. "I can't believe Barry would hold a gun on you," he said. "I know he's an SOB, but still…"

She held up the Hermes box. "The answer might be in here." He reached for it, but she pulled it away. "I think you should let me watch this and I'll report back. From what I've gathered listening to Barry, he doesn't know any more than the rest of us, but he must have suspected there was proof. It wouldn't surprise me if Millicent made a deathbed confession to the award kids. Maybe once he calms down and his knee feels better, he'll really tell you what he knows. Perhaps you can move forward as a family."

Scott crossed his arms and shook his head. "I don't see all of us ever being a family," he retorted.

Ari took a deep breath and looked him in the eye. "Here's how I see it. We both know a lot about loss. We've lost parents and siblings. This past week has been a huge reminder about what I don't have in my life anymore. I can be bitter and angry or I can be grateful for what remains." She shrugged. "I'm choosing the latter." She offered a sad smile and gave him a hug.

As she drove home, she thought about what she'd said to Scott. Did she really believe it? Could she forgive her father for his deception? She decided to keep an open mind, and once the pain of losing Richie dulled again, she might talk with him about it—maybe.

Molly called as she pulled into her driveway. "Were you right?" Ari asked.

"I was, but it was the second scenario. Mackenzie manipulated both Gabrielle and Miguel to get a badge and key, and fortunately, Miguel has no idea that he was unwittingly an accessory to murder. I'm hoping Gabrielle has the same story, and they never connect the dots. It was bad enough explaining it to Eden. She just fell apart."

"So are you on your way over to Mackenzie's school now?"

"Nope. I'm on my way back to the office. Andre's going to interview Gabrielle, and then he'll go arrest Mackenzie."

"You're not going too?" she pressed.

"Nope. This is Andre's show. I imagine Mackenzie will shed a lot of tears and play the victim. She'll probably deny it, so I hope she still has the gun. He's also going to get a CPS worker over there to interview Gabby. Maybe she'll tell the truth about how she really broke her arm. Mackenzie can go to jail for murder *and* child abuse. I'm so disgusted with her that I'd probably sock her in the jaw if I saw her."

Ari chuckled and said, "Then I'm glad you're not going."

Molly cleared her throat. "Now about this crazy brother pulling a gun on you." She stopped abruptly and said, "And you'll notice I'm using the non-judgmental tone Dr. Yee recommended."

"It's all resolved," she said cheerily. "Except I still have a reel of film to watch that could prove Henrietta was murdered. Want to join me?"

"Absolutely! I feel like I owe it to Cousin Glenn."

Molly studied the Hermes box while Ari threaded the projector. "Looks like Millicent gave her husband an expensive handkerchief at some point."

"Expensive was her middle name," Ari replied.

The movie started and they moved to the couch.

It was just before sunrise. Shadows outlined the familiar backyard—the eucalyptus tree, the rose bushes, the walk and the garage. For the first time Ari noticed a porch light outside the sunroom's front door. Suddenly flickers of lightning filled the sky.

"It's raining," Molly whispered.

"August in Phoenix; so it's a monsoon and it's obscuring the picture. There's probably a lot of thunder as well."

The camera remained steady toward the sunrise—until it jerked left and downward.

"He saw something," Ari said.

A figure entered the frame and walked briskly to the staircase. "Damn," Ari said. "I really wanted to be wrong."

Junior Long climbed the staircase slowly, the wind pushing against his ascent, defying him to do what he planned. He stopped a few steps from the top, the glow of the porch light providing ample light for Glenn's movie. He held something white in his left hand and a tin in his right hand. He poured a generous amount of whatever was in the tin on the stair step.

"You asshole," Molly said. "He wanted to make sure when she slipped, it was a good, long fall."

"One that would kill her," Ari murmured. "I'm thinking there's vegetable oil in the tin. That's how they used to package it."

Junior poured some oil on the rag and wiped the railing next to the compromised step. Then he finished his climb and knocked on the door. Glenn zoomed in. Junior pounded on the door and eventually Henrietta answered. She was a sliver of a silhouette in a white nightgown. Junior gestured with his free hand, hiding the tin and the rag behind his back.

"You fucking bastard!" Molly shouted at the movie. "He woke her up. He's created a ruse to get her down the stairs. He's probably saying one of the kids is sick or hurt."

"And it's working," Ari said.

Henrietta disappeared momentarily to get her slippers and robe. She stepped outside and started down the steps. Junior remained behind her, not taking her arm, not offering any assistance. He was no longer her husband or her life partner. He was a desperate man with a failing company, a wife destined to die and a pregnant lover.

As Henrietta approached the fatal step, Ari willed the movie to end differently—and for a brief moment it looked as if it might. Henrietta's foot came down in the oil and slipped. Everything else happened at once. She grabbed for the railing, but her hand landed on the slickest place and she couldn't find purchase. Her body twisted and she managed to grab the railing with her left hand. Her feet tangled and for a horribly long moment she hung suspended in the air, staring at Junior. Ari couldn't make out her face, but she imagined her horrified expression. Junior pried her fingers from the railing. She clung to his hand until he yanked it away and she tumbled down the staircase. Ari and Molly gasped. Although there wasn't any sound, Ari was certain the looming thunder muffled her screams.

Junior turned away. He remained hunched over for several seconds, his shoulders rising and falling while he cried. It rained harder and pulled him from his grief. He wiped down the stair and the railing, removing the excessive oil. He descended the stairs slowly, hovering over Henrietta's body. He bent down and wiped the oil from her hands. He even thought to wipe the bottoms of her slippers. Before he left he scanned the backyard. His gaze looked up and found Scott's window. He froze and stared into the camera.

"He sees the red light," Ari commented. "He knows Glenn is filming."

He jogged to the backdoor, and several seconds later, the screen went white but the whine of the projector continued. Neither of them said anything until the reel's tail flapped a conclusion.

"He probably took the film," Molly said. "Then he put it in his secret drawer." She looked at Ari. "Do you think Millicent knew?"

"Yes. It was probably her idea that she expected him to execute. I'm sure after he went to Glenn and exchanged his film reel, he returned the vegetable oil tin to its spot in the kitchen and disposed of the rag and his handkerchief. Then he walked to work. He probably pulled Millicent aside and told her they were free."

"Did you know it was Junior and not Millicent?"

"I started to wonder after Garrett Beaton told me about his inheritance. I knew Junior was the one who paid them off, not Millicent. Even if he hadn't killed Henrietta, I knew he was complicit. When Mary Bellows said she tried to visit Henrietta, it was clear Junior was cutting her off from the world."

"I don't know how he did it," Molly said flatly. "He looked in her eyes and pulled her hand off that railing."

"I think that moment haunted him for the rest of his life. Scott told me he was never the same after Henrietta's death, even after marrying Millicent and having a second family. There was another clue, too. My dad said he came around to our house sobbing after Richie died. I'm sure everyone else just thought it was grief but really it was guilt."

"Why do you think he kept the film?" Molly asked. "Why didn't he destroy it?"

Ari thought of the Bible verse. "We can only guess, but I think he used it as a way to torture himself. I'll bet he opened that drawer periodically to remind himself of what he'd done."

Molly put an arm around her. "Honey, how will you ever tell Scott?"

She took a deep breath and exhaled. "I have to tell him the truth. He'll decide if he wants to watch it," she said softly. "I'm sure the courts will relook at Millicent's will, especially with some key testimony from Mary Bellows and Cecil Oaks, the bank president." She shrugged. "Hopefully something good can come from this."

Molly turned to face her. "This makes me think of what your dad has kept from you."

She leaned into Molly's comfortable embrace. "I'm not sure what I'll do with that information. Perhaps some secrets are best kept that way."

EPILOGUE

Ari started her spring cleaning at the beginning of May. She'd worked her way through most of the downstairs, and only the cluttered solarium still needed her attention. In the corner sat the Long's old projector and two boxes of Glenn's films. Scott had indefinitely loaned her everything. He'd taken her advice and reached out to Cal and Nobel, his other stepbrothers. Whereas Scott and Carlin decided not to watch the footage, the award kids and Blythe's children did. Ari thought a new level of compassion was a byproduct of witnessing Henrietta's death.

Barry, Cal and Nobel decided everything should be split equally amongst the seven of them, and all of the attorneys were fired. They would work together to rebuild the Fizz brand, and Carlin had decided to move home to Long Manor. He and Garrett, who were roughly the same age, hit it off immediately. As for Barry, a broken kneecap and two days in jail humbled him greatly. His day in court had not arrived, but Ari hoped for some leniency, since she'd never truly felt she was in danger.

She turned away from the boxes and dropped into a chair. She missed Molly who was away on business, wooing more clients. Andre arrested Mackenzie with little fanfare. They had found the .38 in a box on a shelf in her closet. A cousin had loaned it to her for protection. Fortunately she had kept Gabrielle in the dark about the small role she'd played in giving Mackenzie access to the office. Her defense attorney claimed she had a psychotic break as her court date drew closer. She'd attacked the copy machine when she saw the school flyer Brittany Spring had accidentally left on the glass. Although she'd taken Brittany's master copy, since she was connected to the school, she worried the police would know what had been printed, so she destroyed the machine. It was faulty logic at best, but she wasn't logical as evidenced by her psych evaluation. Gabrielle still wouldn't discuss how she'd broken her arm, but the psychologist she was seeing was hopeful.

Ari's gaze floated back to the boxes of Glenn's films. The first box contained all the films she'd watched. They were numbered and she'd noted which ones contained footage of her or Richie. The second box was the one she'd found the day Barry confronted her. She'd never watched them, rationalizing she'd found the film she needed to view. Should she bother to watch the films in the second box, or should she just return it? She'd debated that question every time she passed through the solarium, but she'd quickly banished the thought and moved on. She wasn't sure if her heart could afford another trampling. Now the question demanded an answer.

She sighed and pulled out the box and the projector. She'd just started the first reel as her phone rang. *Jane.* "Hi there," she said cheerfully. "How's the construction going?"

"Can't you hear it in the background? Teri is making it happen!"

Her idea to appease Muriel the health inspector required the installation of a wrap-around counter and losing one of the entrances. Teri Wyatt, Jane's handy dyke friend, said it was an easy job. The added counter space appeased Muriel, but she thought Jane might have thrown a few fringe benefits Muriel's way just to be sure.

"Are you coming by later?" Jane asked.

"Yes, after I go to the movies with my dad and the chief."

Jane laughed. "You're finally meeting her."

"Yup. I just need to get over it."

"What about all that other stuff with your mom and Richie's case?" Jane asked warily.

She smiled. Jane would always be in her corner. She glanced at the screen. Glenn was shopping with Blythe. "I'm letting it go for now. Maybe we'll talk about it eventually."

"Whatever you say, boss."

She signed off as the film ended. She threaded the next one and grabbed the mail, determined to multi-task while she watched. The film began with sunrise over the garage and then moved to cereal for breakfast. She noticed the obvious absence of Henrietta, which explained the glum expressions of her children. When it skipped to a car ride, she watched carefully. She'd learned she and Richie tended to show up in the middle or toward the end when they played together after dinner.

The film skipped again and it was nighttime. The camera focused on a storefront. She recognized it as the 7-Eleven where Richie had been killed. The interior store lights provided a clear view of two customers going up and down the aisles. She guessed Glenn was standing on the dark corner, the parking lot separating him from the store.

Her heart started to pound as a figure on a bicycle approached. Glenn turned the camera to greet Richie, who held up some baseball cards. She didn't need to read the names on the cards. She knew he'd been trying to get the entire 1992 infield for his beloved L.A. Dodgers. He was missing Eric Karros, the first baseman. He said something else, waved and rode across the parking lot to the storefront. He parked his bike and went inside. By then the store and the parking lot were empty, the previous customers having departed while Richie talked to Glenn.

She dropped the mail in her lap. She struggled to breathe as a skinny guy in jeans and a plaid shirt came into the frame and went into the store. She knew that description from the police report she'd memorized, searching for any clues to further the investigation. For a split second he looked over his shoulder, and she saw the face of her brother's killer before the picture disappeared and the reel's tail flapped in time to her galloping heartbeat.

Bella Books, Inc.

Women. Books. Even Better Together.

P.O. Box 10543
Tallahassee, FL 32302

Phone: 800-729-4992
www.bellabooks.com